More Praise for
Talking to the Wolf

"This tale of four friends (one a ghost) takes us across thirty-five years of tumultuous attachment. How alive these women are—including the dead one—and how forever bonded, even with their separate versions of the truth. A terrific book."

—Joan Silber, author of *Secrets of Happiness*

"*Talking to the Wolf* is a stunning, intricate portrayal of close female bonds forged in adolescence. It's a story about how our ideas of success change over time, and the mysterious ways that our deepest friendships both hold us and release us. Rebecca Chace has written an intimate, luminous, and deeply absorbing novel, one that I didn't want to end."

—Rene Steinke, author of *Friendswood*

"Imagine *Mrs. Dalloway* brought into the present and shared four ways, among four women. Rebecca Chace's *Talking to the Wolf* shows us anew how a single day's shape can reveal a whole life's—in work and love, friendship, desire, and even renewed possibilities lurking just beyond the dusk horizon."

—Padma Viswanathan, author of *The Charterhouse of Padma*

"A beautiful, layered, astute novel about friendship and the changes wrought on it by time, success, disappointment, and death that is nevertheless, miraculously, a celebration. You can chalk that up to Rebecca Chace's deep dive into the psyches of her characters and her evocation of both the vanished New York of their young womanhood and the playground of wealth the city is today. Add the pitch-perfect dialogue, narrative suspense, and the sheer heart of Chace's storytelling. I wanted to live in this book."

—Peter Trachtenberg, author of *The Twilight of Bohemia*

Also by Rebecca Chace

Leaving Rock Harbor

June Sparrow and the Million Dollar Penny

Capture the Flag

Chautauqua Summer

Talking to the Wolf

++++

a novel

Rebecca Chace

Red Hen Press | *Pasadena, CA*

Book layout by Ava Morgan

Library of Congress Cataloging-in-Publication Data

Names: Chace, Rebecca author
Title: Talking to the wolf: a novel / Rebecca Chace.
Description: First edition. | Pasadena, CA: Red Hen Press, 2026.
Identifiers: LCCN 2025021043 (print) | LCCN 2025021044 (ebook) | ISBN 9781636284620 paperback | ISBN 9781636284637 library binding | ISBN 9781636284644 ebook
Subjects: LCGFT: Novels | Fiction
Classification: LCC PS3553.H17 T35 2026 (print) | LCC PS3553.H17 (ebook) | DDC 813/.54—dc23/eng/20250625
LC record available at https://lccn.loc.gov/2025021043
LC ebook record available at https://lccn.loc.gov/2025021044

The National Endowment for the Arts, the Los Angeles County Arts Commission, the Ahmanson Foundation, the Dwight Stuart Youth Fund, the Max Factor Family Foundation, the Pasadena Tournament of Roses Foundation, the Pasadena Arts & Culture Commission and the City of Pasadena Cultural Affairs Division, the City of Los Angeles Department of Cultural Affairs, the Audrey & Sydney Irmas Charitable Foundation, the Meta & George Rosenberg Foundation, the Albert and Elaine Borchard Foundation, the Adams Family Foundation, Amazon Literary Partnership, the Sam Francis Foundation, and the Mara W. Breech Foundation partially support Red Hen Press.

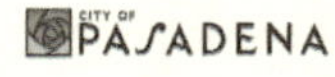

First Edition
Published by Red Hen Press
www.redhen.org

To all of my sisters; you know who you are.

Talking to the Wolf

When she gave me back the notebook, she said, "You're very clever, of course they always give you a ten."

I felt there was no irony, it was a real compliment. Then she added with sudden harshness:

"I don't want to read anything else that you write."

"Why?"

She thought about it.

"Because it hurts me," and she struck her forehead with her hand and burst out laughing.

—Elena Ferrante, *My Brilliant Friend*

cora

I'm so fucking sick of being dead.

I want to shake the walls, rip up the subway tracks, melt those thick metal wires running through the salty dirt beneath the pavement. I know this city as well as my own body and I counted on my body to be smarter than it was—muscles, veins, legs, wrists, fingers, eyes, tongue. I've always been strong. It scared people sometimes, my broad shoulders and muscled arms. Those A & R guys didn't expect a rugby player in heels. It was funny to watch their expressions change, then scramble to cover it up. But I tried not to smile too much at first; it's not my job to help them relax. Just another work dinner and it wasn't raining hard, so I grabbed a Citibike to sweat out the alcohol and sleep better next to the man I didn't want to leave. I knew I'd make the light, standing with the balls of my feet on the pedals to go faster. I was nine years old, pumping up a hill before the long glide down the other side, braids flying back with no helmet. Who carries a helmet in an expensive shoulder bag?

I flew through the light and that taxi just kept coming, tires sliding on wet asphalt like a wall of metal. Blaring horn and bike handles twisting down and away. The accident happened so fast, and ever since my body hit the pavement it's like I'm stuck and unstuck at the same time. I'm caught in the rough first layer of a fresco, lines drawn in that pigment the color of dried blood, my body marked out while the plaster's still wet, trapped in some unknown geometry of movement and the smell of iron.

I want out and I want back in.

Both ways is the only way I want it.

Jeff watching me undress in our bedroom, not listening to me ramble on about my boring dinner because he can't believe his luck. Emma and

Ben asking me to take them to a morning matinee because tomorrow's Saturday and I'm the fun one. The stepmother who buys them popcorn and a box of junior mints for breakfast at the movies. I need to get back to my people, to my own lovely, pumping, agitated flesh.

I can't believe how much time I wasted thinking I was immortal.

Where's Val? She's the only one who might still hear me. We were the ones who always answered the phone, met at the bar with swollen eyes and a pack of cigarettes, moving in and out of love, first periods, last periods, bullying mothers, disappeared fathers, crazy sisters, children unborn, found, or gone, parents dying too fast or too slow, this apartment, that apartment, an eyebrow raised across a crowded room, laughing so hard we had to clench our pussies or wet our pants, and always my heart driving me like an engine until that sudden snapping shift.

This is not my life.

That's right, says the undervoice, speaking in a language only I can understand. It's not your life.

So. I'm fucked.

I have to find Val. Force her to listen to me even if I don't deserve it.

Even after all those years playing in the clubs, she still has the best ear.

val

Val wanted a clean, muffled stop.

She was the only one up late enough to see the snow begin, flecks of mica in the streetlights. She put a spoon under her pillow, face up to catch the snow, the way they all did when they were little. It was supposed to bring a snow day. Val turned out the light and lay on her side watching First Avenue blink out or stay on all night. The night sky lay down tracks between the buildings, stars overdubbed by urban glow. She closed her eyes, hearing the tonal shifts between late-night car tires and the hollow metal door slam from the bar downstairs as someone put garbage bags out on the street, the thump and rattle of glass and a low murmur in Spanish, the scratch flare of a match to the last cigarette of the night.

Sleepless nights came more often than they used to, but Val was afraid to keep medication in the house.

She woke to the sound of garbage trucks with snowplows attached like the prow of a ship. She reached under her pillow and kissed the spoon. It worked. Even in February, a real blizzard seemed improbable; everything should already be slushed down the sewage drains to the harbor. But the sky was stuck on repeat, the east coast gripped by a storm crawling toward New York City, dumping snow instead of moving out to the Atlantic. Val loved the garbage trucks with their headlight eyes, orange cyclops spinning on top and red taillights showing through the static in the air: All clear! All clear! It comforted her to have these lumbering creatures moving purposefully through the city. Maybe it would snow long enough to shut the whole place down for good.

Val kept the bedroom window open since the radiators had to be on full blast or not at all. Cold air dipped under the rising heat, found her bare arm lying on top of the blanket, and every hair shivered up. She pulled the blanket higher with a tiny thrill, inhaling the lovely, metallic, starting-over smell of a real snowfall. Maybe she could just stay in bed and listen to the day unfold six stories below. It was a reprieve to doze like this in her plain white bed with its faded Star Wars pillowcases. She slipped back under the early morning quiet of the neighborhood, spreading her arms over the back of a garbage truck which became an armadillo cradling her through the snow, steam rising up through its scales.

Mornings were always the hardest. Val knew that getting out of bed usually helped, make coffee, get dressed, give the habits of the body a chance to detour from the looming crush of her tilted life. You're not exactly up with the lark, an ex said to her years ago.

No, not exactly.

She hated this long gap between getting up to pee and actually getting out of bed. Mind the gap. Step on the gap and you'll break your mother's back. Crack. Step on the *crack*. A crack can be kind of like a gap though, can't it? Every gap started as a crack. Every mother once broke her back.

This is the kind of thinking that makes it hard to get out of bed.

The sky was lightening the windows in Val's bedroom, blue, gray, pink, orange until the day landed with a thump of white between the buildings across the street. She couldn't stay in bed and she wouldn't—because of the dogs.

She forced herself up and walked to the bathroom, stepping onto the small platform to the toilet. Everything was squeezed into an even smaller space than originally planned in this East Village tenement. The toilet facing a small sink, the mirror above draped with tiny Christmas lights she hadn't bothered to plug in for a while. The poster from that time she opened for the Pogues on the back of the bathroom door, splashed with water marks. Laminated backstage passes hung from the doorknob. She'd painted one bathroom wall poppy red last fall, to change things up, then stopped. It had felt too much like being inside her own digestive system when she was engaged in the act of emptying it.

A can of paint laughed at her from under the bathroom sink.

The bathtub was in the kitchen but it was too much trouble to take the plywood off the top for a quick wash before heading uptown to walk the dogs. They liked her smell. She kept the plywood covered with a Mexican oilcloth printed with blue and red flowers which always made her happy. It was a great apartment. She had been there so long that the rent was cheap, and they couldn't kick her out no matter how hard they tried. She had learned how to spackle and paint for herself and never called the landlord unless it was plumbing. There was room for her old Baldwin upright piano, with her one gold record, "Like A Girl," propped in its plastic case against a publicity shot of her with the band, the Joypoppers. She'd lost her plump lips and ass, age was narrowing her into a weird new beakiness, but she hadn't really changed her hair. A former fan with a hair salon kept Val's roots from showing the gray and never let her pay. Same black hair, same pale skin. I'm turning into a skinny cockatoo, she thought, looking in the full-length mirror on the back of the closet door and fanning her hair up in spikes with her fingers, too lazy to bother with hair gel. She bared her teeth. They were more ivory than white (did she mean yellow?) and she wondered again about buying teeth whitening strips from the drugstore, but the whole kit cost fifty dollars and she couldn't quite bring herself to do it, despite her bottomless vanity.

She'd rather put on a drugstore facemask and lie in the bathtub drinking vodka.

The coffee maker hissed on the stovetop as Val filled a small enamel pot with milk. She loved this little blue pot with its spout and friendly wooden handle. This was her private luxury, taking the time to heat up milk for her coffee. She took her cup to the other end of the apartment where the windows faced First Avenue and her Telecaster leaned against the Gibson in their cases, old rockers in overcoats. Just like me, she thought, sitting in her most comfortable chair and propping her feet up on a stack of books. Fuck 'em if they can't take a joke. But who was she talking to?

Cora. Val had been talking to Cora since she was five years old.

Then Cora stopped talking to Val after that lunch Val overrehearsed for, even though she was Cora's oldest friend; even though Cora had stopped being her manager twenty years ago, when she joined Sony and became a "Suit." Val lost her appetite as soon as she walked into the restaurant. Another French bistro in Tribeca with tables on the sidewalk because it was June. Cora had made a reservation for indoors, red leather booth, white tablecloth, thick napkins. Val kept picking at the edges of her omelet; Cora plowed through her steak frites.

"I've been sending the new songs around," said Val. "I've even tried submitting to contests, though I'm not exactly an 'emerging' artist anymore." She laughed like it didn't matter and Cora waved at the waiter.

"Can I have some more mustard?" Cora never put ketchup on her fries anymore.

"I need a new manager, but everything's changed so much since I left Josh."

"Josh was an asshole." Cora pushed her plate toward Val. "I can't finish these. Want some?"

Val stared at the pile of twisted potatoes, the blood from Cora's steak turning pink on the white oval plate. "It's hard without a manager. People don't even send rejection notes anymore."

"Really? That sucks." Cora looked around the restaurant. "How long does it take to pick up a pot of mustard from the kitchen?"

"Do you guys send rejection notes?" Val couldn't help herself.

Cora's mouth hardened. "My assistant handles all that."

"If you could recommend me to someone it might—I mean, you know, somebody younger who's coming up. Someone you think has good ears."

"At this point in my career . . ." Cora moved a piece of gristle to the side of her plate with her fork. "It's more complicated than that."

The waiter brought the mustard with an apologetic expression. Cora sighed across her plate. "I'm not hungry anymore. You sure you don't want any?"

Cora picked up one long French fry and reached over her plate. She gently stroked Val's closed lips with the pointed tip, as if her frite was an extension of her fingers with their perfect nails. Those fingers had been in Val's mouth before, the two of them pressed tightly against each other in a bathroom stall at the club. Crotch, legs, ass, mouth. In their twenties, they couldn't get enough.

"Open up," said Cora, waving the frite in the air, half-serious, half-joking.

Val batted it away so hard it landed on the floor. Cora laughed and pushed back her chair to go to the bathroom. Val forced herself to stay at the table, watching the ice cubes jostle against each other in her water glass, not crying, listening to Cora talk about nothing as she paid the check.

i need a break, Cora wrote to her the next day. Texting instead of calling.

we don't get breaks! Val texted back, before she understood she wasn't getting an answer.

Cora's break lasted for months, expanded and changed texture. It won't last forever, said Lauren. It's a phase, said Sasha. Was Cora thinking about Val as much as Val thought about her? No, said Sasha; no, said Lauren. Val was too needy, too hungry, she had leaky eyes and a rattling cough. She might be contagious. Who could blame Cora for not wanting to put up with her stench for one more day?

Then came the bicycle and the taxi and Cora stopped breathing on the ninth of October.

As soon as she died, Cora started talking to her again.

Ha ha ha, said Cora.

Now she wouldn't shut up.

If Sasha wasn't hosting the dinner tonight, Val would never show her face at a class reunion. Harrison only mattered because it was where she met Cora in kindergarten, then Lauren and Sasha. They all stuck it out through high school; Val graduated by the skin of her teeth and disowned the place as soon as she could. But never the four of them. Three. The three of them. They hadn't seen each other since the funeral four months ago, so this was their reunion too, in a way. Val used to say that they were the only band she was in that never gigged and never broke up—until Cora broke up with her.

Time to book the reunion tour, said Cora.

Val put her empty coffee mug on the floor. The bright yellow can of Cafe Bustelo shone across the room from the kitchen counter. She had slept in her band T-shirt, so she left that on and walked to the closet to dig out the suit she used to wear when the Joypoppers first started up at the Knitting Factory. Danny had been so pissed when she made everyone in the band wear suits back in the day, but look at him now. Side man for the best of the best and always looking sharp onstage. He would understand why she had put on a suit this morning. She checked herself in the mirror. She must weigh about the same as she did back then, maybe a little less. The jacket still looked good over her T-shirt, but something had happened to her face.

Val opened the front window wide—from six flights up, the street almost disappeared in the snow—and here she was sitting on the edge, legs dangling off the windowsill, almost disappeared herself. She opened her mouth, tongue catching flakes. The heat of her body radiating through the suit pants created a sheen of moisture along the top of her thighs. That familiar distance setting in. Whose hands were these? Whose chapped lips? It was only a quick slip from here to there. Her legs were already not a part of her, they were logs in a forest where snow would drift, accumulate, and melt. In spring, spores would land and fungi would form thick fans, white shell above and soft brown underside below. Leaves flaking and drifting, tiny jaws crunching through the brown and green. All of this happening in slow motion toward mulch, everything feeding something else. It was like that picture book she read over and over when she was little, *What is Soil*? She had crouched on her knees in the park, digging up gray city dirt. She came home and put it in a bowl, adding water from the tap. Mixing her life with a metal spoon.

Good title. There might be a song in it, said Cora.

Val slowly took her hands out of her pockets.

She watched herself climb back inside the apartment, close the window, and hang her suit neatly back in the closet, comforted by the everyday weight of cloth on a hanger. She had made it through the worst of it one more time. She would see Sasha and Lauren tonight, and when everyone else left she'd tell them about hearing Cora's voice and the windowsill. How it was hard to quit the windowsill, but she thought she could do it, like cigarettes. Nobody thought she'd ever quit smoking and then she did, the fingers on her right hand shed their layers of nicotine-stained skin and look how healthy she was now!

Ha, ha ha, said Cora.

Val opened the metal lid of her blackened espresso maker and sniffed the sweet oil of a thousand mornings.

She could still change her mind.

Val piled on long underwear, jeans, sweater, parka, hat, and snow boots. She walked down six flights without seeing any of her neighbors, who were probably taking the day off because of the storm. None of her dog-walking clients had texted that they were staying home. They might prefer to pay someone else to take the dogs out in bad weather. She loved that since they all got smartphones, she didn't have to answer the phone ever again. Plus, now that nobody calls anyone, you don't have to feel bad that the phone never rings. It's perfect.

She walked four nearly empty blocks along Second Avenue to the train, the air soft and cold, not much wind, salt crunching underfoot to keep the humans upright while city dogs limped. The subways were slow and empty, but Val was glad not to miss a day. She needed the money. She always picked Juno up first (come here, baby, here's your treat). He was her favorite, a skinny little city mutt with a funny trick of picking up his back feet and balancing on his front legs when he peed, somehow never spraying urine onto his stomach. Circus dog, she would say to people who noticed, and it could have been true. His owners said he was a rescue, though if he had really been in the circus he might be bored by his new life. Val's walk was one of the highlights of his day. Maybe it didn't matter how much time he spent sleeping in his new family's apartment as long as he could still pee while walking on his hands.

Juno minced along in the snow, looking back at her every few feet for the three-block walk to Sheila and Bertie's, a pair of matching springer spaniels who lived close to Central Park. British names for a colonial breed, she thought, as she snapped on Sheila's leash. At least their owners hadn't docked their tails. Walking out of the building, they pulled at their leads, excited by the slippery white world, ready to melt joyous, bright yellow holes in the snow. Val dipped their paws in a special wax she carried to protect them from the salt the doormen scattered on the sidewalks as if it were a competition. Val was convinced that rubber booties were humiliating for dogs, and she wiped their paws clean when they returned. This was Central Park West, where doormen wore uniforms tucked into rubber boots in bad weather. The apartments where Val's dogs lived were so large there was room for a hardwood foyer before thickly padded carpets pooled out in the living room.

Val had keys to pick up and drop off the dogs, but she never veered from her path between the front door and the kitchen, where the food and water bowls were kept. If she really had to, she used the bathroom or poured herself a glass of tap water, but she was careful to wipe the sink after she washed her hands, never left a glass on the counter, never looked at the bookshelves or sat down on the designer furniture that the dogs jumped on as soon as she let them off the leash. It was best to assume you were on camera all the time and people who lived like this usually had a camera in every room, theoretically in case of robbery, but they were probably never turned off. Some of her clients confessed that they often clicked over to the home cam to watch the dogs from work. Guilty pleasure, a warning that she was being watched, or both. Val figured they must really hate their jobs if they kept flipping their screens back to the dog sleeping or licking its butt. Today, the apartments were hushed and quiet, and she had no idea if anybody was home or not. What did it matter? She was the dog walker.

Val never went to college, never thought much about Harrison until she had to circle back in her late forties, looking for work in the old girl network. Sasha told her to try upscale dog walking to pay the rent "for now" after Val quit teaching music at the community college last fall, burning the earth and sowing salt into the furrows of her life. Sasha put a notice on the alumni listserv with Val's email address and the requests started pouring in. Not all the Harrison families lived near the school, and she split her week between downtown dogs and uptown dogs. Val thought she wouldn't care what these Harrison types thought when she showed up with a baggie full of dog treats, but she was shamed by their identical smiles and perfect teeth, her weekly checks left out on stone countertops signed in a looping cursive that Val would recognize anywhere because she formed her letters the same way, filling her notebooks with scratched out lyrics. Harrison graduates weren't supposed to end up as middle-aged dog walkers.

When had Val stopped recognizing her own life? Was it when Cora cut her off last summer? When Cora died four months later? Or was it when her students called her "Professor" and didn't understand why she started laughing?

All three dogs tugged toward the entrance of the park, sniffed, peed, and smiled back at her, encouraging her to keep up. It was good to be part of a pack. The dogs let Val know exactly what to do, like right now, when she reached down and unsnapped their leads. Bertie and Sheila tore off through the snow, black and white bounders. Joy. Val's feet were cold, and she exchanged a look with Juno, this sweet little dog with the name of a goddess or a car service. They both thought Bertie and Sheila were a little too desperate to be liked, sniffing and wagging at the other dogs, paired silhouettes in the snow until they suddenly burst clear from the group. Juno stayed close to Val, shivering a little, though he wore a plaid coat she had buckled onto him.

"Don't be such a little old man," she told him, her breath turning white in the cold. She started up the hill knowing that Juno would use her footprints as stepping stones. She had a fleece-lined neck warmer she could pull over her nose, but she wanted to feel the air on her face. When she was with the dogs, everything she wore and every object she carried had a purpose. One of her secret projects was that this new, practical Val might stick around if she wore the right costume.

All the dog people were out for off-leash time, bright jackets and strips of neon marking their slow, deliberate movements, bulky as astronauts and strangely endearing. The dogs looped circles around them. Off to the right were ghostly pathways, benches and lamp posts; tall trees marked the cluttered white air in a semaphore she couldn't understand. Maples, elms, and sycamores. Was that Cora walking along the path toward Val through the milky light? *Honestly, I hardly remember why you made me so mad*, Cora would say with her pirate smile, and even though Val knew exactly what Cora had said that day at lunch, she wouldn't remind her. They'd be Mick and Keith again.

My husband's still jealous of you, said Cora.

"He should be," Val said aloud. "He'll never have known you as long as I did."

Juno looked up at her, confused. Even the dog thought she was acting weird.

The psychopharmacologist had told Val that she wasn't schizophrenic, despite the family history.

"Doesn't everyone talk to the dead?" Val had asked.

"Many do, yes," he said. "But for most people, they don't talk back."

Hearing Cora's voice was a result of trauma and grief, the doctor said. It will get better with time. It was getting worse, but she was afraid that if she went back on her meds, she'd never hear Cora's voice again.

Val stopped at what she hoped was a friendly distance from a small clutch of humans. If only I spoke Dog, she thought, then Juno whined, asking to be picked up, and she realized that she did speak Dog. Maybe not fluent, but enough to get around.

Val pretended she was giving into him when she was the one who needed Juno's warm, quivering body next to her chest, his smooth brown head poking out from the top of her parka. She wished she could bring him to the reunion tonight. Maybe she, Lauren, and Sasha would stay after the dinner for a drink and she would tell the truth. Val hadn't meant to avoid the two of them. When Sasha texted them both to make sure they were coming tonight, she said it was four months since the funeral. Val wanted a different calendar. Cora's funeral was yesterday.

Juno licked her ear as Sheila and Bertie ran through the snow with tails curled high. Reasons to live.

Thank you, Cora, she thought automatically, as if those flying dog tails could be a gift from the dead.

cora

It's a lie that the dead can be everywhere at once, or is that God? His eye on the sparrow? I'm keeping my eye on Val. I'm more excited about the reunion than any of them and I need to make sure she gets there. The four of us together. Of course, I'll always look good at the reunions. One of the upsides, I guess. In that photo of us that Val doesn't like to look at anymore, I look pretty good for fifty-two years of allergies, pedicures, haircuts, dye jobs, waxes, pap smears, contraception, fertility treatments, hormone replacement therapy, teeth filled, pulled, straightened, capped, antianxiety, antidepressants, marathons, half-marathons, and work, work, work.

The smell of snow is filling me up today. The Greeks were right when they made burnt offerings to the dead. Smell is our final lust. No touch, no taste, but I can smell the air and hear Val's boots crunching up the hill. Sirens and traffic and all those bodies crashing around when so much depends upon a red wheelbarrow. Val had to memorize that poem for the eighth-grade poetry contest. She turned it into a song and did it a cappella:

so much depends
upon

a red wheel
barrow

glazed with rain
water

beside the white
chickens

I never understood it, but I loved the tune.

What's the hardest working muscle in the body? I want Val to make a guess. She's still a Harrison girl, like it or not, the baddest girl in our class.

That's right. The heart.

Maybe she knew it all along. Val's a music machine.

Here she is, pounding along with her little pack of canines, and I'm the peach pit at the center of the fruit while her flesh keeps sloughing off invisibly between the sheets, under the shower, muscles going soft under papery skin. She might think it sucks to get old, but she needs to wake up. Have sex right now! Even if it's only with herself. I've got smell and hearing, but I want touch, I want taste. I'm pressing up as close as I can. This isn't exactly my idea of eternal life. Val wanted what I had, and now I want what she's got. Trading envy back and forth like marbles.

That last time I saw her, she asked for one more name of one more manager. Another email with my name in the subject heading to get her in the door. She kept pushing, kept asking, kept thinking I held the keys to the kingdom. All I wanted was to stop, take a breath. I rubbed my sneakers over that chalk circle we had crouched over our whole fucking lives, shooting cats eye marbles into the center and knocking everyone, even each other, out of the way. Of course, I was still in the game, so it was easy for me to walk away. At our final lunch (that wasn't supposed to be final), Val was shit out of marbles and I didn't have the bandwidth. The Music Business is a cruel oxymoron, but I didn't make it up.

See the dogs' flying tails in the distance and how everything lifts inside.

Oldest friend, spit sister. Why doesn't she get how lucky she is right now?

sasha

Snow! This could be a disaster, Sasha thought. No, it already was. Her fingers went automatically to the hard, fleshy ball under her right breast, impossible not to keep tracing the perimeters of this newly discovered island. Why didn't she cancel the dinner last week, as soon as she found out? It did no good to squeeze the lump between her fingers like an adolescent pimple, waiting for guilty pleasure and release, washed clean with a sting of witch hazel. Witch hazel was not the recommended cure by the best oncologists in New York, and Sasha believed in science. She believed in research and data. She was a physicist, an expert, even a "genius," according to that embarrassing prize. Facts were the ropes she held onto. This Undeniable Fact underneath her heavy breast was not yet visible but could not be unseen. The tiny coastline her fingers obsessively traced had no regard for the prize Sasha nicknamed the "Genie Award" because it felt like something she'd never be able to put back inside the bottle. The Undeniable knew nothing of prizes and titles. It would shear away the last of her vanity, leaving her stripped to the bone and newly old.

If she was lucky.

She hadn't told Val and Lauren yet. It took her a while to realize they had been avoiding getting together. Instead, they sent group texts with broken heart emojis saying *i love you* or *i miss her.* Sasha invited them both over for dinner a month after the funeral, in case it was easier not to meet in public, but Lauren cancelled at the last minute and Val said she wasn't feeling well (code for too depressed to leave her apartment). Sasha had wanted to be together as much as possible in those first weeks after the accident, but Lauren and Val seemed unable to bear each other's presence without Cora.

Sasha called them intermittently over the past four months, leaving voicemails and receiving reply texts that she answered with the same emojis, trying not to overinterpret the color heart they chose. When Sasha finally got through to Val, there was a long gap, each of them listening to the other breathe, trying not to lose it over the phone. Lauren only picked up when she was on the street, sounding rushed and brittle—can't talk now, wish I could, on my way to a meeting. Big hugs!

Maybe it was too hard to see each other, but wasn't it too lonely not to?

After Sasha found out about the Undeniable, the reunion dinner was her excuse to get Val and Lauren to come over no matter what. She had thought about cancelling the whole thing after the accident, then decided that Cora would have wanted them to gather. Classmates wrote RSVP emails to Sasha about this dinner being in honor of Cora, and now it was too late to cancel—their thirty-fifth, how had they gotten so old? Normally, Sasha wouldn't care if Lauren or Val came to a Harrison event. None of them cared about the school as much as she did. But she couldn't tell them about the surgery in a text (was a crab the cancer emoji?). Lauren and Val would stay after the other women left and help Sasha clean up, the three of them stacking plates in the dishwasher and drinking the good whiskey, gossiping about who was glowing, who was falling apart, who must have had work done, and what Cora would have thought. Then Sasha would tell them about the Undeniable. This would be the real reunion. They could still tell each other the truth, couldn't they?

please tell me you'll come, Sasha put into the group text. *i have to see you. it's important. i can't do this dinner without you.*

She never wrote anything desperate in a text, and it must have made a difference, because they both responded right away that they would be there.

Sasha hardly ever asked for help. Had she ever asked?

She would tell them about her brain turning out the lights on her research, terrified to admit that she was intellectually frozen for the first time in her life. She had blamed the prize, blamed herself, then Cora was killed and the Undeniable arrived. Bad things come in threes, her mother used to say, but only Sasha knew that the prize was an evil Genie who threw open the door, then came Cora, and now cancer was number three. She had the perfect excuse for not being able to focus, but Sasha was a worker bee. When her own mind stopped returning her calls, it was as if some part of her knew that illness and death were lining up to knock on her door. That wasn't true. Her block had started months before Cora's death or the Undeniable. It was all that terrible Genie.

Sasha made a spitting noise over her left shoulder three times fast, pu-pu-pu, like her mother used to do to keep away the evil eye. Old world magic from the steppes of Russia, the Jewish ghetto, Lilith and Baba Yaga.

Bad things come in threes. Annus Horribilus.

The Genie required her to give a semi-annual report on her research to the prize committee. Today. They had extended the deadline when Cora died, out of sympathy for her loss. How pathetic, using Cora's death as an excuse for her own failure to come up with anything new for nine months. Fifty-three years old and unable to meet a deadline, despite a lifetime of overachieving, overcompensating, always doing more than could possibly be expected. Nothing could dissolve that familiar shard inside her chest, reminding Sasha she was only a breath away from being unmasked as brainless, grief struck, and totally screwed.

Cora gone. Cora lost. Cora pitched off her bike by a taxi in the rain, so unlikely that she would go first, the strongest of the four. Now there was nothing but the widening gyre that Cora had made fun of, spinning circles in her dirty white Keds on the linoleum outside of English class, repeating the words from Yeats that she had to memorize for the poetry contest.

Memorizing and forgetting the words of dead white poets seemed so pointless to Sasha now. Hosting the reunion was a terrible idea. She didn't really know any of the other women in her class anymore. Had she ever? Sasha had gone from public school to private school; Queens to Manhattan; all-the-kids-in-the-neighborhood to all-girls. Harrison was a train wreck until the day Cora pulled her up in front of Ms. Anderson's English class to stand in line with Lauren and Val, three back-up singers with all the dance moves, while Cora sang "Stop in the Name of Love" instead of reciting "The Second Coming." (Sasha had never heard of Yeats before and why wasn't his name pronounced the way it was spelled?) In seventh grade, she was soft and short with frizzy hair that never stayed put; but Sasha could dance and she already had big boobs. She was sure they'd get in trouble, but Ms. Anderson only laughed. Who could resist Cora?

Wait, it was Val who first did her poem as a song, wasn't it? When it was Val's turn she stood up and sang the red wheelbarrow poem, slapping her thighs for percussion. Val was all knees and elbows back then, long dark hair and bangs. Then Cora wanted to sing her poem too, with backup dancers.

Val and Cora were twin suns. They copied and competed and hated and loved.

And if Sasha was a planet circling them on her own grand, elliptical orbit, what was Lauren? A black hole? Okay, that was mean, but Lauren was hard to read, and nobody fully understood black holes. Back in the 18th Century, they were called dark stars—that fit better. Lauren was their dark star. Sasha closed her eyes. Could she ever stop applying known systems to human behavior? But it felt good to be loyal, good to not cancel a reunion dinner. Her classmates were right, it was in Cora's honor, who liked any excuse for a party.

The funeral had been held five days after the accident, in the Jewish tradition, even though Jeff, Cora's husband, wasn't observant enough to sit shiva. Sasha was secular, but she wished that he had done it so she could sit beside him in a chair designated for mourning. Maybe a shiva would have made it seem more real. The only person to speak at the funeral home was the rabbi who married them and hardly knew Cora. Jeff stood at the door with his kippah askew, nodding as he held the kids close. Their mother, Jeff's first wife, stood nearby with her second husband, looking as shattered as the rest of them. For the first time, Ben looked older than fifteen, wearing a dark suit and staring through everyone. When Sasha tried to hug her, Emma hid her face in her father's arm.

Kaddish was the only prayer Sasha's father had known by heart:

Yitgadal v'yitkadash sh'mei raba b'alma di-v'ra

She didn't know the English translation, but she knew what it meant.

Sasha forced herself out of bed and pulled up the light-cancelling shades in her bedroom the rest of the way, admiring how they folded back upon themselves like a thick fan. This small pleasure and her protected sleep made it worth the money. Not that money was a problem anymore, but she didn't want to be reckless. She stretched, breathing in and out with her arms, following her breath. This was supposed to align her energy for the day. Sasha knew this might be magical thinking, but there were synapses whirring through the human body, molecules rotating inside leaves and rocks and every particle of snow. An infinite pile of snow molecules this morning. She could tell by the grinding of snowplows twelve floors down, dropping enough salt to re-elect the mayor. One mayor lost an election following a bad cleanup, and now the city plowed at the first flake. This was the first big snowstorm of the year, coming late in February. It might only last for a few hours.

She walked over to the table that she was using as a desk—avoiding the lab and her former advisees when she had nothing to show for her Genie year. There was her yellow legal pad, covered with scribbles, the beginning of thoughts, nothing solid. Could she bullshit her way through the report this afternoon? There were people in her field who hated her for getting the Genie, the fancy apartment, the university chair she inherited when the Great White Male who preceded her finally passed into oblivion.

(That drooling skull of the former department chair pushed back his plate, snapped his jaws, and wiped what remained of his lips on his khaki pants. He knew it would turn out like this if they gave the physics prize to a woman, and wasn't she a bit overweight?)

Breathe. You are having thoughts, Sasha reminded herself. You are not your thoughts. You are having feelings. You are not your feelings.

Sasha forced herself not to touch the lump again. She had an excellent doctor, the surgery was scheduled, nothing else to be done. Today's problem was the brain, not the body. Could she reframe her existing research without revealing that she'd done nothing since she got the Genie? This was only something for their website, their donors—plus all the colleagues who hated her for winning and knew the difference between new and recycled ideas.

(Snap, snap, went the jaws.)

Screw them all. She was from Queens.

She would think of something, she always thought of something when she was up against the wall. All she had to do was trick her mind into thinking about something else. She often had her best ideas in the shower, eyes closed, water pouring down her back. Now all she did was raise an arm over her head to feel the lump under one breast, check the other one, then the lymph nodes under both arms.

Had she rejected the idea of reconstructive surgery too quickly? Her instinct was to have as little done to her as possible, remove the tumor and get out from under the knife. She would never wear a bra-like harness with silicone breasts built in, and wouldn't it be lovely to be free of bras for the rest of her life? She could order up a pair of smaller, younger breasts that hardly needed a bra. They would never sag or give her back pain. Who cared if they were a little too firm to the touch? She would become a runner like Cora, lean and strong. Cora would have wanted to know everything the doctor said, discussed all the possibilities including her dream titties, then gone with Sasha to the next appointment. Cora would have asked to touch the lump herself.

(You are having thoughts. You are not your thoughts. You are having feelings. You are not your feelings.)

Sasha walked over to the window that didn't let in a whisper of air unless she invited it. She watched the snow spin in the updraft from the river and considered gravity, wind, rate, and volume. She tried not to apply physics to every single thing she did, but she couldn't help how her mind worked.

"Let the world be," Val said once, annoyed by some botanical fact Sasha spewed out when they were walking under those flowering trees near the Hudson, dark-barked cherries turning the air pink for one week every spring. Sasha knew what Val meant but wasn't sure that she could do it.

Sasha's drive toward analysis had also been a problem with sex. Impossible to stop noticing the way bodies interacted, the swelling of nipples, penis, clitoris, the manner in which sweat glands, saliva and lubrication responded to arousal. Bodily facts rolled through her head like ticker tape. It was difficult for her to orgasm unless she did it to herself, always had been.

Oh well, that's what sex toys were for.

Sasha didn't feel too old for sex, at least not most of the time. Her dark brown hair was going gray, but she refused to dye it, and usually wore it up or in a braid. She liked her hair, gray or not. It was too curly to look good short, she had learned that years ago when she was trying to be more—what? More chic? More French? More everything she had never been. Thank God, that phase was over. She was Russian peasant stock on both sides, endurance built into her thighs and torso. Her breasts were still quite lovely in her opinion, steaming ahead into their final week before the double lop-off. Fuck reconstruction. She'd get a whole new wardrobe, be as cool as Angelina Jolie. As soon as her brain reported back for duty she would be all systems go, at the peak of her intellectual powers.

The Genie Zoom report was at four-thirty. She could chain herself to her desk until she thought of something intelligent to say, but wasn't that exactly what she had been doing for almost a year? When the prize was announced, Sasha's shock was matched by a sudden inability to feel anything other than gratitude for the check. She remained professional but detached through all the publicity, interviews, and that ridiculous ceremony. After, when she thought she'd finally get to work with an entire year's teaching obligations removed, there was nothing but silence. Five months of puttering and panic.

Then somewhere in the distance came the screech of taxi wheels. The phone rang.

"It's Cora."

"What? What's Cora?"

It was Lucretius with his curtain of atoms descending like rain until that one swerve, a chance moment altering everything that came after. Sasha believed in Lucretius more than God, but she wanted the unpredictable to stay where it belonged, in the lab.

For months, Sasha kept jotting down notes which led to nothing, then she reached up one morning to soap under her breast.

What had her meditation teacher told her?

See the job. Do the job. Get out of the misery.

But the misery of losing Cora? The misery of not being able to work? There was no surgery for this. Sasha loved her research, everything slotting into place when she was really onto something, when her writing became more and more illegible because her hand couldn't keep up with her brain. It was her favorite organ and she wanted it back.

If only they had sex toys for the brain. Maybe they do and it's called espresso. The reward for morning meditation.

She lit a candle, settled onto her cushion, and began repeating her mantra. In and out. In and out.

Thirty-five years was a long time.

lauren

High above the Atlantic on a night flight back from The Hague, noise-cancelled, sleep-masked, blanketed and wide awake, Lauren had no idea that the city was starting to shut down. The problem with cancelling the noise outside was that it only increased the noise inside her head. When her parents were getting ready to sell their apartment in the city, Lauren and her little sister, Diana, had to pack everything up for them before putting it on the market. Her parents lived in Westchester and called the Manhattan apartment their 'pied-a-terre,' which made Lauren clench her jaw, hard.

Taking glasses out of the cabinet, wrapping them in newspaper and drinking a cold Corona from the deli, Lauren found an envelope taped to the inside of one of the kitchen cabinets. *Where Everything Is*, written in her mother's sloping scrawl that Lauren had forged perfectly, writing notes to cut school. Yellowed tape crackled from each corner when Lauren took it down. Inside was a list:

The key to the safety deposit box
The spare apartment keys
The drawer with instructions for her and Daddy's memorial services (same drawer as the keys)
The bank account numbers
The will

There was the computer password so that Diana could search for a file called *Where Everything Is*. The next day at her parents' house, with Diana's two boys running wild and her father enraged at the dining room table, Lauren asked her mother if this envelope had always been there. She nodded as if it was obvious. Didn't everyone have an envelope taped inside the kitchen cabinet in the event of their death?

Diana had taken the envelope from Lauren and put it into her bright yellow folder. Typical Diana, who still assumed that Lauren would lose everything. She handled all their parents' bills and finances now that they had suddenly become old people. At least, her parents' aging felt sudden to Lauren. Diana could recite a monologue about it creeping up in many little ways over the last few years, but all this talk of parents and aging bored the shit out of Lauren.

I need a *Where Everything Is* envelope, thought Lauren, as she pushed up her sleep mask and opened the window shade to the speeding, invisible air.

The place where you will feel at home.

Your ability to love tucked into the back of the sock drawer.

The plane tilted and the night sky turned like a map of itself. The announcement began the beginning of their descent into New York, and the day rose up like a sleek glass tower. Morning meeting at The New York Historical, then mediation with Amy, home to their mocking renovation with the quartzite counters and stainless-steel refrigerator.

Why had they agreed to make everything cold and hard? Is that why they might be breaking up?

The lights of the city came up as the plane banked low over the Atlantic. She brushed the corners of her eyes, telling herself that the leaking was sleeplessness, not age or grief. As the ground appeared through the clouds, she saw the snow and her heart lifted automatically. Snow meant that she could take Masha sledding. Masha, her sweet girl that she bought stupid presents for in the airport gift shop. Her only uncomplicated love. She wished that she could have woken up at home this morning. Did Amy remember to tell Masha to put a spoon under her pillow for a snow day?

The plane bumped onto the tarmac and the sound of landing gear broke through her headphones as gravity took hold one more time.

She called as soon as the plane landed. It was early, but she knew that Amy would be awake, sitting with her hands wrapped around a mug of tea in the tender quiet before the children, the day, and Lauren herself, with her moods and ambition and lost patience. All she wanted right now was to lay her head on Amy's lap as she drank her morning tea.

"I just landed," she said into her phone, hoping that Amy would sound happy about this.

"Good. Was it an easy flight?"

Amy was never happy anymore. Why did Amy marry her? Lauren had never been able to fully love anyone until they had Masha. Even now, she was trying to hide her failure from Amy. She wanted to stay married.

"No snow day," Amy said. "I checked. It started last night, but they say it may taper off by the afternoon."

"Poor Masha," said Lauren.

"Poor us!" Amy said. "It would have been nice to have an excuse."

An excuse for what? Skipping mediation? Putting Masha in front of a movie and sneaking off to bed in the middle of the day? Lauren could distract her with sex if Amy would only give her the chance. Lauren wouldn't disappoint her in bed, but Amy's desire could no longer be assumed. What was that line in the Chekhov play? About the girl being like a locked piano? Lauren took Russian Literature when she was a senior at Harrison, and she forgot nearly everything but that one scene in *The Three Sisters*.

"She doesn't understand it herself," Mrs. Francelli had said. "She'll marry the baron but never love him. If she could only find that lost key, she could unlock herself."

"She can't find it because she stopped looking," said Lauren, who had read the part of Irina in class. Francelli stopped and considered her. Lauren had said something more insightful than expected from this sloppy, detached girl who always arrived late to class. It had been a small moment of triumph. Lauren never forgot that Chekhov scene. But who was Irina? Lauren or Amy? She still had her old copy of the play; she would reread it when she got home.

No, she wouldn't—Lauren was the locked piano, always had been. The gender roles momentarily fooled her into thinking that she was the baron. Lauren might be more butch than Amy, but she was the one who turned the key and locked the piano.

"Are you coming home or going straight to work?" asked Amy.

"I have a morning meeting, so straight to the office."

Coward. Coward. She could claim jet lag and skip the morning meeting, but if she arrived home after Amy left to drop off Masha at kindergarten, she might run into Ash (the pain in the ass formerly known as Shoshana), who woke late and almost never left the apartment. Even Amy was starting to wonder if her adult child would always circle back home. (Like Diana, Lauren pointed out needlessly.) Ash was Amy's child from her previous life, and of course there was nothing unusual about their twenty-something living at home after some failed attempts at jobs and roommates. Lauren couldn't care less what gender Ash was, and she had finally learned to say *they* every time, though she secretly thought all this anxiety about pronouns was a waste of time, even though it was a symbol of the patriarchy. Lauren didn't tell Amy that, of course. It would make her sound old, and she was already ten years older than Amy. Besides, the lesbian couple not accepting new pronouns wasn't exactly getting with the program.

Cora would have told Lauren to grow up and keep her mouth shut. Val and Sasha could laugh about it and tell her that she needed to ease up on Ash. She was so impatient with Ash and so patient with Masha. Was it biological? She had wanted to love Ash from the moment she saw them, but the years of hostility had worn her down. The last time she came home from a work trip, she could hear Ash and Masha dancing and singing to some Disney song through the door, Amy giggling as she took a video. When Lauren walked into the apartment, Ash stopped singing and left the room. Amy looked apologetic as Masha ran in for a hug. Lauren knew that she was supposed to be one of the adults, but all she wanted to do was bolt.

You're the problem, not Ash, Cora would say. Lauren could take it from her because Cora loved her with all her failings—and Cora told the truth.

Through the phone, she could hear Amy opening the refrigerator, the crackle of Masha's brown paper lunch bag they had drawn on together the night before. Stars and moons and witches. Masha wanted to be a witch when she grew up; she practiced flying in the hallway.

"She's not awake yet?"

"Not yet."

"And our thing is at noon?"

"Yes. I'll see you there, then."

Amy's voice lifted in the way it did when she wanted to get off the phone. No, stay here with me, Lauren thought, as the airplane lumbered toward the gate and the cabin lights revealed the worst of everyone.

"Give Masha a kiss for me. Tell her I'll pick her up after school, take her sledding."

"She has Girl Power after school, unless they cancel because of the snow."

"Oh, right. Well—"

"I'll see you at mediation."

Amy hung up. When did their conversations become mechanized? Lauren had wanted a child so much, and Amy finally said yes, even though she already had Ash. Lauren was convinced that Masha would knit them into a family. Instead, the baby split them into two separate triangles, with Amy at the apex of both. The Queen Mother. Did this make Lauren the Royal Consort? She liked that title a lot more than Evil Stepmother, but if she and Amy didn't have sex anymore, were they still lovers?

Masha changed everything, just not in the ways Lauren thought. She was utterly slain by this fully formed human with straight black hair who stared from one mother to the other, then wriggled up to Amy's milky breasts. Sweet water pearls that leaked into Lauren's mouth when she made love to her before they weaned the baby. They spent months choosing a sperm donor for this child who somehow looked like both of them, and now, after all that time, money, and effortful exchange of fluids, Masha was the only one who wasn't disappointed. Lauren had thought that having a baby would fix her, make her better for Amy. Why had she ever thought that Ash would learn to love her?

Lauren clicked off the phone and closed her eyes.

This reunion was such a bad idea. How could they have a class reunion without Cora? Even Amy thought that four months was too soon after Cora's funeral, and she was the nice one. The one with the ability to love them all.

cora

We didn't know it was snowing the night the Joypoppers played the eleven o'clock set at the Rainbow. By the time the gig was over, I'd been inside the club so long I forgot what outside air smelled like. Shahzad from Slaughterhouse Records had called to say he was coming down to hear the band, and even though he kept saying that and not showing up, I had a feeling this was the night. It was the perfect time slot for the band. Nobody wanted to be there before 10:00, and after 2:00 a.m. the players that mattered went home. Record execs have to get up in the morning even though 9:00 a.m. in New York is 6:00 a.m. in LA.

I kind of hated them even though I wanted to be them.

I spent all afternoon on the phone making sure that narrow bar with tippy tables was packed. It used to be a Ukrainian social club, and the room opened out into a linoleum dance floor. The Rainbow was our living room and we thought it would last forever—probably what the old school Ukrainians thought before it turned into a rock club. I miss that shitty back room with the plaid armchair and wooden table with cigarette burns striping the edges. I even miss the tiny bathroom with band stickers all over the walls and the seat left up because girls didn't matter. That night, I paid Chrissy out of my own pocket to get her to tend bar. She was a fan, knew the words to Val's songs, and could serve and sing at the same time. Plus, those arms, those eyes, those tits.

I told Lauren and Sasha to get there around 10:30. They knew how to make an entrance. Sasha teased her hair up into a cloud and wore fishnets under short shorts. Lauren always made you look twice in her Joypoppers T, high cheekbones and boy cut from the barber shop on Astor Place. They would rule the dance floor as long as Val was onstage.

Every single one of us was fucking gorgeous.

Slaughterhouse was where I wanted the Joypoppers to land, and my magnet was turned up so high Shahzad didn't have a chance. Val could tell I was hyped. She didn't want to be told when someone big was coming to a show, but she always knew. I told her to move "Like A Girl" to the top of the set list. Danny fought me on that, but I knew this was our hit single before it happened. I needed his guitar to knock it out of the room right from the start. Danny never liked me. He never forgot that one night I wouldn't fuck him when we had the chance. Now I wish I had. At twenty, he looked like Rimbaud, but he belonged to Val. She was the writer and he was the player. She was great on rhythm but couldn't do it without Danny playing lead. Her band, her boy. We all knew the rules and pretended there weren't any.

Shahzad walked in right when I wanted him to. Val's long bangs falling over that mouth we all wanted to kiss. "Fuck like a man and talk like a girl," she sang in that dreamy, driving chorus and every single person in the room knew what she was talking about. The dance floor was packed with Sasha down front, dancing only for Val. Lauren cruised the room and pulled some new babe into the whirlpool. I watched Shahzad tap his foot on the bar stool and signaled Chrissy to get him another top-shelf whiskey on the rocks. She sang along with the chorus as she pushed his glass across the bar and we had him. We had Slaughterhouse.

Val tipped over the mic stand in an almost ironic rock 'n' roll move, dark nipples showing through her lucky shirt. She pulled the mic closer so we wouldn't miss a word. Even I wanted her, and I'd already had her.

When the four of us finally tumbled out of the bar, it was snowing, and Shahzad had signed the band. Val lay down on her back in Tompkins Square Park to scrape an angel in the first thin layer of snow. When she got up, she pointed at me.

"You're the angel tonight."

"You did it, Val! Not me."

But she was right, and so was I. We walked through the park toward her apartment, snowfall like glitter. Next to one of the shuttered restaurants on First Avenue, a cardboard flat was left out on the sidewalk. Val put down her guitar case and brushed snow off the top of the box.

"Val! That's gross!" said Sasha. "The restaurant threw it out."

"I thought we were going to the Odessa," said Lauren.

"Look!" said Val, tipping up the front so we could see. "Raspberries."

There must have been twenty plastic boxes filled with berries, closed neatly and double-stacked.

"They must have dropped them when they were carrying them in," said Val. "Somebody grab my guitar."

We'd never had that many raspberries before. Back at Val's place, I smashed them into the bottom of our glasses, adding lemon juice, vodka, and snow from the fire escape. Sasha and Lauren made scrambled eggs and toast with raspberries. Val sat down at the piano, her fingers stained berry red, that natural spotlight pouring off her until the downstairs neighbors banged on their ceiling with a broom. Even the sky turned raspberry as the sun came up.

The Gods were smiling.

val

Val stayed in the park as long as she could, trying to feel lucky. The reunion was plowing toward her. No matter what Cora said, Val still had time to grow a carapace or back out at the last minute. She'd rather throw snowballs for Sheila and Bertie. When she said her usual goodbye to Juno inside his front hall, she let him keep licking her face until he whined and looked at her with eyebrows raised. He was right, she wasn't having a good day (oh, why couldn't she bring Juno home with her when he knew her best of all?). She closed the apartment door and locked it, cameras recording every move, talk radio the soundtrack for doggie solitude.

Juno, Sheila, and Bertie were the only creatures she didn't have to pretend to be happy for, and now she only had to remember three names instead of the twenty-five in her ear-training classes. She had liked her students at the community college, but every time Val walked into the classroom, she felt like a fraud. The has-been rocker teaching music as an adjunct, no tenure, no health insurance, too old to be the lowest of the low on the academic ladder. Students only took her class because they thought it sounded easy (it wasn't), or were biding their time before dropping their next song, which they figured would go viral and rocket them to stardom. When fame arrived, they told her, they wouldn't need to know how to sing on key.

That might be true. What did she know about auto-tune except that it was a fucking cop out?

But she loved the confidence in their beautiful faces and laughed with them as she led their vocal exercises with some of the notes she couldn't hit anymore except on the piano. She told them to imagine they were singing in an arc, that the windowpanes in the classroom were a ladder and they should place each note on one of the rungs, up and down. She told them that even in a big hall (and yes, she had played big venues, but they never asked) you can always find the exit sign at the back. Aim your voice at the exit, arc as high as the ceiling. In an outdoor venue, use the curve of sky to the horizon. The throat, jaw, and lungs are the three most important parts of your instrument, she told them. Vocal cords are the strings and your skull is the resonator. But they won't do you any good without ears.

Some of them worked hard and some didn't, some improved and some never really changed. You can't teach talent, one of her less than brilliant colleagues said, but what was talent? Val had the talent to crash back into her own outdated ideas of herself as soon as she woke up in the morning.

Val didn't decide to stop teaching; she simply never went back after the required faculty training session for live shooters on campus. It was her fifth year of adjunct teaching, and she had meant to keep her job, but couldn't help herself.

The auditorium was filled with faculty and staff on folding chairs because attendance at these sessions was required and you had to sign in, which meant the Dean's office was keeping track of names. Val thought signing in was a good idea for once. There were so many shootings now, at least the college was trying to respond. Tenured faculty still blew it off, but Val felt a surge of civic pride as she took her seat, until the security guard stood up to introduce the video.

He was the one who had walked up to Jamilla at the music department's graduation event and accused her of being drunk. Nobody was noticeably drunk and everyone was over twenty-one. Jamilla was the only person wearing a headscarf; she might also have been the only person there who didn't drink. Val intervened, and after she convinced the guard to walk away, Jamilla kept trying to reassure Val that she wasn't offended.

"This kind of shit happens all the time, let's celebrate graduation!" She tugged Val toward the dance floor.

Val went to the head of HR the next day, who nodded, registered Val's complaint, and nothing happened. Everyone knew the adjuncts were only there to keep the bottom feeder classes running. Now, this same security guard was telling people that school shootings were certainly a hard thing to think about, but best to be prepared and thank you for coming to this training session.

Val wanted to get up and leave, but she was afraid of the *pop pop* of gunfire down the hall. There were no closets in their classrooms. There were no locks on the classroom doors.

The video opened with the words: *RUN - HIDE - FIGHT*

A white man wearing sunglasses and a backpack walked into a campus building which looked eerily like the college. Why did everything look alike now? Even the actor looked like every other shooter she had seen on the news, but of course, that was the point. The dramatization had all the production value of bad porn.

Sometimes bad people do bad things, the voiceover droned. The man dropped his backpack, pulled out an automatic weapon, and started firing. Bodies fell to the floor. The BMCC auditorium was silent. Nobody leaned over to whisper to their neighbor or look at their phones as they did in the monthly faculty meetings.

This was the perfect place for a shooter to come right now, all of them seated in rows like metal ducks at a midway firing range. Irony didn't help. Val poured sweat.

RUN. Leave your belongings. Call 911. Run zig-zag away from the building. Do not scream or point.

Would she remember to run zig-zag?

HIDE. The campus buildings will be locked automatically when there is an active shooter.

If the doors were locked, how could anyone get out to run zig-zag? Val could feel her neck flushing that mottled red she hated. Hot flash or panic sweat? She curled her fingers around the bottom of her folding chair. People in the video who looked too much like the people in this room were running into a small office. They were pushing a desk in front of the door.

Turn off the lights. Silence your phone. Lock the door if possible. Be quiet.

The shooter wants the maximum number of kills. Stay silent. The bathroom is not a good choice.

It's not? She remembered hiding on top of the toilet at Harrison with Cora, locking the stall and pulling up their feet so it looked like nobody was there. Some dumb prank before there were any newsworthy school shootings.

Silence the vibration on your phone. Bury yourself.

FIGHT. Now the video showed a middle-aged man picking up a folding chair as the shooter burst through the door.

Improvise weapons.

Really? A folding chair? Like the ones they were sitting on right now?

Val didn't remember how she got out of the auditorium. The large, rectangular windows facing into the classrooms appeared to shatter as she walked down the hall, but the only sound was her own footsteps. She pushed open the door to the street and headed instinctively toward the river. The pedestrian walkway over the West Side highway was a dingy metal cage, enclosed all the way around to protect from the weather and discourage jumpers, though jumping from a low bridge into a traffic snarl at the base of Manhattan was a highly ambiguous choice.

You want to make sure it works, Val thought, walking above the honking cars. That's when Val knew she wasn't going to teach anymore. She didn't want to die inside a utility closet that smelled like bleach.

Stepping off the bridge into Battery Park City felt like leaving Manhattan. A private nurse pushed a woman with a stricken gaze along the sidewalk in a wheelchair, swathed to the chin in a beige fur jacket. Even the flowers planted in beds around the trees grew to the exact same height. It was a public area, but you could feel the surveillance. Doormen, security guards, cameras. The people who lived here paid high maintenance fees and the sidewalks were emptier than most city blocks.

She walked by an enclosed cement dog run, where a uniformed man was hosing down the floor. Two tennis balls, one green, one orange, bobbled in the stream of water, trapped against a chain link fence. Dogs would have to skid to a stop before they hit the end of the run. A dog walker opened the gate and unleashed two Corgis. Not Val's favorite breed, but it wasn't their fault they looked rich and stupid. They were so happy to be off the leash, circling and sniffing the wet tennis balls. She wished they could dig their claws into dirt under those well-trimmed rhododendrons, but at least they were outside.

She quit BMCC that afternoon and made about the same money as a dog walker for the rich, off the books. It was a relief to be back outside the system, and she didn't miss the students as much as she thought she would. Teaching had been a performance and she was good onstage, but she didn't have to convince the dogs of anything.

Then Cora died, and Val couldn't bear to be with anyone except the dogs.

When the new year flipped, the Joypoppers showed up in some annual roundup of influential bands from the eighties. There was going to be a show in a Lower East Side gallery, with archived video from one of their gigs. It was good, it was something, it might lead to some press about the band. It was only a little storefront gallery on Orchard Street, but that was still a hip neighborhood, a little past its prime, but who wasn't? At least somebody cared about the Joypoppers. She hadn't told Lauren and Sasha about the show yet—what if they were the only ones there? Danny acted like it was no big deal, he might or might not make it to the opening, and she pretended to agree. But she knew that she would go with or without him, and if anyone asked, the answer was yes, she was still writing songs.

Reasons to live.

sasha

Sasha peeked at her Insights timer while she meditated. There suddenly seemed like a lot to do for the party, even though she had hired a caterer, plus her two favorite grad students to serve drinks and clear plates away as needed. Maybe some people wouldn't come because of the storm and then she would have ordered too much food. She had to pick up the flowers. Check the weather. Is this all that remained? Repeating lists of errands? Was she simply too old? Was that what the Genie was here to show her? Never was so much fought over so little, as her PhD advisor used to say. Prizes are meaningless and hateful; there should be a ban on all prizes!

I am feeling angry, I am feeling sad. I am not my anger. I am not my sadness.

Sasha was relieved when the timer went off, told herself that it counted even when she felt less relaxed after meditation, put on her white terry robe, and walked into the living room. It still surprised her that she actually had an apartment overlooking Riverside Park. The snow was turning the branches of the elms into a photograph of New York City. This was why she loved this apartment. She had held out for it when the university offered her other places without the view, and when Cambridge tried to steal her away, they caved. So much green in spring and summer, small ice floes moving steadily past the Jersey shoreline in winter. She had gotten more of what she wanted than she ever thought she could. Her mother and father were gone before they could see it happen. No kids, no husband, but Sasha had tenure, she had the prize, and they could never take the apartment away. She always pictured her parents' escape from Europe as a lithograph she had seen of children being lowered from the side of a boat onto a raft in the middle of the ocean. Now, Sasha was living twelve floors up in a doorman building overlooking the river, courtesy of Columbia University.

Sasha pressed her forehead against the window, murmuring something that could have been a prayer if she knew any. Her parents left the shtetl and religion behind when they landed in New York via London, and Sasha knew no Hebrew, just an inarticulate yearning that rose up now and then. She gave thanks to the building, the treetops, the lampposts, and even the snow that might ruin her dinner. It felt like a kiss, and why not? Sasha pressed her lips to the glass then wiped it clean with her sleeve. This was why she liked living alone. She leaned her forehead against the window and closed her eyes, cool and damp.

Twenty-four people coming tonight, not bad out of a class of fifty. Some would blow it off because of the weather, and there were the former classmates who simply disappeared from the list. Not everybody who passed the test to get in had the slightest affection for Harrison.

The acting secretary of the alumni association had pestered Sasha with texts about the RSVPs to the reunion dinner.

hi Sasha 😊 *have you heard back from Sydney Harris or Louisa St. John?*

nope

OK just let me know, we're reaching out 🙏

Sasha didn't bother to reply to the embedded racism in "reaching out" to the only two Black girls in their class. What could Sasha know about what Harrison was like for Louisa or Sydney? She hadn't known either of them well at school, and they weren't the only ones who never responded to the class emails that grew more frequent as their generation's parents began to die off. The school was trying to respond to long-overdue charges of racism from current and former students, too little too late, and littered with missteps more public than a text to Sasha. When the alumni board asked Sasha to be on the committee to address racial injustice, she said no. She had to attend to her own racist institution, thank you very much.

Other than Miss Pierce (who changed her life), Harrison paid no attention to Sasha before the Genie. Weighing in on the new science labs was as far as her loyalty stretched beyond this dinner party. Thank

God the gyre was widening. Let the twenty-first century slouch toward Harrison and swallow it whole.

Of course, she would never have learned the Yeats if she hadn't gone to Harrison.

Plus Cora, Val, and Lauren.

Was it unusual that only one of the girls in their class had died? Sasha had two other friends who died early (cancer both times). But Cora was the only one from their year, one of those nightmare deaths that frightened everyone because it was so easy to imagine a bike accident in the city. Sasha had her own private list: heart attack in a public place, trapped in a fire, pushed in front of a subway train. Sasha knew that it would have been worse for Cora if she lived, given what happened to her spine. What was Cora thinking, biking at night in the rain without a helmet? Probably had a few drinks, though nobody talked about it. Poor Cora. Stupid Cora! Her stupid, reckless ego, still pretending she was in her twenties. All her own fault.

And why had Cora ghosted Val those last few months? Sasha would never understand it. And now Cora was a real ghost. Whatever Val said to Cora, was it really so terrible that she had to stop speaking to her? Val could be exhausting and Cora had a mean streak. Plus, they were both in the music business, which was more like a nasty clubhouse than a business. Just like academia, Cora used to say, but with more money and better music. All Cora told her about the break was that Val had asked for one too many favors. Cora was Val's first manager, then she moved up the corporate ladder and dropped Val and the band. Val was pissed off at first, but the Joypoppers were still hot and everyone was on the rise. Val had gone through a few managers since then, jazzed and hopeful every single time—and who knows how these things work? It was depressing to see someone as good as Val playing singer/songwriter open mics after another band broke up, hard to laugh at her desperate, cheerful banter between songs. Cora was defensive and Val was fragile. Their vectors moved in opposite directions.

Still.

"I just can't deal with Val right now," Cora had said to Sasha last summer. "I'm taking a break." Then she changed the subject.

At the time, it was impossible to push Cora about it. Truth? Sasha was scared to push. Cora got Val her first record deal back in the day, but she never held back. If she thought one of Val's songs wasn't any good, she'd shrug. "It's fine." Or she'd say it to Val's face and watch her crumble. When Sasha asked Val, she'd say at least Cora was honest, and they should take that song off the set list. But even after she got married and bicoastal, Cora was the one who made sure they knew about Val's gigs and pushed Sasha and Lauren to choose a night for them all to go together; share a car service home from Bushwick on the company dime.

Val was completely undone by the accident. They all were, but Val most of all. Cora hadn't spoken to Val for months, then came this swerve in the fundamental order and Cora was deleted, wiped clean from the face of the earth.

Rage couldn't touch the gap of grief.

cora

I want to tell Sasha that everything will be all right, but even the dead can't see the future.

On her first day at Harrison, Sasha was the new girl and Mr. Anderson put her desk next to mine in those four-desk squares that were supposed to help us work "independently together" or something. It took until the first snow day for us to become friends. It's not like I hadn't noticed that she got all the questions right, especially in math. I wanted to keep sitting next to Sasha so I could copy the answers; I could tell she wasn't going to rat me out. When school let out early because of the storm, I thought I'd try being friendly to the new girl.

She was standing in those dumb snow boots in the lobby, looking like she didn't know what to do if school got out before 3:20.

"Want to come to the park?" I asked.

Sasha's face got all scared and thrilled and I knew we could do whatever we wanted with her. Val and Lauren were coming over since I lived close to school. I might have wanted to scare her, show the new girl who's boss. Even the teachers said our names in a chant: Cora, Val, and Lauren. I loved it. I used to string them together in my head as one name, Miss Cora ValandLauren, like the old Dutch colony names we had to learn in social studies. Val gave me a look when I invited Sasha along, but it was my house, so I was the decider. Lauren acted like she didn't care, which meant she cared the most. We left our backpacks at my apartment and went to the park, the twins slowing us down as usual. Mom always made me bring them even though they were only eight and a total pain in the butt.

"The snow is almost never deep enough for Dead Man's hill," Val said.

We ditched the boys on the baby hill with their dumb friends. We were younger than anyone else sledding on Dead Man's. All those loud teenagers, boys landing hard on their stomachs and girls who went in seated doubles. We didn't know how the lineup worked, but we acted like we were supposed to be there. It was all Val's idea.

"You go first," I said, shoving Sasha in front of me. Now, I'm sorry I did it, but I was scared to go down, and it was easy to be mean to her before I knew her. Did Val ever write a song called "Easy to be Mean"? She should. Dedicate it to me in memoriam. I could be mean, but I'm loyal.

"Are you good at sports?" I asked. Sasha shrugged, holding onto the sled rope and looking at the ski jumps the big kids had built up, everybody screaming over the bump. Now the park puts hay bales in front of the trees on the big hills, but nobody paid attention back then. Lauren held onto the back of the sled runners as Sasha lay down on her stomach, hands gripping the steering bar.

"Ready?"

I didn't hear Sasha say anything, but Lauren pushed her off and the sled slammed down the hill, then lifted over the first jump. She landed hard, but she was doing it! She steered around the big tree, heading straight for a park bench and shot underneath, slamming into that cyclone fence at the bottom, tossed back like a trampoline. The sled glided to a stop. Sasha didn't move. I started running down the side of the hill. "I killed her!" I yelled, slipping and falling in the snow. It was all my fault that she was dead.

When I got there, Sasha was lying completely still. Was there blood anywhere? Then her eyes popped open. "We've got bigger hills in Queens."

I stood there feeling like an asshole until she started laughing, cheeks bright red. "I'm kidding. I just thought it sounded good 'cause you don't know anything about Queens."

She handed me the sled rope and marched right up the side of the hill while I tried to keep up, yanking my steed behind us by its rope bridle. Sasha always thinks it's the other way around with me, but she's the one who sees windmills in the invisible air. I'm the company manager pulling a pack mule along the rocky trail, making campfires and counting heads.

The dinner's going to be great tonight. I can't wait to see everyone and I'm hungry all the time now. Not really fair since my body has left the building, but I'm going to take what I can get. Sasha's still sweating and eating and shitting and pissing, even if her beautiful breasts get thrown into a metal pail and she never sees them again. She should make herself cum more, really. Who cares?

I wish I could still make her laugh, but what I really want to tell her is that everything will be okay. Her breasts will drop away and her brain will unlock. There will be time to forget what it's like to be inside her skin right now.

sasha

Sasha turned away from the window overlooking the park and circled the living room, though there was nothing to clean. She had built a long seat over the radiators; the upholstery was dark red with blue patterns that picked up the colors of her Turkish rug. Tonight, people could sit along the window seat, her favorite place to read. She moved her framed photo of the four of them to a more central place on the low bookshelves. Val, Cora, Sasha, and Lauren, arms around each other on a park bench, each of them unironically happy about getting their picture taken. Sasha ran her finger along the top of the silver frame. *If you live alone and have a cleaning person once a week, there's no dust*, her mother would say.

The photo might upset Val, and she didn't want to rub it in her face, but Cora should be seen tonight.

Most of these people hadn't been in the same room since the funeral.

Sasha made her green shake and drank it down while the radio delivered its daily report. First came the snowstorm, then another murder of an unarmed Black man by the police, two mass shootings. She turned the radio off, decided that was irresponsible and turned it back on. It was impossible to tell if anyone was really in charge of the government.

Sasha needed to get outside as quickly as possible. There is something wrong with me, she thought. It's the end of the world and I still want to buy wine and flowers. Matter cannot be destroyed or created, she chanted silently as she pressed the elevator button. It was too late to cancel the dinner or the report. Her work with quantum cognition theory had already made its way into the world. According to the prize committee, it could be a key to one of the locked rooms humanity had built around itself, and the powers that be would have to settle for that.

One door, one key, it might be the best she could do.

Sasha saw herself standing at the doorsill of this one imagined room, clutching her precious key while a whole series of other rooms tumbled off into smoke and air. The west coast was on fire; the polar ice was melting. What did one idea matter, even if there was a prize for it? She had given most of the Genie money away to climate change research as quickly as possible. The money made her feel guilty. She had a good retirement fund, no children, and her parents were dead. The only purpose of the prize was to make her forever indispensable to the university. She bought herself a very expensive dress to wear to the ceremony. She felt like a paper cut out when she gave her speech, but what had she expected?

Besides.

It was thrilling to win.

She mentioned Miss Pierce in her remarks, along with her parents and MIT. She knew that being seen by Cora and Miss Pierce, truly seen for the first time in her life, had started the internal clockwork of her theory, what civilians called psychological physics, classical physicists called bullshit, and Silicon Valley called the holy grail. The tech bros wanted probability theory applied to human behavior—if you could use theoretical physics to predict what might make a person reach for their wallet, there was money to be made. Real money, as people who already had money liked to say.

None of that had been the goal of Sasha's research, who still called physics the Invisible World, because that's what Miss Pierce called quantum mechanics in eleventh grade. The Invisible World was what made Sasha kiss the window. But hadn't she always wanted to win that prize? Be officially named one of the best of the best?

(Snap, snap, went the department chair's drooling jaws.)

Today was Saturday. Her double mastectomy was scheduled for next Friday. Another perfect excuse to put off the committee report, but she wasn't going to use it. Would a man think about this if he had prostate cancer? He wouldn't hesitate to get another extension. Not Sasha. Her body was none of their damn business. Sasha stepped into the elevator, glad it was empty. She didn't want to make small talk with a neighbor walking a dog; she found it so much harder to concentrate these days.

What was it about her secret obsession with unlocking the clockwork of the human brain? It could all be jibber-jabber, or it could be a new pathway through the labyrinth, her hands running over stones laid in a grid below the surface, holding onto a filament pouring out of her core like a spider. Arachne, Ariadne, marking a path from monster to daylight. She kept her seventh-grade paperback of Greek mythology in the stack on her bedside table for comfort reading in the middle of the night, next to a bottle of CBD sleep gummies. Only a Harrison girl would reach for the Gods with their familiar jealousies and foolishness, not to mention sex and violence. She caught herself smiling at her own reflection in the elevator door. All this nostalgia welling up before the reunion even began.

Ridiculous!

She was going to come through this surgery lopped but cancer free, and then her brain would reboot. She had recently listened to a podcast that advised everyone to spend some time every day meditating upon their mortality, so she was right on schedule. Hadn't there been an article somewhere about your fifties being the most creative time after your twenties? She would have to look it up.

lauren

In the car Lauren took into Manhattan, the driver took surface roads through Queens and Brooklyn, driving carefully on the plowed streets below the highway. Low buildings with scrap yards half covered by corrugated green plastic were slowly changing shape beneath the heavy snowfall. The driver took his time. They chatted a bit about the weather. He was from the Cote D'Ivoire and indulged her when she asked if they could speak French instead of English. After all those years in French class, Lauren could just manage to hold a conversation. Only Harrison would have pushed French more than Spanish, though her sister had told her the school finally added Mandarin and Arabic.

Lauren and Amy agreed from the start that Masha would never go to Harrison.

The driver had been in New York for eighteen years. He went back to Abidjan once a year to visit family. When she asked which city he preferred, he shrugged.

"I'll move back when I'm ready to retire."

I'll never retire, Lauren thought. They'll have to force me out. She had spent her whole working life at The New York Historical Society, starting as an unpaid intern. She was at the helm when they knocked "society" off the title. When her friends spoke about retirement she pretended not to hear them. There had already been too many times in her life when the only thing keeping her going was work, and if Amy really left her—

No.

She would never stop working, but she got out of breath tugging her roller bag up the slippery steps to The New York Historical, gripping the iron railing hard with her other hand. She had to stop and rest inside the vestibule. It took a minute for her eyes to adjust to the dim interior. She was fine, the snowstorm had slowed everything down, that's all. Lauren's assistant, Naomi, whose flawlessness she didn't quite trust, covered for her in the meeting after Lauren said something about jet lag. This worked for now, when all she could think about was the clock marching steadily toward mediation with Amy. She wished she still smoked.

She felt her watch vibrate with WhatsApp messages from the Netherlands as snow kept falling past the large windows of the conference room. What time was it in The Hague? Yesterday, she had been deep in the Dutch archives of the first colonial settlement of New York, working with a translator, choosing which papers they would ask the Dutch government to loan for an exhibit that was still two years away. She forced herself not to check her smart watch. She was the one who had forbidden phones on the conference table during a meeting. Pointless, really, since you couldn't exactly tell people to take off their watches.

She tried counting her breaths. Focus. Work.

"Go ahead and leave early today if you need to," said Lauren as the staff meeting came to a close. "Because of the storm."

Everyone looked surprised.

"Oh, we're closing early," Naomi said quickly. "Thank you all for coming in despite the weather."

"Right. Of course, thank you," said Lauren.

She hadn't remembered the Slack message about closing early due to weather, though Naomi would have framed it as if the decision came from Lauren. Had she approved it? Probably. She had no idea. From the conference room window the snow looked like static on an old black-and-white television screen. Lauren was the only person in the room old enough to know what that looked like.

She decided to walk all the way downtown to the mediation appointment in Tribeca. She could leave her carry-on in her office, pick it up tomorrow. She had her boots and the exercise would calm her. She was still hoping these sessions with Amy would transform from an exit ramp to a portal, but mostly, she hated everything about it. She wasn't as tired now that the meeting was over, the coffee and pastries that Naomi ordered had helped. Lauren walked everywhere, long walks after Masha was asleep or early departures from work to give herself time to grab a drink at the downstairs bar. Amy knew that exercise kept her wife from turning into a monster with three heads, but Lauren logged more miles than she used to. The apartment she already thought of as Amy's had become unbearable. Was it really because of Ash or was it the way Amy looked at her now? What would her own place look like if it came to that? A one- or two-bedroom for her and Masha, somewhere near her new school. Maybe one of those high rises with a balcony facing the East River. Would a balcony be safe with a small child? What about the nights when she didn't have Masha? She had lived on take-out before she met Amy.

Some tourists were taking selfies with the statue of Alexander Hamilton in the lobby, gun raised for his final duel. They had braved the snow to get here and now it was closing early. Lauren reminded herself to smile at them. The Broadway musical was good for their brand and some of the tourists even stayed to look at the exhibits. She liked this statue more than before. He was a workaholic who didn't deserve his wife and loved his children, just like her.

Lauren zipped her coat up tight, glad she brought it on the trip, though Northern European rain was nothing like this snowstorm. Black umbrellas pulled people along as if the umbrellas were running the show, lifting, flipping, popping inside out, crows with metal ribs wheeling down the sidewalk. All these bodies, cars, buses, and umbrellas performed their own choreography as the snow kept shaking down. What a glorious hassle. Lauren walked down Central Park West and veered left onto Sixth Avenue, past one of the upscale malls invading the city, a two-story green space set behind glass. People were drinking coffee, speaking into their phones. Some were collapsed onto the small metal cafe tables, head down on crossed arms as if they were enduring a long flight.

Two men played chess, a slow moving, live-action window display. The girls used to play checkers in the park after school, nickels versus dimes. Sasha almost always won, Cora was wildly competitive, and Lauren tried not to care. Val passed a joint of pot mixed with tobacco because she really didn't care. According to Val's cousin, that was how they smoked pot in Amsterdam. Getting high made Lauren feel even more disengaged than usual, but going home meant Diana practicing her pirouettes in the living room while her mother dropped the needle on the same track from *The Nutcracker* again and again. Diana would beg Lauren to push her leg up toward her ear as she stood on one foot with her back pressed against the doorframe. She nagged until Lauren did it, holding her breath against the cloying, chalky smell of her sister's tights and leotard. Diana didn't really have the right body for ballet, but their parents insisted she could do anything. Maybe this was Diana's problem: she was good at too many things. Lauren didn't take any after-school classes except for Hebrew School, and exited stage left after her bat mitzvah.

She was an escape artist by thirteen, pockets stuffed with twenty-dollar bills from the cash drawer her parents kept in the kitchen to cover tips and babysitters. If the mall at Columbus Circle had been there when Lauren was a teenager, she would have ended up under those fake hedges trained against a sheer wall. Most of the people sitting inside had too many bags gathered around their feet to be passing through. How full did these new spaces get in a storm, and where did people go when they were kicked out? There seemed to be a hive-mind acceptance that the hundreds of people sleeping, eating, and overseeing their children's homework in the subway cars might as well ride all night, though savvy New Yorkers avoided the cars which smelled too strongly of survival, empty even at rush hour. People were mostly silent about this, as they were silent about the dogs on the subway who were getting larger and more frequent. No longer kept in dog carriers, they trotted right under the turnstiles. Lauren was fairly certain she had seen a timber wolf on the D train.

When Lauren arrived at the mediator's office, a third-floor walk-up she resented for the money she was paying to walk through the door, Amy was already in the small waiting room. If things were good with them, they would have joked that this was the antechamber to hell.

Amy's long, silver hair fell over her cheeks, concealing the side of her face. Amy hadn't changed that much in seven years. Long legs, no makeup, an expensive, oversize sweater, and snow boots. These were the cumulative symbols of Amy: practical, fragile, and sturdier than she looked. Lauren wanted to peel everything off her in a room that nobody else was allowed to enter. She wanted to say *let's get out of here, legal mediation is just a code word for divorce. No matter what, this woman will convince us that we're never going to make it.* Instead, she hurried out of her coat, brushing off the snow and blathering on about the weather and her flight until Teresa opened the door to her office and they walked over to her familiar couch, placing themselves carefully on the green upholstery. They had recently transitioned from couples therapy to legal mediation. It was confusing because Teresa was licensed for both. Lauren was sure it was a scam, but Amy loved Teresa.

"You've just had some time apart," Teresa said.

"Five days," said Lauren, at the same moment that Amy said, "a week."

Amy was right, of course, if you counted the travel days. Oh, how to live up to the person who was always right?

"I told Lauren that I needed more responses to my texts when she was traveling, and—"

"I did! It was the time difference—"

"You still don't get how lonely it is with the kids. I've started letting Ash bring their phone to the table."

"We talked about that. When I'm home—"

"When you're home, Ash doesn't come to the table."

"But if you let them stare at their phone all the time, you're just giving up, letting them bully you."

Teresa held up her hand. "I think we were talking about Amy's need for more contact when you're away, Lauren."

"We had contact! I was texting you all the time, it's—"

"Six hours ahead. I know."

Apparently, Teresa wasn't going to fill the silence.

"I feel like I live alone, when I actually live with my wife and children," said Amy. "If I *did* live alone—with the kids, I mean—I wouldn't mind so much."

"And what about you, Lauren?"

Lauren hated Teresa's voice, especially now. So phony. As if she cared.

"I don't want to live alone," Lauren said. "We have a daughter. Two children, I mean. I want to live with my family. I only travel for work."

Amy looked at Lauren as if she didn't quite know who she was anymore, and Teresa's impatience grew more obvious. It was Lauren's trust fund and higher salary that made it possible for them to raise a child and scaffold a young adult in New York, while Amy freelanced. Why did none of this seem to matter?

Amy looked down. "I want a separation."

Why was Lauren the only one surprised?

"What's the difference between separation and divorce?" Lauren asked. Teresa seemed to be answering her, but nothing made sense.

"Amy? We don't have to do this. I have to see Masha!"

"Nobody is going to stop you from seeing your daughter," said Teresa.

"You're throwing me out? Is this what you're doing, Amy? It's my home, too!" Lauren was on her feet, watching herself shout like her father.

"We are only talking about taking a break to feel what it's like to live separately," Teresa said. "Isn't that right, Amy?"

Amy nodded, unable to speak.

"Lauren, please sit down," Teresa said.

Lauren sat, legs trembling.

"Masha needs me to come home."

Amy wouldn't look at her. The rest of the session blurred into a dull roar of tissues and appeasement, then they were in the downstairs lobby of Teresa's building.

"It's just a trial separation," Amy said.

"I don't like either of those words."

"Me neither."

"I want to come home."

"It's just for a little while."

"Really?"

"I think so. I don't know."

"Fuck therapy and mediation, you know?" Lauren reached out for Amy's hands, her fingers lay between Lauren's palms like sleeping birds. "Let's go on a trip instead, somewhere warm with snorkeling and hammocks, just the two of us, your pick. This separation is all Teresa's idea. We don't have to do it."

"It's not."

"What's not?"

"It's not all her idea."

And Lauren was flattened by the girl she loved standing there with her eyes on the floor. Lauren had failed her like she knew she would. If she let Amy have whatever she wanted, would she let her back in?

"I don't need anything from home." Lauren was determined to speak quietly. "I left my suitcase at the office. I can sleep there, or get a hotel."

"What about the reunion?"

"What?"

"Isn't the class dinner tonight? At Sasha's?"

"I don't give a shit about the reunion." Lauren was not the kind of person who cried in the entrance to a building.

"You should stay over at Sasha's tonight."

"I didn't come home for the reunion. I came home because I live here, with you and Masha."

Amy's eyes flicked, "And Ash."

"And Ash. Amy, listen—"

Amy walked out the door while she was still talking.

Lauren leaned against the plaster wall next to the mailboxes and covered her face with her elbow.

She was surprised by how much the lobby echoed.

cora

It's like the night of the hurricane, when Lauren lived on East Seventh Street and people all over the city put big Xs on the windows with masking tape. Only now I'm putting my body in the shape of an X right here in the lobby. I'm with her in the walls and the mailboxes and the echo.

Strength and endurance training are my thing. Lauren's windows will hold.

I think the hurricane was in August, 1980-something. We were trying to do what they said on the radio, on TV, at the bodega on the corner, but it seemed like such a joke. If there was a hurricane strong enough to blow out all the windows in New York City, would masking tape save us? The hardware stores ran out, and Lauren asked me to bring some over—my super had extra. That's why all the hardware stores were out, because of the supers. When she opened the door and saw me with a roll of masking tape slung over each wrist, Lauren looked both ways and pulled me inside the building.

"You could get mugged for those."

I followed her up four flights to that tiny apartment she shared with Angela, and when she pushed the door open, I saw why she really wanted me to come over. Boxes half full of books and clothes were all over the bed.

"Angela's keeping the apartment," she said.

"Ah. Shit." Lauren was the only one who thought it would last forever with Angela, but I wasn't about to tell her that. "Let's go out on the fire escape," I said.

We smoked cigarettes as spindly trees whipped green below our feet.

I counted how many windows were taped up across the street while she told me that Angela was doing some showcase in LA, and Lauren thought she was too busy to call until she found the love letters on rice paper with a beautifully inked red stamp in the corner. Angela was sloppy. Her name and address were written in calligraphy on the envelopes.

"Calligraphy? For real?"

"And it's a guy! Can you believe it? They're playing opposite each other, of course. I thought, since it was a man—"

"How come she gets the apartment?"

"Both of our names are on the lease and I've got more money. I can afford to move but I can't do it, Cora. I thought I was so good at leaving, but this time—"

"You can stay at my place."

"I love her."

"Really? Do you really, Lauren?"

The expression on her face almost made me wish I hadn't said that. Almost. Somebody had to say it, but what do I know about love? I handed her another cigarette and crawled back through the window into the apartment. "Should've brought packing tape instead of masking," I said, loud enough for her to hear over the wind. "I'm calling Val and Sasha."

"No, don't."

Val came over with a joint and Sasha brought two bottles of red wine. We packed and Lauren smoked on the fire escape until the wind started tipping over the metal barrels on the corner, spinning trash into tiny tornadoes.

"Like I need another metaphor!" Lauren yelled.

Val stuck her head out the window. "Get in here, we need your help."

Lauren came in from the fire escape and we drank all the wine.

"Angela's got some tequila under the sink," she said.

Sasha shook her head. "We never liked her."

"You loved it when she came to your gigs," Lauren said to Val, who was lying on the bed, looking like a rock star with spiky hair and Viva Glam lips. We were smoking inside now because Angela hated the smell. "You told me to bring her every time."

"Only to make you happy. Plus, she's a great dancer, looks good to have her down front."

Val tapped her ash onto the bedspread Lauren was leaving behind.

"She looks real good down front," I said, grabbing my own tits, then Val got up from the bed and we started grinding like cartoon characters. Val banged her crotch against my ass with her hands on my hips, moaning loudly.

"Stop!" Lauren said. She was lying on the floor between the moving boxes on that nice yellow rug she paid too much for when she and Angela were first playing house. I didn't want Angela to keep the rug.

"I love her!"

"Oh, shut the fuck up. You love *us.*"

Lauren grabbed the bedspread and wrapped herself up in it. She was trying not to smile under there, I knew it. Oh Lauren, my sweet drama queen, so hard to believe this was us in our youth.

We rolled up the rug, used all the masking tape, and sat in that living room for the last time, watching the sky turn mauve. Nobody's windows blew out. Thirty years gone and I still want to pull the blanket off Lauren's head and tell her this is love, right here, right now. She's always had a bolting problem. She needs to be with Sasha and Val tonight. Go back to Amy if she can. I'm here. Not here. Here.

lauren

Lauren walked blindly uptown, knowing only that she had to get out of this neighborhood. Should she have followed Amy? She was such a coward. The snow began to fall again as she crossed West Broadway, whooshing taxis and black cars churning through icy gray pools on every corner. Did Amy mean it? Was she giving Lauren exactly what she wanted? Cora had warned her not to push Amy to choose between her and Ash.

"The parent will always choose the child," Cora said. "Ash will grow up eventually, and what will happen to Masha?"

"Maybe I'm happier with my daughter than my wife." This was the week before Cora's accident, when they met at an Irish pub near Lauren's apartment. She liked the dark wood bar with a jar of pickled eggs next to an old-fashioned plastic box stocked with olives, lemons, limes and pearl onions. The bartender was friendly but didn't talk too much. The rest of the bars in her neighborhood were for the Wall Street types and closed early.

"Kids grow up," Cora said. "They leave."

Cora pulled out her company card and nodded to the bartender. She scrawled her signature and left a big tip. Every drink was a meeting for Sony, but it was hard for Cora to go out as much since her job got so big and she married the most boring man on earth. Cora liked saying, "I gotta be with Jeff and the kids," more than Lauren liked hearing it. Why wasn't she bored? But her stepchildren loved her, and Jeff wasn't going to leave her or fuck around like the usual assholes she picked. Once she hit her forties, Cora decided to get married to a Suit. What was surprising about that?

"Don't let Ash get to you so much," Cora said, when she leaned in for their goodbye hug.

"She's lost in her twenties, just like we were."

"They," Lauren corrected.

"*They* will get easier," Cora said. "And Amy is the best."

Were those the last words Cora said to her? Lauren still had some voicemails that she couldn't erase or listen to. The only person Lauren hadn't disappointed was Masha, and even that was debatable. Lauren had walked home from the bar that night knowing she'd missed Masha's bedtime again. She told Amy that her dinner with a board member went late, which wasn't a total lie, since Cora was now on the board of The New York Historical. Amy liked Cora, but it was easier to lie.

"Most people choose fight or flight," Amy had said when they first started couples therapy. "You choose both."

Amy volunteered for the Audubon society every anniversary of 9/11. The huge spotlights streaming upward from the site were beautiful until you got close. September was migration season and thousands of birds were drawn into the beams, mostly songbirds and fledglings that circled endlessly, disoriented by the blue-white light. Until the volunteers started counting them, it was impossible to know how many tiny corpses fell to the street, swept up by maintenance men the next morning, or dragged away by urban predators. Amy was part of a team that counted birds in shifts all night long. As soon as they reached 1,000, or if even one bird fell from the sky, the lights were turned off for twenty minutes so the birds could find their way south again. Amy told her that from the ground the birds looked like insects fluttering around a porch light. In the video she showed Lauren, birds showed up on film as white streaks across a bar of blue light. They seemed to be falling up instead of tumbling down to an island of fill dirt as thin as icing. Lauren had taught Masha never to walk on the metal sidewalk grates that exhaled hot air, a New Yorker's terror of the whole thing giving way.

When Lauren hesitated about living downtown, near the site, at the conflux of two tidal rivers that would eventually fill the mouth of the city, Amy only shrugged. "People live in Venice, we might be dead by then."

She's still so young, Lauren had thought, though their ten-year age gap didn't feel like much when they first got together. Amy had left Minneapolis for a graphic design job in New York without telling the man she barely knew that she was pregnant at twenty-two. After Ash was born, she got in touch to reassure him that he didn't have to be involved. She did everything on her own before she met Lauren. She and Lauren got married in a hot rush, flying out to San Francisco when gay marriage first became legal. Big gestures at a new life.

Lauren didn't know that Ash would become their own twenty-something tidal estuary, flooding back and forth every few months, carrying garbage bags stretched with rage and dirty laundry. She hadn't expected Amy's helplessness in the face of her child's anger; she hadn't expected her own failure as a step-parent. Lauren started booking more work trips and ate alone at the pub, covering her tracks as if she was having an affair, wondering for the first time what she might do if the opportunity came along. One night, when Amy was out and Lauren was putting Masha to bed, a backpacked kid and two others trooped into Ash's room and shut the door, barely acknowledging her presence. Lauren waited in the kitchen until they left, then leaned against the door to Ash's room.

"What?" Ash had Amy's eyes. It was disorienting the way those same eyes could look right through Lauren. They "blanked" her as the kids said.

"I'm from New York, Ash. Not Minnesota. I don't want your fucking dealers in the house, got it?"

Ash shrugged. "They're cool."

"Not here. You pay for your shit at the door or on the street."

"Okay."

Ash was high, of course. Getting tough with them was like punching a marshmallow, but this was the moment, after years of trying to make friends, that Lauren stopped bothering with Ash and started hating herself.

She bolted.

She attended conferences about how to apply contemporary archival practices to the ongoing refugee crisis, focusing on New York harbor's historical role in the migration patterns of the "Empire of the United

States," as her interns called it. She had spent her whole career collecting facts about New York history that nobody cared much about. "I'm pouring water into a bucket with so many holes hammered through the bottom, it's only a circle of air." She told her interns, a revolving group of young people she never had drinks with. They didn't think of Manhattan as an island off the coast of America. Spalding Gray had thrown himself off the Staten Island Ferry years ago (they had never heard of him). As far they were concerned, New York City existed as a target and a shield to the rest of the world. They were right, but for the kind of person who applied for an internship at The New York Historical—a high-strung, self-obsessed, secretly bookish kind of person (a person like Lauren)—there was nowhere better to live. If you couldn't get a job in Berlin, why not stay in Ridgewood?

Lauren appreciated the cynicism of the young, but part of her longed for a final, epic battle instead of this slow, brutal collapse. Fast or slow, empires always left a pile of scattered remains, so this was where she did her work, one historical fact at a time. But it was getting harder to believe that archiving humanity still mattered. How many had avoided the shelters last night, afraid of being robbed, abused, or deported? Lauren had never been more aware of the turning screw of history working in concert with every aspect of her life. System collapse.

Was this really the moment when she would lose Amy? When she had already lost Cora? Could she live without Sasha and Val? Maybe. She didn't want to endure the way they all looked at each other now that Cora was gone.

It was a terrible time to be alone.

Canal Street surged away to her right. The red pagoda roofs of the Chinatown banks looked like a better idea in the snow, every downtown artery clogged by the medicated rich avoiding the unmedicated poor. Most people Lauren knew lived in a semi-dulled, ongoing state of panic. Everyone was on some kind of drug except Amy, who laughed easily with their children and found solace in helping birds.

Without her, Lauren felt certain that she would never sleep again.

sasha

Sasha stepped out of the elevator just as a dog walker was coming in the lobby. Four snowy beasts, five counting the dog walker. The huge Bernese Mountain Dog belonged to a plastic surgeon who lived on the fourth floor. A totally irrational dog for the city. Sasha walked a wide circle around them, hoping the friendly Bernese wouldn't jump up while the man holding four leashes talked weather with the doorman. How could Val stand being a dog walker, and why was she still doing it? Sasha had suggested it as a temporary fix but Val claimed to like it more than teaching. Thank God she got that rent stabilized apartment back in the eighties. Crappy apartment turned safe haven, but it still felt depressing to Sasha, though the block had come up a lot since the crack house days. Oh, what did it matter? Val loved her apartment. She filled her bird feeder and planted her window boxes on the fire escape every spring.

sorry i missed your call i was in the garden, she would text.

Was that even true? Val regularly disappeared. Even before Cora died, she stopped answering texts or emails, her voicemail filled up, and finally one of them (usually Sasha) couldn't stand it anymore and went all the way downtown to ring her bell.

Val would answer the door looking too thin, wearing an old band T-shirt and underwear, maybe a robe and socks in winter. She'd make coffee and say she'd been down the rabbit hole. She was sorry to have worried anyone. "It's my last bad habit," she'd say, quit smoking, no drugs, hardly any drinking. The only thing left was her vanishing act. Sasha could tell she meant it. So many side conversations with Cora about Val, and then, after Cora ghosted her, Val only wanted to talk about Cora. It was exhausting, but Val seemed so lonely now. She refused to take antidepressants because it might stop her from writing, but when was the last time she wrote a song that anybody heard? Whenever Sasha came to check on her, Val was childishly pleased that someone had bothered to find out if she was alive or dead. Lauren's theory was that some part of her wanted to keep them guessing.

Val's problem was that they had all thought Val was going to be famous, and she almost was. When "Like A Girl" went gold, everybody wanted her. *Interview* magazine did a profile, Slaughterhouse Records signed her, then Val dropped them in a huff over the second record. Cora said that Val acted up more than she should have. But Val was supposed to be a rock star. Rock stars act up. The only fact Sasha knew was that it was all a really long time ago.

Sasha stepped out into the snow and walked carefully along the shoveled part of the sidewalk. She felt more fragile with the Undeniable branching and growing with every step, every breath. When she reached the curb, the streetlight showed a distant red hand in the muffled light. Her block was usually busy in the morning, runners in superhero Lycra and children trooping toward the school bus or the park. The elderly who still read a newspaper made from paper carrying coffee from the deli, heading for their favorite bench.

Why had she assumed that she would get old? Her parents hadn't gotten old. Cora hadn't gotten old.

Sasha looked up at the tall apartment buildings, all those kitchens suspended one over the other. Was it a snow day with the parents taking it slow for once? Hot chocolate and mini marshmallows with the breakfast cereal. Table lamps set near a window signaled *home* through the storm. The only vehicles on the road were school buses (no snow day, too bad), taxis, and SUVs with energetic wiper blades. Did the wealthy really think that an all-terrain vehicle was enough to keep them safe? The world was all chaos and probabilities, and no matter how much equipment you buy, you can still wake up to a lump under your breast. It's a medical procedure, not a physics equation, she told herself. She still needed to come up with something smart to say by four-thirty.

How about restating the obvious: frightened people buying expensive cars so they don't have to think about death is good for the economy.

I'm good for the economy, Sasha thought, pressing the doorbell at the florist shop. Academy Florist had so far survived the changing neighborhood, where gentrification meant more closed storefronts. Marie, the florist, still lived upstairs in the apartment that came with the shop. Old school. She opened the door holding a cup of tea and moved quickly to let Sasha inside, wind whipping around the doorframe. Marie was older than Sasha, somewhere between sixty and seventy. Her close-cropped white hair and tailored smock made her look fashionable even at this time of day. Marie practiced Tai Chi every morning, another thing Sasha meant to do. Maybe she should tell Marie about the Unavoidable, practice for telling Lauren and Val. It would be easier with Marie, whom she would never ask to help her with anything.

Sasha gave Marie quick kisses which didn't land. Marie was from Paris, and Sasha knew to only pretend to touch both cheeks.

"Would you like a cup of tea?" asked Marie.

"No, thanks." said Sasha. This felt impolite considering that Marie had opened early for her, but the tea smelled strong and earthy. Actually, it smelled like dirt. Sasha wondered if Marie was taking Chinese herbs for some ailment, but then, why wouldn't a florist drink dirt in hot water? It was green and moist inside the shop, blossoms lit the room with whites, yellows, purples, and blues. The loamy smell overwhelmed Sasha. They were standing inside a terrarium, looking out at the world through steamed glass.

She would tell Marie. She would tell a stranger first.

"Snow is my favorite weather." Marie looked out the window. "I know that's funny because my work is all about keeping things warm and growing, but if there were more flowers that grew in the snow, I would stock them." She pointed to some bare branches near the door, spray painted white for decoration. "Those don't count of course. We have holly branches and winter berries. But you're here for flowers. It's a big party tonight, yes?"

"Yes. No." Sasha was embarrassed by her social ambitions in front of Marie, who was sleek and self-contained. "Twenty-four people, but they're all old friends, or they're old, anyway. It's a class reunion."

"Ah, school reunions. We don't do those so much in France."

"I hope they'll come in this weather," Sasha said, suddenly deflated.

But why deflated? If everyone stayed home because of the snow she would still have the flowers. What happened to her resolution to be kinder to herself after Cora died? Why was it still so hard to believe that she was worthy of fresh flowers?

Marie walked over to a refrigerated case filled with stalks of irises, phlox, lilies, hydrangeas, and roses.

"Maybe all white? For the snow day?"

"Perfect," said Sasha. "No roses."

"Of course not. Roses are depressing unless they are in the garden." Marie laid white hydrangeas side by side on her large table at the back of the shop. "Do you want two large bouquets, or several smaller ones throughout the house?"

"I'm not sure. We'll be in the dining room and the living room, buffet style."

"I think two larger ones," said Marie. "A centerpiece for the table, and perhaps something taller for the living room? We can add a few smaller arrangements in shorter vases." Marie held up a rectangle of thick, milky glass, and quickly chopped down several stalks.

"Yes, perfect. Thank you so much."

"Would you like to wait, or shall I have them delivered when Alfred comes in?"

"I'll wait."

"Good. You sit right here."

Sasha sat in the only other chair in the store, upholstered with a faded pattern and curved armrests. She would tell her now.

"How hot is your apartment? Keep the window open a crack, near the flowers."

"It won't look like a funeral?"

"No." Marie ripped butcher paper from the long roll at the edge of her worktable. "It will look like snow."

Why wasn't Sasha a florist? It would be so peaceful to be in this shop all day long. The radio played music instead of the news. Every job had a clear beginning and end. Precise, thoughtful work with petals and stems.

White skulls, white flowers. They all had to wear white dresses to their graduation at Harrison. Vestal virgins on the altar of education, though Sasha was the only one of their group still a virgin by twelfth grade. Val wrote a petition protesting the rule of white dresses, but the majority of the class didn't sign, which enraged Val, who threatened to skip graduation. Sasha signed but didn't see why it mattered. They could wear any style of dress they wanted as long as it was white and no more than four inches above the knee. That last constraint was absurd. They'd been rolling up their gym skirts at the waist since middle school.

Sasha didn't care about her dress. All she remembered was that it was long and embroidered. She was more worried about her parents embarrassing her with their repetitive pride, as if she was the only person in the world who ever graduated from Harrison. Val wore a white minidress with thigh high white boots. When she stalked across the stage to get her diploma, the principal gave her such a dirty look they all started giggling, which only made it worse. But Principal Bancroft was onstage in front of hundreds of parents (except Val's mother, who never came to school assemblies, not even graduation). Bancroft handed off the diploma and Val strode back to her seat in a blaze of glory.

She was good onstage.

Sasha's parents' friends thought her mother was a snob for sending her daughter to a private school. Scholarships were a shameful admission of lack. Nobody in the neighborhood went to school in Manhattan until high school. It was exhausting just getting your kids through middle school, confirmations, quinceaneras, bar and bat mitzvahs. They didn't want their children taking the subway alone. Why leave the neighborhood? Her mother shrugged it off, *she's home before dark*. But Sasha wasn't always; there were after-school activities and in her second year at Harrison she started spending more nights at Cora's.

She never told her mother about the night she and Cora spent at Val's house. It was supposed to be only Cora, because Val never invited anyone else over, but Sasha was helping Cora with her seventh-grade science report when Val called to ask if she'd come for a sleepover. Sasha worried that Val would feel stuck with her, but Cora wanted her to come.

"You won't believe her house," Cora said, as they walked to the uptown subway. "It's kind of cool, but weird."

"How?"

"You'll see."

"What's her mom like?"

"I like her," Cora said, and changed the subject. When they got off the train at 168th Street, Sasha realized that she knew Manhattan as little as her friends knew Queens. She had never been anywhere except the Upper West Side and Central Park, near Harrison. Washington Heights was near the George Washington Bridge, steep hills led up from avenues filled with street vendors selling Italian ices or Mexican food. She heard more Spanish than in her neighborhood. The women called each other "mami."

"Is this Spanish Harlem?" she asked Cora, who laughed.

"Washington Heights, where the Cloisters are."

This didn't look anything like the park with the monastery where their class rode a chartered bus to see the unicorn tapestries.

"Val can go see the unicorn whenever she wants," Cora said.

Lucky Val, thought Sasha. Why hadn't Val told them that on the trip? Val didn't talk much about her house or her mom. Sasha had made her own mother into a character for the other girls. They liked the funny things her mom said, how a spoon under their pillow would bring a snow day.

When they got to Val's block, Cora slowed down. "Her name's Miriam," she said. "And she might be sitting on the stoop, so don't act weird around her."

"I'm not going to act weird! You're the one acting weird."

Cora ignored her, and when they got to the last building on the block, a woman in a light blue coat and ankle boots was sitting on the stoop drinking a cup of tea, despite the sharp wind off the river.

"Hi Miriam," said Cora. "I brought another girl from our class over."

The woman's face lit up. She was too glamorous to be anyone's mom. Red lipstick and long dark hair piled on top of her head, a few tendrils curled down as if they just happened to land that way. "Cora! So glad to see you."

Cora went up the steps two at a time to hug her.

"And you are?" Val's mother started to stand up, then sat back down and held out her hand. Sasha was standing one step below Miriam. It felt like she was greeting a princess. She wondered if she should kiss her hand.

"I'm Sasha," she said. "Nice to meet you, Mrs. Stone."

Val's mother laughed. Sasha liked her already. "You have to call me Miriam. All the girls do, right, Cora?"

Sasha would have said something, but when Val's mother let go of her hand and moved one of her legs, Sasha could see right up her coat. She wasn't wearing anything underneath. No dress, not even underpants. Sasha never saw her own mother naked.

"Come on," Cora said.

"Val's upstairs," said Miriam, smiling at them both. "You going to watch TV or something? You should order some pizza."

"We will, thanks, Miriam."

Cora rang the bell for Val's apartment. When the two of them were buzzed into the lobby, Cora turned on her.

"What is wrong with you? You were so rude!"

"I didn't mean to—"

"I knew you'd act weird."

"She wasn't wearing any clothes!"

"She's obviously wearing clothes. She looks nice!"

"She's not wearing anything underneath," Sasha whispered.

Cora stopped. "Nothing at all?"

"Not even underpants." Sasha looked up the stairway, afraid that Val might hear them. Was she coming down to get them? What if she lived on the first floor?

"Well, you know." Cora made her thumb into a bottle and tipped it back like a drunk. "It's not really tea." Cora giggled. Sasha had never seen her parents drunk. Never naked, never drunk.

"Is she crazy?" Sasha asked.

Cora shrugged. She looked through the glass front door at Miriam, who was leaning back with her beautiful legs crossed high and bare, one foot bobbing in the air. "It's cold out," she said.

"Should we say anything?" asked Sasha.

Cora gave her a look that was kind of sad and kind of sorry.

"Hey!" Val was four flights up, leaning over the bannister. "Come up, already. We've got to order the pizza."

Cora hooked her pinky around Sasha's. She didn't have to say anything.

They panted up four flights to Val who was sitting on the top step, glaring. "What took you so long? I'm starving!"

Val ended up in the graduation photos with Sasha and her family, which her mother loved, since Sasha was always staying over in Manhattan at her friends' houses instead of bringing them back to Queens. The photo with Val proved that Sasha did have school friends, even if her mother hadn't met their parents.

The girls were told to carry small bouquets for graduation. That morning, her mother handed a white cardboard box to Sasha. She was shocked by how professional it looked. White ribbons looped and trailed from lilacs, lily of the valley and tiny ferns.

"How much did it cost?"

Sasha had assumed her mother would make the graduation bouquet herself. The flowers didn't matter to Sasha any more than the dress. She knew that she wouldn't look glamorous in the graduation pictures, still too short and round (what Cora called curvy) and she couldn't handle her hair. But she was the only one in the class going to MIT, full scholarship. Her mother refused to tell Sasha how much the flowers cost, only that she went to a florist near work, which meant Manhattan and money.

"It's called a nosegay," her mother said, and for once, her voice was so quiet that Sasha had to lean in close. Her mother pulled Sasha into a tight hug, laughed, and wiped her eyes with the back of her hand, yelling at her father that he'd better be ready, it takes an hour to get there and they don't want to be late. Sasha didn't know until that morning how much her mother, who shouted down all the union guys around their kitchen table, wanted to see her daughter looking like a bride.

When Val arrived at graduation without flowers and asked if she could take one of Sasha's blossoms from the nosegay, Sasha said no.

Marie held up the first bouquet for Sasha's approval. "Yes?"

Sasha tried to speak around the sudden stop in her throat. Marie extended the flowers for her to sniff.

"Mock Orange," said Marie.

"I think I *will* get them delivered," said Sasha, getting to her feet.

"Good idea." Marie took a sip of tea. "It's slippery out there."

val

Snow drifted through the sidewalk grates while Val waited for the subway home from Juno's house, wondering if she could cancel her coffee with Danny. He was just back from tour, and always reached out. He was on the road or playing studio gigs nearly all the time now. They had been in love with each other for a little while. Danny was always in love with the unattainable woman. She had been his impossible crush and when she became possible, he said no. Now, she didn't know how she had ever felt that way about him, but they were still crucial to each other. She loved the way he played, but he tired her out in a way he never did when they were in bands together. Had he changed? Or had she gotten to know him too well?

She peeled off her dog clothes, removed the plywood board, and got into the tub. There was no real shower in her apartment, but she had switched out her old fixtures for some fancy French faucets Lauren passed along when she and Amy were doing their renovation. Val now had a spray attachment that went from the main tub faucet, instead of the old shower above the tub that was so small the shower curtain stuck to her legs. The spray attachment was a beautiful object, Val loved the heft of it every time she picked it up from its stainless-steel cradle. The faucet handles were white porcelain marked *Chaud* and *Froid*. She liked pretending that she was in France.

She had cancelled her evening dog walks to get to Sasha's on time, which made it look a lot like she was going. Val closed her eyes, dipping her head under the warm water to rinse off the dog smell. There was some vast hand twisting the tuning pegs inside her body, her spine a guitar string stretching all the way from her bathtub to Sasha's apartment.

When the lights went down and the place was packed, there was no choice but to walk onstage.

Make 'em love, make 'em hate, make 'em wait, said Cora.

"James Brown," Val said out loud. "You got that from me, Cora."

Val put her head underwater, hair webbing out around her skull as her body sank. She imagined a camera overhead, how strange her nakedness looked in the steamy light. Her breasts were less full than she pretended, nipples breaking the surface at the end of two narrow ski jumps. They leaned in different directions, periscopes circled by curled hairs she didn't bother to pluck anymore. Her belly was its own grand island with her belly button a tiny lake at the top. Soft ground of a rising hill that would never disappear from her landscape, no matter how far she walked or how much she weighed. She used to be able to see her furred sex when she looked down the front of her body, but now she rested on her elbows and pushed her pubus into the air. There were kinky strands of white mixed in with the brown curls. She didn't want to shape it with a razor or get waxed anymore.

Her mother used to call Val into the bathroom to refill her glass when she drank in the tub. Her mother flaunted her body to the end, rejecting modesty as an American neurosis, though she had only been to Europe once, an exchange student in the sixties. She told Val about the topless women of all ages on the beach, who tanned their low-slung breasts and let their armpit hair grow. It sounded sexier than it looked on her mother, and Val never lingered to speak with her in the bath, though now she wished she hadn't turned away so fast. Val had outlived her by seven years, her own body tracing her mother's belly, thighs, and multicolored thatch. Val tucked herself into a ball and her buttocks went sunny side up, revealing stretch marks she had traced with her finger the last time she strained her head around and took a good look in the mirror. Privacy was her reward for solitude. Val could occasionally glimpse herself as this woman who took it all a lot less seriously, unconcerned about wandering nipples and pooching belly. That Val was floating above the bathtub, careless and free.

It's lighter than you think, said Cora, quoting from Sister Corita Kent's "Ten Rules for Students and Teachers," which was still taped inside Val's guitar case. Val's thoughts were collaging with Cora's voice now, or was this her own voice, repeating the rules backstage like a prayer before she went on? John Cage. Sister Corita Kent. It didn't matter who said what anymore.

Val sipped air between her lips and let her body float upward.

The snow was on pause and lit-up buses lumbered up First Avenue when Val went to meet Danny. The shoveling had begun. Building owners got fined if the sidewalks in front weren't shoveled. There was always the chance that a slip on the pavement would lead to a lawsuit, and this was how the city made sure the pavements got cleared. The supers were standing on stoops and doorways, watching day laborers scrape it down to cement, tossing shovelfuls into slushy traffic lanes. Men with shovels appeared for hire when it snowed, the same men who sold cheap umbrellas when it rained. It was easy to find someone to do the work that was scorned by people who had been here longer. Some of these men had agreements with the supers to sweep up the daily garbage from the sidewalk in the front of the building. Some walked the streets with a shovel over their shoulder.

Val hurried past her own super, Harold, as if she was late for a meeting. He threw more salt as she went down the steps, to prove he was on top of the storm or to throw something at her, she wasn't sure. It had taken her a little while to realize that he was a total asshole. But she had been in the building longer than him, so he mostly left her alone. A man she'd never seen before was shoveling the sidewalk. The guys in the neighborhood didn't keep working for Harold.

The restaurant where she and Danny used to meet got cool, got famous, closed down and made a comeback. They could all relate. When that place closed for good, Val went out of her way not to walk by the white wine and seafood joint which replaced it. Now she and Danny went to the Odessa, a twenty-four-hour Ukrainian diner that was one of the last holdouts. The food wasn't as good, but it was real. Val turned down Tenth Street, her favorite east/west corridor. The street got progressively wealthier as you walked west toward the center of the island, peaking just north of Washington Square, where the old chess club kept its bay windows open in summer to the clink of moving pieces and timing bells.

Walking east from Val's building there were boutiques and cafes rippling out from the former hipness of Avenue A. The laundromat was open, steamed-up windows with figures moving bundles inside a blurred aquarium. The laundromat had closed only once, after Hurricane Sandy. Val was surprised by how relieved she was when they reopened a month later. She didn't know the name of the owner, and by now she was too embarrassed to ask. The laundromat was one of the last havens in the neighborhood. You could read a magazine with pages softened by the humidity, waiting for the *ping* of the dryer. The owner (what was her name?) had opened up this morning despite the snow.

Val had liked the first days of Hurricane Sandy when they were all thrown together. The months got hard. She lost most of her archives in that storage place near the river. Danny had helped her peel things apart, no gloves or masks. They didn't think of that until later. Nobody could prove the rising water made them sick. Val was almost never sick and Danny was a hypochondriac. Separating her old gig posters and pages of lyrics was a surgical process, hieroglyphs spread out on the cement floor of the storage unit like wet skin. If it wasn't for Danny, she would have tossed all of it. Danny was there because it was his story too. She was the fool who wrote it all down.

She turned the corner onto Avenue A, where a young man was shoveling the sidewalk in front of the Odessa. He wore old-school headphones and Val could hear a pounding bass line. When she reached him, he spun the shovel and saluted Val in her black pea coat and striped stocking cap. She kicked right into performance mode, snowlight instead of spotlight. She held out her hand as if they'd rehearsed it, and the kid—must be an underemployed dancer—pushed the shovel handle toward her. She caught it and dipped; Fred Astaire and Ginger Rogers, then spun the shovel's waist and passed it back. The kid dipped, clapped, and whooped. It was the old improv rules: yes and—yes and—yes! Everything expanding with their matching grins.

"You must be a dancer," said the kid.

"Not really. Back in the day, I did some stuff."

"You still got the moves."

He held the door open and she swept into the Odessa as if it were the Grammys.

Danny took obsessive care of his health and looked the same as he always had, though sometimes Val realized that wasn't true. He wasn't the skinny, handsome boy in a black T-shirt hauling an amp up the back stairs of the club. He still hauled his instrument cases, but now he wore suits when he played. She would tell him to get a haircut.

Val had no idea what she looked like either. Maybe she never had, despite backstage mirrors and photo shoots. Who cared? The kid shoveling out front thought she still had it.

Danny started talking right away like he always did.

"Things went well in Brussels after a rough start. You want tea? They actually have a really nice green tea now."

"Lipton's." Val said. "Milk and sugar."

"You should try the green sometime, it's better for you." Val shrugged. "Okay. Be right back."

Were they really going to age like this? Bickering like an old couple without ever having had sex? They used to play together all the time. He was with the Joypoppers when she got the record deal. But then came that walk on a day that smelled like vomit from Gingko trees dropping their fruit. When she said she was interested in writing the libretto for an opera they had talked about for months, he changed the subject. Danny was working with famous people now, she knew that, but he also knew she was good.

After that silence, she stopped talking to him about her work, which he may not have noticed. She had talked to Danny about everything over the years: her break ups, her pathetic bank account, the imperative of life as a musician. But when she stopped sharing her side of the conversation, he didn't notice. She was moody as hell, okay, fine, but he just kept talking and something *had* changed. She didn't call him on it because she wasn't sure she could bear what he would say. Silence is an answer. Ghosting is a reply. Just ask Cora.

She didn't tell Danny that ever since Cora died, she wouldn't shut up.

Danny always thought I was a bitch, said Cora, making Val laugh out loud as she waited for Danny to bring her tea. A man at the counter turned to look. Was it possible to get too weird for the Odessa?

Danny carried their two cups over to the booth, then went back to the counter for a small metal pitcher of milk. It was slow because of the snow, and the owner, Kestutis, wouldn't ask them to move if they weren't ordering food.

"You never change," said Danny, watching her rip open a packet of sugar.

"Neither do you."

"We workshopped the show in Brussels, then went to Luxembourg for the opening. It was hard because the sound wasn't right, and the music director didn't really get it."

"I thought you were the Music Director?"

"I was the MD in Brussels, but it was this local guy in Luxembourg. Beautiful space, but all that time inside the theater really got to me. When we came out at night it was cold and rainy. I wasn't feeling well, but then I started drinking apple cider vinegar every morning in hot water, before I did my stretches. I mean, now my stomach is pretty good, but at first—also, Monica didn't really know, I mean she knew, but she wasn't totally clear on what she wanted to hear, and there was a lot of new material."

Every time he said Monica his lips trembled slightly because she was famous, and Danny was pretending it didn't matter.

"We only had three weeks prep, two with the musicians before all the tech came in. It was intense, switching between classical and electric guitar, plus I was playing mandolin and even penny whistle for one of the pieces. Crazy. It was a small pit, well, not really a pit, the musicians were onstage the whole time. Which bugged Monica, who didn't want us to pull focus, but we were playing, you know? We had to be able to read the music. I mean, it took a while to figure out. But then I started feeling better. I just kept telling myself, let go, let go. But maybe I let go of too much, you know? I mean, it's her piece, but there has to be some kind of integrity."

Danny dropped his gaze to his teacup and tried to lift the bag with a small wooden stirrer. It kept slipping back into the hot water. Val pushed her spoon across the table. This was the Danny she loved, the man who could switch between four instruments onstage but couldn't manage a teabag. She wanted to talk to him about the gallery show with the Joypoppers. It was happening in a month and he had to come with her. They were bandmates.

He picked up her spoon and smiled at her. There was something jazzed about him.

"Kalia was there," he said. Now she got it. The one he was so obsessed with two years ago. Danny's energy swirled like he was back on speed, which was what brought on all his stomach trouble in the first place. Kalia was married, lived in Prague or Rome. She was part of the architecture around Monica. Far from home for the gig, and of course she was a beauty and very talented, maybe twenty years younger than Danny. But who cared? Two years ago, every text from Kalia, every beat in their communication, gripped him like a new addiction. Val drank a lot of Lipton's at the Odessa pulling him out of that sinkhole.

"I know, I know," he said, holding up his hand. "But I'm okay, I mean, it was good. We were really—there's a connection there that's—we spent a lot of time together. I mean, we didn't have sex, but there was a lot of holding each other. On the last night, after the show moved to Amsterdam, we walked around the streets until four in the morning. I don't know her situation." His face was lit. Maybe he had never stopped with Kalia, maybe he dabbled all along. Snorting instead of shooting.

"Why don't you fuck her?" Val said suddenly. "Just grab her and fuck her. She'd probably love it."

"No, no, it's not like that."

"Why not?"

Danny spread his hands out, trying to explain his helplessness for the hundredth time. "What we have is—it gives me this taste, I mean, it's not everything I want, but—"

"Really?" Val interrupted. "Maybe it is."

Danny finally looked at her. He took a sip of his tea. "I don't have a lot of time. I've got the podcast and that thing with the quartet. I let all that go for the show, and now it's like, *now*. Plus, I played last night and I'm playing tomorrow, so I've really got to do some arrangements today or I am well and truly fucked."

"When's the last time you were well and truly fucked, Danny?" she asked. "Get some more hot water for your tea bag, otherwise, it's all you, and we have to take turns."

Danny stared as if he could see snakes writhing on her head. He had never listened to her—he used her like reverb. Did she want to turn him to stone? Her envy was so close to the surface, the enlightened woman over the bathtub nowhere in sight. Danny was one of her oldest friends. He let her stay at his place when she had bedbugs. He helped her when her archives were destroyed by the hurricane. She tried to slow her breath into four-four time while Danny picked up both of their cups and came back with another round.

"They didn't charge for the refill," he said quietly. "What's going on?"

It felt as if everyone in the Odessa was turning to hear her reply. The silence buzzed loud; noon was early for this neighborhood. But in fact, the cafe clatter was rising up and down, it was only quiet at their table. Danny cocked his head like he did when he was trying to really hear a piece of music.

"I'm fine," Val said. "I've been getting up early, walking the dogs. I like the dogs. My guitar keeps looking at me and I can't seem to walk over to the piano. I think I need more structure, a deadline. The dogs help, pays the bills, gives me two things a day I can't blow off or there'll be piss and shit all over the carpet. I miss Cora." She was afraid to look in his eyes because then she'd know what he thought of her. "I'm going to the reunion tonight, which will be—I mean, I don't know what it will be, but I don't want to go."

"What reunion?" He thought she meant a band reunion.

"Harrison." It kind of *was* a band reunion, but Cora couldn't make it.

"So don't go," said Danny. "No rules."

That used to be their code for everything. Relationships, jobs, bad behavior, good behavior. No rules.

"I have to go."

Danny reached across the table and took her hand. "Don't go."

"I have to."

"Why?"

"Sasha's hosting this dinner and I told Lauren that she had to go with me. We haven't seen each other since Cora's funeral."

"Who gives a fuck? They'll understand or they won't. Nobody loved Cora more than you, not that she deserved it—rest in peace." He let go of her hand.

"I do, okay? I give a fuck. I don't want to go because I haven't had a gig in way too long and I'm a dog walker. Seeing Lauren and Sasha only makes me feel worse about Cora."

Danny wasn't listening. His eyes were on her face, but he wasn't listening. He was thinking about Kalia, or the notations and arrangements he had to finish by tomorrow, maybe flipping between the two. Val listened for Cora's voice, fighting the urge to turn around and look for her. Is this how everything falls apart?

Take it to the bridge, said Cora.

Right. James Brown. Mine again.

Val watched Danny focus. "You should go," he said. "It will probably be fun."

sasha

Sasha's mother used to say that bad things always happen in cold weather. Sasha had immediately listed all the terrible things that happened in the height of summer, starting with the atom bomb on August sixth. Her mother laughed. "What do you know of bad things?" she said, turning back to her checklist for the union, vermin in the workplace, overtime, unpaid sick leave, workman's comp.

Nothing could live up to her mother's list. The wooden table and mismatched chairs inside the yellow kitchen of their sunny two-bedroom in Rego Park were gone. You don't keep real estate in New York, Sasha told herself sternly, you only borrow it. She owned the smell of burnt garlic and the view of silver painted roofs with TV antennas holding their own like prehistoric birds. She owned the back of her mother's head bent over paperwork; the sleeves of her flower print shirt stretched to bursting by her strong arms.

What did she know of bad things?

She resisted the urge to call Val or Lauren and blurt out her news. Wait until tonight, in person. They used to talk nearly every day, though that slowed down after Lauren and Cora got married. Their families brought a harried exultation into their rushed conversations and they both interrupted themselves constantly to answer the children, assuming that Sasha would understand she had to wait, she must have more time than they did because she lived alone. She didn't understand and she didn't have more time.

Sasha hadn't been allowed to interrupt when her mother was on the phone unless it was an injury involving blood, but her own generation seemed to privilege their offspring's chitter-chatter without question.

Sometimes, Sasha got sick of waiting and hung up. Cora didn't have Jeff's kids all the time, but Lauren seemed to assume that Sasha would call her back, and mostly she did, telling herself this wasn't a test of friendship. Sasha's mother used to call her best friend every day, the rippled cord from the red wall phone gently bouncing across the kitchen. Sasha had to duck under it to get to the refrigerator. Her mother and their friends talked nonstop about nothing. But now it felt needy to call and talk about nothing the way they did in their twenties, and hardly anyone answered the phone unless she texted first to ask if this was a good time.

It was exhausting.

She went into the bedroom and picked up her notes for the report. She would go to a coffee shop and put together a final outline as if she were still in graduate school. If she stayed home, all she'd think about was the reunion dinner. Work would keep her sane. She shoved the legal pad into her shoulder bag, zipping it tight against the weather. Out the door before she could change her mind.

More people were on the street, bundled for the storm when Sasha emerged for the second time. The badger steps bravely forth from its den, she told herself. Anthony, the doorman, nodded from behind the desk in the lobby.

"We're sending up a coat rack this afternoon," he said, to reassure her that they hadn't forgotten about the party.

"Thank you, Anthony," she said.

"Too bad about the weather," he said, meaning for her party.

She shrugged and smiled. Was it too bad? Not while it kept softening the world. Everyone was forced to walk more slowly, maybe even talk to each other. It was supposed to snow in February! She missed the blizzards that covered the cars and shut down the city completely. She had once skied ten blocks to the video store, though now there were no more video stores and she couldn't remember which boyfriend had the skis, or where exactly he lived.

But hadn't it snowed for three whole days? Lots of time for sex.

She missed the way the four of them used to hurl themselves into events like snowstorms, concerts, road trips, even sex, until the thing itself took over, large and wordless. Drugs were like that too, though

Sasha had only taken the smallest amount, afraid of injuring her favorite organ. Val used to tease her about her fear of drugs, placing Sasha back outside the circle. Cora was kind of in love with Val back when they were snorting lines off a hand mirror in the bathroom, but wasn't everybody? Though anything sexual between them was just a high school thing, right? They all cared more about their careers than sex at this point (right?).

She still didn't know if Val had slept with both Cora and Lauren.

"Sleeping together is an exaggeration," Lauren had said.

We've all tipped over since Cora died, thought Sasha. Aging in step with the sixth extinction. Last breaths were the only ones remaining, but daily life necessitated a kind of blindness. It was a joy to inhale the sharp, falling snow and watch the children's neon jackets, scarves, and hats light up the sidewalk. Nobody used sleds with metal runners anymore, gone with the heavy snows of childhood. These children tugged blow-up rafts and small plastic toboggans with pink nylon rope. Wood, hemp, and metal replaced by glowing plastic that would outlast them all. A father and daughter pulled their large, embarrassed dog past her front door on a plastic disc.

Sasha loved her block.

A young girl ran past as if everyone was invisible except for two other girls at the corner. Maybe the parochial and private schools had closed for the storm. Or maybe their mom was like Cora's mom, Jessie, who declared "mental health days" when it was obvious that going to school and work was a rotten idea.

Sasha pulled up the hood of her parka. She always thought that she would have one small child all her own, hopefully a girl, but she never stopped using birth control until she didn't need it anymore. Men became so much less interesting over the years, and though she tried, Sasha couldn't manufacture attraction to women. Lauren had Masha and Ash, even if Ash hardly counted. Val had abortions. Cora had Jeff's kids in the end. The chosen family was the system that mattered, not the biological one. The four of them chose each other.

"Wait up!" The girl on the street yelled to her friends. She had lost her hat, dark braids matted with snow. She looked the same age as Sasha on that first snow day, when Cora invited her to come sledding and none of them knew what would happen.

Cora had met them at the Central Park bandshell on a hot July day when something bad really did happen. She was sitting on a park bench with Val when Sasha got there. Val had a bottle in a brown paper bag, but her whole bad girl punk thing looked off. Cora was dressed like an executive even if Val still looked rock 'n' roll. They were in their early-forties. Day drinking in the park didn't look that fun anymore. Or was Sasha getting too straight? Boozy brunches only made her feel guilty, and this was a weekday. Sasha was teaching summer session that year and had checked Cora's voicemail after class: *meet me at the bandshell, I'm leaving work early*. It was too hot for the park. Besides, the bandshell was a teenage hang, a tourist hang, it wasn't where Sasha wanted to go after work to talk through some drama about Cora's wedding (all three were bridesmaids). Probably a stupid fight with stupid Jeff over something Cora thought was the end of the world.

Sasha knew it was bad when she saw Cora's face.

Lauren rode up on one of those Razor scooters before Sasha could ask what was wrong. Lauren had a new girlfriend and the glow of good sex.

"Amy said I love you last night for the first time." Lauren hopped off the scooter, then stopped. "What is it?"

"I lost the baby," Cora reached for the bottle tucked between Val's thighs. "It's been three months since I had a drink."

They crammed onto the bench, wrapping Cora in a nest of arms and legs.

"It's too hot!" said Cora, but nobody got up and Sasha started crying. Cora shook her head. "I'm the one who should be crying, you big dummy." She was already kind of drunk.

Cora and Jeff had decided to push up the wedding and get married before she showed, but nobody else knew why they changed the date.

"I started bleeding last night. The doctor said there was nothing to do but wait, rest, and it might taper off. Remember when you got your period, Val, and called to tell me? I asked what you were doing about it and you said you were 'letting it bleed,' like the Stones album." Cora laughed. "The only good thing is that we didn't tell the kids I was pregnant."

Emma and Ben were five and three. When she first met Jeff, Cora told Sasha she didn't know who she loved more, him or the kids. She even loved his ex-wife, who told Cora that she was the best thing that ever happened to Jeff. Sasha had kept her mouth shut.

"I don't want to see anybody but you guys." Cora passed along the bottle and they all took a sip. The whiskey was warm and cheap. It was like the time they pricked their fingers and rubbed the blood together to be soul sisters before they all started bleeding every month.

"Let's get a boat," said Val.

"What are you talking about?" Cora didn't look like she wanted an adventure.

Val stood up and pointed at the rowboats on the lake, beyond the Bethesda fountain. "We're taking you on a cruise."

"Oh, shut up. That's for tourists!" But there was a *yes* in Cora's voice and Val was right: something was better than nothing. It was too hot to stay on this bench. Sasha wondered if Cora wasn't better off at home in bed with the air conditioning on, but that also sounded like hell on earth. Cora should buy a new mattress and bundle the bloodstained sheets down the incinerator.

They untangled their octopus arms and started walking. A metal rowboat banged as the rental man held it close to the dock for them, smiling as if this was any other day. Val took the middle seat with the oars, Lauren sat in the bow, and Sasha and Cora sat together in the stern. Their combined weight tipped it so far down Sasha thought they'd go under. But the guy pushed them off like it was nothing to toss four middle-aged women into a flat-bottomed boat without life preservers. Nobody ever drowned in the boat pond. Val started rowing toward the middle of the lake as if she knew what she was doing (when did Val learn how to row?). Cora leaned against Sasha, trailing her hand through the green water as they splashed past well-equipped tourists with sunhats, cameras, and water bottles.

"This is the kind of thing we'd do if we were visiting another city," said Lauren.

"Why don't we ever go anywhere together?" asked Cora. "Just the four of us."

Nobody said anything.

(Because I'm working all the time.)

(Because I want to go places with Amy.)

(You know I can't afford it unless I'm on tour.)

"We used to skate here in the winter," said Cora, reaching for the bottle. "Mom took me and the boys. We'd sneak onto the ice when it was thick enough, not like anybody cared."

"How did you know if it was thick enough?" asked Lauren.

"Mom would throw a stick out on the ice for a big dog. If a Great Dane went through, we stayed off," Cora laughed.

"That's horrible." Val stopped rowing. "*¡Peligro! ¡Hielo Fino!*" she exclaimed.

"They didn't have those signs back then. The dogs were fine, Mom couldn't throw that far."

"I always wanted to steal one of those signs," said Val. "Make a great album cover."

"You don't have to steal one for it to be an album cover!" Sasha was feeling the whiskey and wishing she had a bottle of water.

"Yeah, I do."

Then Cora saw the bridge of brides. Three women shimmered above them in white lace, too pretty to be real. One held a parasol while a man with three cameras around his neck snapped photos for a bridal magazine. *Turn around*, Sasha mouthed at Val, but it was too late. This was a terrible idea. The worst idea. They should have left the park for a dive bar on Third Avenue. Cora gripped Sasha's shoulder and puked into the water.

"Oh, Jesus," said Val.

"Anybody bring water?" Sasha was trying not to pull away from Cora and the smell.

"Fuck it," said Cora, and splashed her face with water from the lake.

"Ugh! Don't drink it," said Sasha.

Cora cupped some with her hand, swished it around in her mouth then spit it out. "Can't blame it on morning sickness."

Val started rowing hard under the bridge, away from the small pool of vomit. The turtles and fish would take care of it.

"Stop," said Cora.

Val backed the oars. Camera shutters clicked overhead.

"Where did you learn to row?" asked Lauren.

"Berlin."

Cora leaned her head back, staring up the girls' long dresses between the wooden slats of the bridge.

"You can still get married," said Sasha.

"No. I can't."

"You fucking well can." Val started rowing again. "I mean, if you want to."

"We set the date because of the baby."

"So change the date."

"We already put down our deposit."

"Don't change the date," said Lauren, leaning around Val so Cora could see her. "Nobody knows you were pregnant except us, right?"

"And Jeff."

"He doesn't count," said Lauren and Val at the same time.

Cora stared at them. "You think he doesn't count?" Cora laughed and couldn't stop. Val slapped an oar against the water, splashing Sasha and Cora.

"That water's disgusting!" Sasha screamed.

"No, it's not! Cora's puke is way back there!"

Val flailed the oars soaking their shirts in the hot sun, boobs on parade. Tourists pulled their boats away as fast as they could. The paper bag around the whiskey bottle came apart in pieces in the water on the bottom of the boat and Sasha picked up her feet, trying to save her strappy sandals. The bottle rolled under the seats toward the back and Cora grabbed for it, breathing hard.

"Okay. Okay." Cora unscrewed the top, took a sip, winced. "But I'm exchanging the dress." She rested her head on Sasha's shoulder. "I think I need to go home."

"There, there," said Sasha, shielding Cora's face from the sun as Val rowed them in a slow circle back to dock. The four of them subsided, their clothes stiffening with pond silt.

There, there.

Every family is a chance operation, Sasha thought, stepping out from under the awning of her building, head down against tiny needles of snow.

"I laughed when they told me I was pregnant at forty," her mother had told her. "Like Sarah and Abraham."

Sasha was still trying to get away from both of her parents when they died in their mid-sixties, cancer (colon and prostate, not breast), only a year apart. At the time she thought that twenty-four was too young to be an orphan, not that her parents were too young to die. Now that the Undeniable was nudging her in her early fifties, Sasha might die younger than her parents. If that's the way the genetics played out, it was better that she never had children.

Val's father disappeared when she was a baby and her mother overdosed on sleeping pills when Val was in her late twenties—terrible, but not exactly unexpected—her mother had tried so many times. Cora had said it was almost worth it since Val wrote a whole album of great songs out of it. "Kiss Off" was Val's last album with the Joypoppers. Sasha found it hard to listen to. All those sad, angry songs.

Lauren's parents were still alive, safely tucked away in Westchester. Cora's mother, Jessie, was the only parent that Sasha ever saw.

Jessie!

Sasha was only two blocks from the nursing home. She could tell Jessie everything, then she'd be able to think straight past the Undeniable into the invisible world she knew so much better. Wasn't that the purpose of confession?

What a noble way to procrastinate.

The lobby of the nursing home was lined with books, good books because it was close to the university. Cora and the twins had done their research. This was a good place, one of the best in the city. There was a friendly person at the reception desk and a gym for physical therapy. Once you took the elevator upstairs to the actual rooms, it looked like a hospital. Beige linoleum floor and pleated curtains on wheels. All the memory care patients had single rooms that were locked from the outside. The only hope was that the patients were beyond embarrassment.

Outside of each room was a small plexiglass box where families placed optimistic photos of the patient with their family members to remind them that this was their room. Inside Jessie's box was a photo of Cora with her mother from her wedding to Jeff. Cora was wearing that sexy red dress she exchanged for the white one. "I'm too old to have kids, I'm too old to get married," she moaned over cocktails.

"Oh, shut the fuck up," said Val the night before the wedding, when they all stayed over at Sasha's house, getting drunk and gifting Cora with lingerie. "You're getting married."

Cora stretched a bright pink thong over her head and stuck her tongue out at them.

"It's a good dress," Sasha whispered to the photo before knocking on Jessie's door.

I can never grow old, she thought, looking at the gold bubble letters spelling out Jessie's name on the door as if it were a child's birthday party. The real Jessie respected five-year-olds too much to spell out their names in ugly cardboard letters. Maybe there was an app that could tell you when to take your overdose and avoid this part.

Sasha was wrong to come here, snow or no snow. Seeing Cora's mother wouldn't make Cora appear in her living room tonight. It wasn't going to solve her Zoom talk or make the Undeniable disappear before next week's surgery.

She opened the door.

Jessie was in her recliner in front of the window. She hadn't spoken since the last stroke, though the caregivers were sure that she understood everything. She had a private room and a button she could press if she needed anything. She was knitting, which was shockingly domestic for Jessie. She was dressed like a grandmother, too, short white hair, glasses, and a multicolored afghan draped over her shoulders. When Cora and the twins moved her into the home, Sasha helped them decorate Jessie's room with a nautical theme. Jessie had always wanted to take a cruise around the world when she retired, so they made it look like she was actually living on a boat despite the landlocked view. The plastic water glasses had sailboats on them. Jessie seemed to like it, but Sasha couldn't tell if Jessie was humoring them or they were humoring her. Maybe it didn't matter.

"Hi, Captain Jessie, how are you doing?"

Jessie put down her knitting. Nothing wrong with her hearing. Hard to tell if she knew who Sasha was, though the fact that Sasha called her captain was a big hint. Jessie was good at covering when she couldn't remember people or things. Cora had asked Sasha to come to some of Jessie's neurology appointments with her when one of the twins couldn't do it. Jessie was less difficult at these appointments when it wasn't only Cora, so Sasha was there to smooth the ribbon, as her father used to say. The neurologist would say three words: table, garden, flag, at the beginning of each visit, and ask Jessie to remember them. About fifteen or twenty minutes later, she would ask if Jessie remembered the words. Sasha panicked when she forgot the words herself.

Table. Garden. Flag.

Cora and Sasha started using this as a code for losing it. "Table, garden, flag!" Cora would say if Sasha called her work phone at Sony, just to make her laugh.

After Cora died, nobody asked Jessie to remember anything.

Sasha hung her coat on an anchor-shaped hook on the back of the door and walked over to the visitor's armchair. She kissed Jessie's cheek—the feeling of lips to paper, a comforting smell of baby powder.

"That's a nice sweatshirt," said Sasha. "Nice and comfy."

Jessie stroked the sweatshirt pooching over her stomach.

"The blue looks good on you. Are you cold? I think it's hot in here, but that's fine. Still snowing out. It's cold but nice. Looks pretty, doesn't it?"

Jessie stared out the window without smiling.

"Hey, Jessie, it looks like you've stopped wearing bras. Have they stopped helping you put on your bra?"

Jessie shrugged.

"Well, who cares, right? Remember how big my boobs were in seventh grade? Cora thought it was so unfair."

Sasha glanced at Jessie's face. Should she have said Cora's name? No sign of recognition.

"Yeah, well, the boobs aren't turning out to be such faithful friends after all. Getting them lopped off next week."

Jessie nodded, still looking straight ahead. Maybe that was the best way to respond. No need to say anything more about it.

"It's our thirty-fifth high school reunion. Can you believe that? Val's coming tonight, and Lauren. I don't see them as much as I see you, to be honest. Everyone's so busy. I thought I'd stop by and see you first, tell the girls how you're doing."

Jessie picked up her knitting.

"It looks a little weird to see you without a bra, honestly, but you should be comfortable. I'll tell Helena to make sure you put one on if you're wearing a lighter shirt to go to the music events or the game room, okay?"

Jessie didn't look up.

"Your generation was like, Burn the bra! Right? Burn the bra and now I'm worried about you looking unkempt without it. Don't you love that word? Unkempt? I mean, what about kempt? Sounds like a Yiddish word. I am extremely unkempt on the inside, don't be fooled by the bra. It's good that you don't remember things the way you used to. You've got what everyone is looking for. You're fully in the moment, like the Buddha."

Jessie smiled, actually looking a little bit like the Dalai Lama, despite the dopey sweatshirt and knitting needles. Sasha leaned in though there was no need to whisper. "I never used to talk to anyone like this, not even Cora. But I can tell you the truth because it might just disappear, right?"

Jessie kept knitting.

"Am I talking too much? Would you rather just sit quietly? I can be quiet, believe it or not."

Jessie put the needles down and patted her hand.

"I'm actually really messing up right now, Jessie. Ever since I got the Genie, I have no more ideas. There, I said it. All this pressure to be brilliant. I think my brain just stopped functioning. You get that, right? You're the only one who knows how that can happen."

Jessie picked up her knitting again. *Click clack, click clack.* Was Sasha being cruel? Did Jessie even know she had Alzheimer's? Nobody ever used that word around her. What was the point?

"Anyway, I've got this talk coming up this afternoon and I've got nothing. I feel like we're all pretending that the committee didn't make a terrible mistake. What will happen if I'm just—done? I've been faking it my whole life, and because of the Genie, everyone's too scared to ask what I'm working on, but what if I'm really one of those pathetic people hanging around the lab and taking up all the air in the room? The ones who stopped producing anything interesting years ago. The ones who froze. It's the biggest check I've ever seen."

Jessie raised her eyebrows.

"I got the Genie for taking baby steps and now I've got nothing but obsessions and an unfinished outline. It's kind of hard to explain, but the main idea is a predictive system for human behavior using quantum mechanics. Kind of a trap, like the Theory of Everything, but I can't stop thinking about it. I can't even discuss this with my colleagues without sounding like a crazy person."

Should she say "crazy person" in a place like this? Jessie didn't seem to notice. It was a private room.

"Nobody respects what I do because it's this really new field, and now they hate me. They all thought I was digging my own grave by looking at macro results using micro tools, developing a science-based system about psychological choices. Does this make any sense to you? The problem, of course, is that I'm not a neurologist or a psychologist and nothing's more impossible to predict than human behavior. Kind of like the chaos that we're used to predicting on a particle level, which is what gave me the idea in the first place."

Jessie started a new row.

"I know this is incredibly dense, but it turns out that a lot of people are interested in predicting human behavior. The people who give out these prizes know a lot more about Silicon Valley than I do, and they think my work might help them invent some kind of quantum computer that codes human behavior so they can sell things faster and better than anyone else. Which disgusts me, since the whole point is to buy less, not more. I never knew that this was the most interesting part to them until I got the prize. It's like I just looked up from the lab table for the first time in thirty years and I don't know where I am. There's no magic formula, we're all just acting out our lives without really telling each other anything. I have this huge urge to rip away the veil, you know? In daily conversation. An incredibly bad idea, but I get so impatient, no—bored. I get really bored sometimes—no, not just bored, angry. I have the freedom to research whatever I want because of this big deal prize, and all I feel is trapped. I don't want to help make some supercomputer code. I want to see if there's a pattern in the random forces driving all of us, and if there is, how do we steer it in the direction of life on the planet? For example, getting that prize was largely a matter of chance, anyone who's ever gotten it knows that there are a lot of people who deserved it just as much—well, several—definitely a handful, that's just a fact. So the prize is like a swerve that upset the probabilities of my life. In my case, a lucky swerve, but there's also swerves like Cora."

Still no response to Cora's name.

"What it really means is that I have no idea how to talk about this without questioning everything they awarded me for. Something I'll have to do in about four hours, so I guess this is kind of a practice run. Is that okay with you?"

Jessie frowned and picked up a dropped stitch. Maybe all these names, even Cora's, were just snow falling past Jessie's window. Maybe Jessie thinks I'm a recorded book, thought Sasha. One of those audiobooks the caregivers play for her to pass the time. Cora had given Jessie a collection of Penguin Classics, old-school CD discs, but Jessie couldn't remember how to work the machine.

Jessie smiled at Sasha as if she wanted to encourage this nice middle-aged lady to keep talking. Sasha opened the CD player and pressed play on the first disc of *David Copperfield*. The same disc that had been there on her last visit. "Whether I shall turn out to be the hero of my own life . . ." They listened to the first chapter until Helena came to take Jessie to the cafeteria. Helena and Sasha knew each other by now and didn't have to talk much. Weather. Fine. You too. Cora's twin brothers made all the decisions now.

Helena waited for Jessie to finish her row, knit one, purl one, then checked that Jessie's slippers were pulled up tight over the back of her heels before she got out of her chair. The smell of school lunches steamed down the hall.

So many heroes, thought Sasha.

lauren

Lauren knew she was crashing when a bag of hot peanuts from a food cart on the corner of Bowery and Canal smelled like it could save her life. How long had it been since she ate anything? She had that low-blood-sugar tremble. The peanut man nodded in a way that didn't invite much. He had to be desperate to work his cart in a snowstorm, wool hat pulled down to his eyes, fingerless gloves holding a long-handled spoon, stirring up warmth from a blackened wok crusted with sugar.

"Cashew or peanut?" The nuts were warm inside their wax packets, and Lauren opened the bag right away, despite her self-consciousness about eating on the subway or the street. She huddled under the cart's big yellow umbrella, not sure if he minded her staying this close but too hungry to care. She felt his eyes on her. When she looked up, he looked away.

Everyone in the city survived by pretending not to see each other performing private acts in public. The woman sitting across from Lauren on the subway, holding her own hands so tight the knuckles shone. The man leaning against a building on West Broadway, stiff white shirt cuff hiding his crumpled face as tourists streamed by like a nightmare of insects. A teenager opening a can of cold soda with an audible snap as the whole bus flared with longing. Lauren was the middle-aged woman eating at the peanut stand in a snowstorm, unable to take another step.

"Hungry," said the peanut man. It wasn't a question.

Lauren was embarrassed by her fingers shoving the sticky mess into her mouth, but her body was running the show. Amy had tried to train her to carry a protein bar for these moments, knowing how she forgot to eat, then needed to grip the edge of her desk when she stood up too quickly.

How could Amy want a separation when they were already so far apart?

The man held out another wax packet. "No charge."

Lauren shook her head. She reached for her wallet and pulled out two more dollars. He was right, Amy was right, she should eat more.

"No charge," he said again. "You have far to go?"

"No, please, take it," Lauren said, waving the dollar bills toward him. "It's very cold out here."

Just as she said it, she realized that she was being rude. He was offering her a gift. She hadn't known her weakness was so apparent. She crumpled the bills into her pocket. "Thank you."

He handed packet number two over the metal counter. Why was it so hard to accept kindness? Shackled if beholden. Her mother had taught her that and it ruined her.

Inside this packet were dark brown chestnuts, their husks slightly blackened from the coals underneath the iron wok. She hadn't known these were part of his larder. He pulled a chestnut from his coat pocket (did he keep a bag there to warm his hands?) and cracked the soft meat into his mouth, spitting the husk out onto the street. It was comforting to share this awkward spitting of shells, though they still didn't look each other in the eye. The mealy flavor stilled her trembling in a way that sugar peanuts hadn't. The flapping yellow umbrella formed a tent of heat and light. They were no longer strangers.

"What part of China is your family from?" She asked.

"I'm from Sunset Park, Brooklyn."

Idiot.

Cora would have rolled her eyes at him, mocking Lauren in a way that pulled the three of them together. Where are you? Lauren wanted to yell to Cora through the thick white sky. She shook her head at the man instead, acknowledging her own stupidity, murmuring "sorry," but it was hard to tell what he was thinking. If Cora were here, he might have been able to forgive Lauren. She cracked another hot chestnut between her teeth. All she really wanted was to go home to Amy and take a jet-lag nap. Masha would pounce on the bed when she came home from school, all hard hugs and elbow jabs, wanting to tell her about everything, everything, everything!

Lauren could still pick Masha up after school. She was her mother and could take her out of her after-school program for one day—they would celebrate Lauren's return from a work trip, have a snowball fight, donuts, and hot chocolate. They would come home together, stomping snow boots on the doormat outside the apartment. Lauren would smile when Ash sloped their way through the living room. She and Amy would read Masha's bedtime story together, long legs overflowing Masha's big-girl bed.

Lauren would never have agreed to couples therapy if she thought it was the road to mediation. Was it really so important to be truthful with each other? Long relationships had bumps in the road. Like Cora and Val. Cora overreacted to whatever Val said to her at that lunch, but Lauren knew they'd get over it like they always did. Cora had iced Val out for too long, it was cruel, but it wasn't supposed to be forever. Was divorce what Amy wanted? Masha was only six and Lauren could support them all with child support and alimony. Ash loved their little sister but was much happier with Amy before Lauren came along. The two of them had survived without a father or husband, and the three of them would be fine without Lauren. Amy would make sure of that. She always did. The little fur family in the hollow tree. That was Masha's favorite book when she was in pre-school because of the soft brown fur glued on the cover. A book covered with teddy bear fur was like a magic trick.

Lauren's watch buzzed: two o'clock in New York, eight o'clock in the Hague. No wonder she couldn't think straight. She had to get something more in her belly to hold herself together.

"Thank you," Lauren said to the peanut man, who smiled politely. Gusts of snow were rearranging the city like one long wedding gown. Lauren put her head down and started walking, keeping her eye out for delivery guys on motorbikes going the wrong way down the street. She had gotten more careful since Cora, always looked both ways, no more superhero moves—her life belonged to Masha.

Lauren wanted to be both inside and outside the hollow tree.

She pulled her scarf over her face. Spicy noodles would save her life. Soup noodles, pork dumplings, then she would pick up Masha. Lauren walked past awnings gathering snow above rows of staring fish. Stacked purple eggplant behind mounds of lychee nuts, passionfruit, bok choi, lemongrass, ginger, and daikon root. Maybe Lauren should buy loads of vegetables and a whole red snapper, then turn right around for home. Cook a big meal and watch Amy's mouth moisten with cooking oil while Masha prattled on, drowning a second helping of rice with soy sauce until Amy reached out a hand for the bottle. *Slow down, baby, it'll get too salty.* Ash would shovel in food as quickly as they could and Lauren wouldn't mind that they never said a word. Lauren would cook a meal good enough to banish this terrible new formality between them that only Masha could ignore because she was the one everybody loved.

White and gold kitties waved mechanical paws in the restaurant window for luck. Lauren pulled open the door to the smell of oil, meat, and hot pepper. There were two women behind the counter, a little girl coloring at one of the empty tables, two teenage boys leaning against the drinks cooler looking at their phones. Everyone stopped talking when Lauren walked in. She had been there often and wanted to be welcomed as a regular, but they were open, they would feed her. It was enough.

How could they know that she felt like an intruder everywhere she went today?

The place was tiny, plastic tables and chairs squeezed between the counter and the front window. The food came quickly in a plastic bowl. A bouquet of throwaway chopsticks sat on the table. Lauren closed her eyes and breathed in the spices from a bowl of meat and noodles so generous she would never be able to finish it, unexpectedly grateful for the invisibility of a middle-aged woman eating alone. She tipped noodles into her mouth and tried not to slurp, though the radio was going and the teenagers talked loudly back and forth in Mandarin. The little girl hummed as she colored at the next table. Lauren and Amy loved taking Masha out to a local place where the tables were covered with paper. Small buckets of crayons were next to the salt and pepper, and everyone could draw as much as they wanted. Lauren bought a roll of white paper at a craft store and they covered the dining table so that Masha could draw at dinner. Lauren had helped her cut out her drawings and tape them onto a long strip of butcher paper thumbtacked to the wall in Masha's bedroom. A map of her world. This fall, Masha had changed her room when she was getting ready to start kindergarten at a new school. A fluffy orange rug, a desk with drawers, her own alarm clock. More girl, less child.

Lauren stopped coming home as much for dinner. More woman, less mom? She looked away from the coloring child and pressed a paper napkin against her eyes.

One of the women brought over a pitcher of water and a Styrofoam cup along with a pile of napkins. "Too spicy?"

Lauren shook her head, gulping water. She wanted to say, thank you for taking me in, thank you for water and spicy broth, noodles, meat, and bone. Thank you for your little girl coloring. She took some deep breaths. This was the second time she had cried in public today—Lauren, who never cried. What if her family scattered into a pile of sticks and straw like the houses in *The Three Little Pigs*? Masha giggled about the wolf because she lived in a house made of bricks. Masha was too old for nursery tales, but Lauren wasn't. She had to keep Masha safe for as long as she could. This was the love that could break her.

Lauren would curl like a dog at the foot of their marriage bed. Rub Amy's feet with oil, then massage her calves and thighs, as far up as she was permitted to go until—the crayon the little girl was using snapped in two. She was pressing hard on a yellow sun with thick stripes. The girl looked surprised, then picked up the broken piece and kept humming as the sun got bigger and bigger. She didn't care that she was going to make a hole in the paper. Lauren wanted to be just like her. She would make a hole for their bright yellow sun with whatever remained in her fist.

She would not allow her life to become all cash and loneliness.

Amy had wanted Cora at the birth.

"Why Cora?" Lauren didn't know why they needed a third person there at all.

"She loves us both, and she'll be there for you when I can't be. Also, she really wanted a baby, and this is as close as you can come. I mean, she might not want to be at the birth because of that. But ask her, okay? You need backup and she's the strongest of all your friends."

"You think? I mean, she's the strongest physically, but Sasha—"

"I want Cora because she does triathlons for fun."

"But we'll be in a hospital, with nurses, our midwife, the doctor on call—"

"Not the same. It's not natural to have only one woman attending a birth, that's never how it was done before male doctors took over."

"What about hiring a doula? Or your sisters—"

"Which sister? The one who never gets in touch unless she needs something? Or the one who thinks I have everything, and she has nothing?"

"I just mean—"

"I do have everything." Amy reached out her arms. "Kiss me!"

"Yes, Goddess Queen."

Lauren moved carefully onto their bed, afraid of jostling the baby free before its time. But Amy was ready, skin furred and taut as a ripe peach. She slept for shorter and shorter stretches. It was hard for Lauren to wait for the unimaginable to arrive. She could buy all the things they were supposed to have for a baby, but when she felt Amy's belly ripple as this creature moved inside her, she realized that she only had ideas of babies, a meaningless collage of plump bottoms and big eyes.

"Why can't we just undo the zipper and let the baby out here," Lauren said, kissing the top of the brown stripe on Amy's belly that went from navel to pubis. She would miss that stripe when it joined the pale tributaries from Amy's first pregnancy with Ash. How could there have been a first pregnancy without Lauren? If she had been there, Ash would love her now.

"We might end up taking the baby out by zipper." Amy closed her eyes. "The sooner the better."

Lauren kissed her on the lips, and when Amy opened up for her tongue, wanting more, Lauren felt the baby move.

"Don't be scared," Amy giggled. "It doesn't know what we're doing."

But maybe stirring the pot did make a difference because Amy's water broke that night. Val came over to stay with Ash. "Don't worry about it, we'll get stoned together," she said to Lauren. Cora picked them up in a town car, and all three of them bundled into the back seat. Amy lay across their laps and pushed her feet against the door when the contractions came, streetlights flying by on the west side highway. Amy said that she was going to throw up because of the air freshener in the vehicle. Lauren kept telling the driver to slow down. Cora looked Lauren in the eye and told her they were doing great.

Leslie, the nurse midwife, was already waiting for them at the hospital with the speculum she always warmed up before insertion. There would be a doctor on call just in case. When Amy had to stop and press her hand against the wall of the building to wait for a contraction near the hospital entrance, she saw Lauren's expensive 35mm camera slung over her shoulder.

"I said no birthing pictures!" Amy yelled. The case opened and the camera fell out onto the sidewalk. The three of them stared.

"Did that just happen?" asked Cora.

"I only brought it for after, I promise!" Lauren said. "Only after, and not if you don't want it." Lauren picked up the camera, then looked at Amy. "How did you do that?"

"I'm a witch goddess," Amy smiled. "No need to shout."

"Better be careful," Cora told Lauren as the hospital doors slid open.

Amy grabbed for Lauren's arm and took a breath. "Superpowers intact."

After that, it was all witch, goddess, and superhero. Amy was right: they needed Cora through that long, sleepless time, filled with Amy's deep breathing, walking, and hoarse curses. The midwife came and went, checking vitals, checking the baby's heartbeat. Amy gripped Lauren's wrists so hard they turned white, then purple. Lauren tried to do everything they learned in their birthing classes, until Amy said, "Fuck the breathing and fuck the bathtub. Get this baby out!"

They never lit their special candle or remembered the playlist. Cora brought juice and water and the midwife checked Amy's cervix. Amy was begging for an epidural, and when that didn't stop the pain, she asked for the zipper, but the midwife said it wasn't necessary. Amy was dilating just fine, soon it would be over. Then Amy went past language and everything was animal, blood, and mucus and the midwife saying *push*!

Lauren could see the baby's head stretching Amy's vulva into a nightmare cartoon, her sex looked flayed open and it couldn't go on and hands reached and pulled and there was Masha! Long, slippery, terrifying. A bulbous eel with clenched eyes, fingers and toes like a real human being. The midwife that Lauren no longer recognized held out scissors for Lauren to cut the cord. She stared at that thick, pulsing rope and thought she might throw up. Cora held her elbow steady. Amy's swollen eyes opened as someone put this stranger to her breasts which had grown ten sizes overnight.

"Who's going to take care of this baby?" said Amy, nearly gone with exhaustion.

"Me," said Lauren, nudging her child's gums toward Amy's long nipple while Cora sat at the foot of the bed, crying and smiling. Lauren watched her daughter's hands waving like underwater sea fans, the back of the baby's skull pulsing in the newfound air. Everything was suddenly biblical, three women circling mother and child. The baby latched on, and Amy plucked off the newborn beanie with her teeth to smell the crown of her daughter's head, the rest of her tightly swaddled in striped blue and white cloth that appeared out of nowhere. Cora and Lauren looked at each other without speaking as Masha snorted and sucked and all the Gods in all the heavens sang that it was good, it was good, it was very, very good.

Then everyone fell asleep.

val

Val was cold. Damp socks in cowboy boots is what she got for wanting to look cool. But if she went home before the reunion, she would never leave. She should've eaten something at the Odessa; she loved the borscht and it was cheap. But she had been too angry to eat. She had veered toward anorexia in high school and struggled with bulimia in her twenties. Her stomach still closed up shop when she was down the rabbit hole. But you could never be too skinny for rock 'n' roll.

Yes, you could. Throwing up in the bathroom, smoking instead of eating. At least she had survived the drug wars and quit smoking. Not everyone made it out of the eighties. AIDS took longer (sometimes): Raymond, Maddy, Tito, Curtis, Dano, Tommy. All these bodies disappearing fast or slow and always thinking she would be next in the backdraft of scythes cutting through their twenties. The night Tommy told her he was positive after they'd been having sex for months. She got tested, tested again, and brought him food until he got too sick for it to make a difference.

Tommy had looked out the window when he told her, sitting with the sheets wrapped around his knees, afraid she would be angry.

She was angry, then she wasn't, then he was gone. She volunteered with God's Love We Deliver, Act Up, and GMHC. These men looked almost transparent and thanked her too profusely when she dropped off a meal, turning out to be not much older than her. She got behind on her deliveries because talk was easier than food. Names kept getting crossed off the list and the band did benefit shows. The winter light outside her window was the same as it was in 1987, as far as she could tell.

She trudged across Fourteenth Street when the light turned green.

Val had always scorned people who stood at the corner waiting for the light, but jaywalking with three dogs was hard, and she had gotten into the habit of waiting even without the dogs. I don't have sex, don't do drugs, don't even jaywalk, she thought. Am I boring? Is it fatal? She was more terrified of being boring than being old. She was already older than she ever thought she would be. Hadn't she resisted the windowsill for good reason? A few cars swished carefully along the wide, two-way street, chains rattling on tires. The red brick Quaker meeting house on Sixteenth Street colored itself in through the snow. She loved that building even though she had attended too many memorials there.

Not mine. (Cora wouldn't stop talking.)

Cora's memorial was uptown at Riverside Chapel. Val was unable to play or sing at the funeral, though Jeff had asked.

You could've played the one you wrote for Tommy, said Cora.

No, I couldn't.

Maybe Val's memorial could be at the Quaker meeting house if someone could afford to rent it. Lauren might do it, and Danny would kick in something. Maybe St. Mark's Church would be better, or maybe nothing would be best. They used to talk about where to have their memorials all the time in the eighties, over soup and buttered challah at the counter of the Veselka. The ones who were really sick spooned up the chicken broth and left the matzo ball behind. When Val was young she wasn't afraid of death or what came after, but now she wondered, where was the enlightenment hiding? Would it come in the shape of a woman over the bathtub? Could Cora reach down a hand to guide her or was her voice only a projection, like the doctor said?

Months of silence and now this nonstop talking. Hearing voices was something Val was used to, listening for words at the piano, but this was different. This was either going to kill her or heal her.

I'm working on your song, Cora. It's just not here yet.

cora

When Val realized Danny wasn't listening at the Odessa, I was eating her rage for breakfast. Danny loves Val, he really does. But why does she only love selfish men? Talented narcissists, just like her. When I stopped talking to her last summer, she told the others I'd gotten mean. But who got how, when? How far back does she want to go?

Val used to be a lot more fun, and I'm way past mean.

Val hears the world, but I see it. That's how I got so good at my job. Who was worth the investment, the promotion? Who was worth me? I got pretty good at betting on the right ones. I mean, there's always the tick tock. How long will this song be exactly right? Maybe five minutes. How long until this human burns up their life? Maybe ten.

I bet on Val, and I'm almost never wrong. She's the real thing.

She got her five minutes, not fifteen, that's how it goes for most of the nightfish. I love Val but musicians are such babies. Hard work and perseverance are beside the point. They were wrong about that at Harrison, like they were about so many things. Nobody taught us about the triumph of chance. What were the odds of me riding that Citibike across Ninth Avenue without looking downtown? What were the odds of that taxi? Chance with no music, though Val might've been able to hear something I missed.

A long high note with the rain turned down.

I wasn't mean to Val, not really. She just exhausted me and I said some things she didn't want to hear. She knows I'm honest and it can hurt sometimes. But that was always our deal.

Look at the snow coming down like chunks of time.

I'd take another day. Hey, I'd take another thirty seconds. I'd sit on the floor and run my hands over my body, starting at my feet and rubbing scented oil all the way up to my scalp. I'd spend some time with my fingers between my legs. I'd eat a whole chocolate bar by myself.

She's not the only one who can't stand the way things turned out.

Val has to pay attention to the dogs, keep following them all the way uptown to Sasha's. I'm going to talk to her as long as necessary. I'm stuck on a bed beneath the ice, watching it melt and looking for the exit sign.

She's got to wrestle with the angel until one of us lets go.

val

Val caught a blur of blue in the corner of her eye. Cora!

It was a man in a blue parka the same color as a Citibike walking a large white dog. This was a creature bred for blizzards. Maybe he was big enough to shut out the sound of Cora's voice.

The dog snuffled up, black nose, dark eyes, thick fur covered in snow, white on white. The man pulled the dog back.

"What's its name?"

"Olaf," the man said. "My daughter named him." Olaf pressed his heavy head against Val's hip, wagging.

"He likes you," the man said.

"He knows where the treats are kept." Val pulled off her gloves. She had a small bag of doggie crack in her coat pocket. Olaf started to wag even more.

"Sit!"

Olaf did not sit, Olaf wagged harder.

"Sit, Olaf!" The man was a little embarrassed and Olaf grinned at them both, pink tongue lolling. "He's not very good, I mean, not very well trained."

"Oh, he's perfect." Val held out her hand, flat palmed as if she were feeding a horse. Olaf licked up the freeze-dried beef and sat, hoping for more. Val and the man caught eyes and laughed. Lauren and Sasha were right, she should get a dog, but musicians had to travel, no pets, no kids. A gig might come up and she couldn't afford a dog sitter. She knew exactly what someone like her would cost. Olaf sniffed at the snow hoping for beef crumbs.

"He lives for this weather," the man said.

"Is he a Samoyed?"

"A mix. Mostly Samoyed."

"You have a big place?"

"Oh no, we have a tiny apartment, but we inherited Olaf, so here he is."

Val liked anyone who would keep a dog so obviously wrong for the city. She rubbed Olaf behind the ear. She wished she could curl up inside that warm pocket of fur.

"You must get asked all the time."

"He belonged to my ex-wife's mother. After she died, we ended up with him. My wife didn't want to keep him, but our daughter's nine, and well, he's a lot of dog, but he's Olaf."

Val kneeled down and held Olaf's big face between her hands. "Olaf," she whispered. "You are a lot of dog." She got to her feet and started walking.

"Wait!"

Val turned, wind whipping her hair around her face.

"You're Val Stone, from the Joypoppers, right?"

"No, not me."

"But I used to see you guys all the time, down at the old Knitting Factory—"

"Must be someone that looks just like me."

She let him take in her hatchet face, heavy pea coat, crappy boots and who-knows-what expression on her face.

"Nice to meet you," he said, as Olaf tugged the leash toward Val, wanting more treats.

"Nice to meet you both." She started walking north as if she had to be somewhere.

"Stay warm!"

She waved without turning around. She was so ashamed, there was a siren going off in her head. Why did she have to keep bumping into everything she used to want?

'Better keep moving so you don't fall down,' she heard Cora say. *That was a good song, one of your best.*

Val wished the sidewalk wasn't so slippery. She wanted to run. She wanted to get on the A train to Rockaway. The beach in a blizzard wearing cowboy boots sounded better than going to this stupid reunion, but it would be really cold at the beach. Maybe she was getting too old for that shit.

Ha ha ha.

"Shut up, Cora!" Val said out loud, glad to live in a city where nobody looked twice. She cut over to Irving Place, a street that existed for only six blocks. More people were coming outside now, one step, two step, salt and snow. Was Val going to walk all the way to Sasha's house? She didn't want to arrive early, hobbling into Sasha's fancy apartment in her wet boots like a crazy person. She had never belonged at Harrison where family money was a protective pelt, like Olaf's white undercoat. Val was the scholarship kid, same as Sasha, only not as book smart. Val might have made money if she had stopped waiting around for her big break, writing songs, trying to keep another band together. Producers, reviews, managers, the business side that she fucked up over and over.

You didn't care enough about the money, said Cora.

That's not true. She cared about money, she just wasn't good at anything but music. Nobody forced her to spend her life hanging out in back rooms playing unpaid gigs.

Yeah, well, too late now, motherfuckers, Cora laughed.

Change the record, change the track, just keep breathing and the noise inside her head would ease up. That's what her former shrink called Cora's conversation with Val. Noise. Maybe Sasha was right, she should go back on her meds, but when you spend some time looking at a bottle full of pills, that becomes its own very bad idea. There should be a daily dispensary, like a methadone clinic, for your antidepressant cocktail. If they had that kind of clinic, her mother might still be alive.

Of course, there's a very good chance your mother was better off dead.

You think I don't know that? She liked you, you know.

I liked her.

Val had called the Bellevue hotline once. *If you are having thoughts of self-harm, you should hang up and dial 911 or go to the nearest emergency room,* said the robot.

She called 911 when she found her mother on the floor of her bathroom, though she must have been lying there for at least twenty-four hours.

She called Cora next, who got in a taxi and did the talking for her. All three of the girls helped her pack up Miriam's apartment, then Danny came with the van and they moved everything into storage. After it was done, they got very drunk. Val tried to erase how her mother had looked when she walked into the bathroom calling her name.

A hundred years ago.

Val missed the jelled, quivering cans of Campbell's tomato soup that her mother used to dump into a pot on the stove without adding water like the directions said. Her mother poured the gloppy mess over white toast and called it Warhol's Blushing Bunny. She used to smoke hand-rolled cigarettes and watch Val eat, sipping vodka out of her favorite English teacup. The teacup meant that she could keep drinking out on the front stoop and watch the neighborhood. Val never thought this was unusual until she started going to other people's houses for dinner. Most parents drank in the living room before they sat down to eat with the kids. They smoked after the meal and never drank alcohol out of teacups. It only made sense if you were on the stoop.

A little dog burst out of a coffeeshop in the arms of a gangly girl who didn't notice Val, but the dog blinked at her, all cozy inside its red plaid coat. It was a sign. Val stepped inside. Steam from the espresso maker softened the air as Val scanned the specials board written in looping chalk letters. Could she afford the tomato soup? It wouldn't be as good as Blushing Bunny, but it came with bread. She wanted to stay in this warm place, it got harder to find a safe corner the further you went uptown. It cost at least ten dollars to sit down anywhere, and Val had worked in so many restaurants that she tipped big, no matter what. Val could ask for a pat of butter on the side, make it last.

"Regular coffee and tomato soup for here," she heard herself say. It would be twelve dollars, not ten, but sitting in a strange coffee shop on Irving Place felt like boarding a ship to ride out the storm.

Val found a table near the window, wrote "Ship City" in her notebook, then drew circles and ships around those two words, adding Olaf's big head in profile. The margins of her notebooks were covered with cityscapes, dogs, and mountain ranges for the dogs to run. She added a river coming down the mountain, so they could swim. This cafe was faux arty with two schoolroom clocks on the wall, matching white faces and long black hands. One of them was circling counterclockwise with the individual clock hands spinning backwards as well. It was hard to pull your eyes away even though it was only the same idea twice. When she looked at the clock whose hands appeared to be still, it was two-thirty. No wonder she was so hungry.

Her soup arrived with two pieces of bread. Val blew on the tasteful sprinkle of chives in her soup bowl, small green dashes floating on a perfect red circle. She hesitated, spoon suspended.

You shouldn't have ordered tomato, it won't taste like the Warhol.

Cora sounded world-weary. Can you be weary of the world when you're dead? That would really suck.

Cora laughed, and Val smiled into her soup.

They could still make each other laugh.

sasha

"Will you please take me home?" an old man asked Sasha as she walked through the lobby of the nursing home. His eyes were desperate though he was neatly groomed and dressed. Had he forgotten why he was here?

"I'm sorry," said Sasha, walking heartlessly into the snowy afternoon. So many people longing for home. Sasha longed for home and she had a very nice apartment.

"You can't save the whole world," her mother used to say when Sasha brought home half-dead starlings, fallen from the nest in early spring.

"But how do you choose which part to save?" Sasha asked.

Her mother shrugged. "Up to you."

Those young birds hardly ate no matter what Sasha tried feeding them. They usually lasted about a week until she found them with their feet curled up on the bottom of her old guinea pig cage. She stroked each bird's iridescent green-black feathers now that they couldn't be frightened by her. No more opening and closing their beaks with tiny pink tongues craving something Sasha couldn't provide. If she didn't want them thrown down the garbage incinerator, she would have to bury them that very day, because the Jewish tradition was to bury their dead as quickly as possible.

"How do we know it's Jewish?" She asked her mother.

"In this house, all the birds are Jewish. Now go bury it in the park."

After her father came home, he put the bird in a paper bag and helped her dig a shallow hole with the trowel her mother used for their window boxes. He put his wool scarf over his head like the tallit he didn't own and recited the Kaddish by heart. It was the only time she saw him cry. Every single time.

Once, Sasha brought home a pigeon dragging its wing along the sidewalk. She wrapped the bird in her coat and placed it in the cage on fresh wood shavings and strips of newspaper. She macramèd a tiny collar with a leash made of string and told her parents she would hold the string as the pigeon flew beside her, the envy of the neighborhood. But the pigeon had to get better before her mother would let her try on the collar.

"Leave it be," her mother said. "It's a tough old street bird, like me."

"It's a rat with wings," said her father, to make Sasha shriek, "No! She's a rock dove and her name is Cleopatra!"

Cleopatra ate everything Sasha gave her. A month later, when they went to the roof and opened the top of the cage, Cleopatra flew out, landed a few feet away, leapt into the air, and was gone.

"I thought she was a homing pigeon," Sasha cried. "I thought pigeons came home!"

"This isn't her home," her mother said, knowing better than to take Sasha in her arms when she was too sad to be touched. Sasha looked for Cleopatra in the neighborhood all afternoon. She'd know her if she saw her.

"That bird wasn't anything special to look at, but she was smart," her mother said, sitting on the edge of Sasha's bed that night, the shadow of her ponytail making wriggly lines on the wall.

"How do you know she was smart?"

"She let you bring her home, didn't she? She took care of herself and then went back to work."

"What work?" Sasha was exhausted by tears.

"The work of staying alive."

Sasha missed her mother every day. She thought of her whenever she saw a pigeon walking purposefully along the sidewalk.

Sasha looked at her watch. She had walked a distance of 2.9 miles, taken 7,497 steps, and climbed three flights of stairs—she hadn't actually climbed any stairs, though it made her feel better to believe her watch. Her watch could tell her the temperature and wind speed if she asked it to, but why ask?

The nursing home was opposite the Cathedral of St. John the Divine.

In the snow, it looked like one of Monet's paintings of Rouen. Sasha saw them at one of the museums in Paris—not the Louvre, which she was finally old enough to give herself permission to dislike. Monet did so many studies at different times of day because he wasn't really painting the cathedral, he was painting light. Today, the light was gray and white, outlining the statues of the saints, wide stone steps spread out below like a terraced garden. The middle section was shoveled and salted into a white carpet leading up to the big carved doors. There was still order in the world.

She would skate along the surface of her outline for the Zoom call, then change her clothes and get ready for the party. Could she tell the committee that she had spent her life working in the invisible world because she didn't know which parts of the visible world to choose?

Her mother chose the ground in front of her, working for the union that gave her and Sasha's father a pension for an old age they never reached. Small, reliable checks arrived each month in Sasha's bank account, just as they had intended on their careful, handwritten beneficiary forms. Sasha chose abstract thinking and now it had finally let her down. She touched her breast surreptitiously through her down coat, nothing to feel, nothing to do but what she was already doing. The Undeniable could only be seen in black and white through a huge machine. Light was also invisible, and Monet spent his whole life painting it.

What if there was nothing left for her brain to formulate?

Breathe, she told herself, stepping carefully on the salted parts of the sidewalk. Today was not a day to slip and fall. She was fifty-three years old. This made her smile because she didn't really believe it, though the numbers don't lie, as Miss Pierce used to say. An idea would come as she walked and the wind was lessening now, snow blowing from trees and rooftops in random bursts. No wonder they rounded up the intellectuals in every revolution. Helpless people like Sasha only knew how to swim through lexicons, adding to the pile of books to be burned for the new society.

If her mother was alive now, would she be proud or ashamed?

It all tired her out, but walking was thinking, and she had to think no matter what—more steps on her watch, less time to prepare. She stopped at the window of one of the last little repair shops. A perfect miniature snow drift rested on the window ledge below the typewriters and vacuum cleaners. A hand-lettered sign read *We Repair VCRs*. How long could they last? Forever, please forever, though in fact the two men who worked inside were cranky and skeptical when she brought them her old vacuum cleaner. New Yorkers were supposed to be skeptical, not sleek and fit, living on smoothies and green drinks. She had gotten through grad school on bagels and coffee—but this morning? Coffee and a green drink.

Sasha turned down a side street toward Broadway. She hadn't started chemo and could still eat whatever she wanted. No breasts + no hair = no death! She'd get a cup of coffee and a bagel for luck. There was always an open deli, even in the worst weather. A toasted bagel and coffee-regular-to-go solved all the problems of the world.

The first deli she walked into had a grill and smelled of eggs and grease, instant gratification. Two men were talking to the man behind the counter. Arabic? Farsi? Sasha only knew English and Spanish, though she was planning on learning Arabic or Mandarin, maybe Italian if she was too lazy for a new alphabet. She could audit any class she wanted at the university, but she was afraid to be seen sitting at the back of a class outside of her field. Taking a language class might look like a retirement move.

Knowing that Harrison taught her that kind of thinking didn't mean she could escape it.

The man behind the counter smiled. "May I help you?"

What she really wanted was a blueberry muffin grilled in butter, but she didn't dare the sugar, despite the coming strip-down, lop-off, lock-down.

"I'll take a toasted bagel with butter," she said. "And coffee, regular."

"What kind of bagel?"

"You have an everything?"

The two men moved to the back of the store as the deli guy's gloved fingers flipped through the pile. "You got the last everything bagel on the Upper West Side," he said triumphantly.

Sasha laughed. The deli guy cut her bagel in half and slapped it onto the same kind of toaster they had in the university dining hall. She loved watching the heating elements turn orange, the familiar scent of toasted onion and garlic. Who would ever want to leave this deli?

Fuck the Zoom and the reunion dinner. All she wanted was to spend the rest of her life in every place of business she went into today.

"Coffee, regular?" The deli guy was making sure.

"Regular."

He spooned in the sinful sugar, then a splash of real milk from an open container in the small refrigerator behind the counter. A precaution against the unhoused, who might fill a paper cup with milk and walk out without paying. He handed her the coffee while she waited for the bagel.

Three snow-covered boys burst in, "Salam, alaykum!"

"Wa alaykum salam," the men chorused back.

The kids jostled each other. One of the men leaning against a stack of boxes at the back said something which made the youngest run up and punch him in the stomach. The man groaned and pulled a face as if he were really hurt, while the little one looked proudly at the older boys, who ignored him. The man behind the counter laughed and the boys began to grab snacks. Everyone watched this cyclone of boyhood whirl around the shop. One small bag of chips each, three sodas that the oldest carefully selected for the rest. They lined up in front of the deli guy, who packed all their things into one bag, each time ringing up a zero.

The three of them swirled out of the store, "Masalama! Masalama!"

The door closed with the jangle of a bell hung on a wire, and in the sudden quiet, Sasha could hear music playing softly. One of the men at the back of the store sighed, the deli guy shook his head, then caught Sasha's eye.

"Your bagel!" He turned his back and wrapped white paper around her bagel: onion, garlic, poppy seed, sesame, salt and pepper. Once upon a time, some genius rolled a hot bagel in all the leftover toppings.

That's the genius who should have gotten a big prize.

The deli guy handed it to her in a brown paper bag with a paper napkin tucked inside. The register rang up four dollars and seventy-two cents.

She handed over a five and risked asking, even though she wasn't a regular, "Are they your boys?"

He shook his head and smiled. "No. They're off to school and need a snack."

"School starts this late? Is it because of the snow?"

"They have religious school," he said.

"Ah, of course." Her own parents never went to schul, but they fought over whether to send Sasha to Hebrew school on Saturdays (her mother won: no bat mitzvah, no memorized prayers, no pile of small checks). Sasha tucked the warm paper bag into her purse, then stopped. Where would she eat it? Her bagel would be cold by the time she walked home and it would never taste as good again.

Sasha's cell phone rang. Her oncologist's office. She stared at the screen until it rang again and forced herself to answer.

"Hello? Yes, this is Sasha."

"Hi, this is Patty from Doctor Sanchez's office. I'm sorry to bother you, but the doctor would like to change the date of your surgery to this coming Wednesday instead of Friday. Will that work for you?"

"Oh. Sure, I mean, do you know why? Is there something new I need to know about?"

"No, no. She has an opening for surgery on Wednesday and thought it best to get you in as soon as possible."

"Oh, okay. I mean, yes, that's fine. May I speak with Doctor Sanchez? Just to make sure there's nothing—"

"I'm afraid she's not available today. This is really just about her surgery schedule. She thinks the sooner the better, if that works for you?"

"Yes, that's fine. Wednesday's fine."

"Good, I'll let her know, and I'll be sending you an email about the prep, and what time to arrive at the hospital on Wednesday morning."

"Okay. Sure."

"Have a nice weekend. Stay warm! It's crazy out there."

"Thanks, Patty, you too."

She ended the call and stared at her phone. Was it really only about the schedule? Had they seen something new on her scans?

Sasha pushed the door open against the wind, her hand tucked around the warm bagel in her pocket.

She was only a few blocks from Miss Pierce's house. What if she did what New Yorkers never do? Ring the bell without calling first. The snow would be her excuse. Last minute, but so what? Sasha could tell her everything. Before she could change her mind, she walked two blocks to one of the few addresses she would never forget. The name *Pierce* under the buzzer was the same, raised white lettering on green plastic tape made by one of those label guns they all used to have. Sasha created labels for everything until her mother made her stop at the utensil drawer. *I can remember where I keep the can opener!* A pigeon flew in and settled on the ledge above the door of Miss Pierce's brownstone, blinking sideways and fluffing its feathers for warmth.

"Hello, Cleopatra," said Sasha, and pressed the bell.

There was a long pause. Should she ring again?

Sasha opened the bag and shoved a piece of bagel into her mouth. She was chewing as fast as she could. Maybe she could use Miss Pierce's doorway as a place to eat her bagel out of the storm. How rude would it be to ring a second time?

She pressed the doorbell again.

The first time Sasha saw Miss Pierce's doorway it was snowing almost as hard as it was right now. She and Cora were twelve years old, and Miss Pierce was younger than Sasha was now, no grey hair, no cancer, no warm bagel in the snow.

"Cora! Hurry up!" Sasha had yelled at Cora's window. Sasha left home at 6:30 instead of 7:00 so she could pick up Cora on the way to school. Sasha envied Cora's sleep as she walked three blocks to the subway in Rego Park to sit in a rattling train car with her textbook flipped open. It was her second year at Harrison. Sasha's mother had made her apply because she didn't like the local middle school, didn't want her to go to Jewish Day School, and Harrison had the biggest endowment in the city. Her mother's plan worked. Sasha was accepted on full scholarship. She hated it. Her neighborhood friends dumped her. None of her clothes fit right. The Harrison girls were smooth and sleek, even their pimples looked like freckles. Her mother kept saying that Sasha only had to stay through eighth grade, then she could test into Bronx Science High School (God Willing, Kinehora).

Then came Cora, Val, and Lauren, and by her second year at Harrison, even though her mother yelled every morning that she needed more sleep, Sasha set her alarm and rode the slowest local train in the city all the way to Times Square with the first wave of commuters, then took the uptown express to Seventy-Second Street so she could ring Cora's bell, four blocks away from school.

She didn't want to go to Bronx Science anymore.

Cora's bedroom window was on the second floor facing the street. The doorman, whom Sasha didn't call Benny because she wasn't supposed to call adults by their first names, opened the door for her with a smile. He wore a fur trimmed leather hat and a black wool overcoat with gold buttons and winter boots. He had gray hair with a boyish face and looked like most of the men in her neighborhood.

"Why do you think all the adults in the building call him Benny, and he calls them Mister, Missus or Miss?" Sasha's mother asked.

"To ask the question is to answer it," said her father, without looking up from the crossword.

"But Benny's so nice. He likes everyone in the building, or at least he likes Cora's family."

"Does he have a union card? The doormen and the supers have a good union."

Sasha said hello, goodbye, and thank you to Benny. She didn't call him anything.

Sasha took the stairs to the second floor and pulled off her snow boots in the hallway outside Cora's apartment before pushing open the door, which was always left unlocked. Sasha's building had a courtyard where the old people sat on benches and kids played Foursquare. The super knew everybody, but they always locked their doors. In Cora's building, the apartment door was left open and the doormen gave liver-flavored biscuits to every dog in the building. Jessie was the only mother she had ever met who insisted that Sasha call her by her first name. Sasha knew people without fathers but hadn't met anyone whose parents were divorced before Harrison, where nearly everybody shuttled back and forth between their father and mother's houses. They must have the money for two apartments. Cora hardly ever saw her father, who had a swimming pool in California. She showed Sasha a picture of him once and it was true that he looked like a movie star, though Cora said he wasn't.

"Cora! Boots!" Jessie yelled from deep in the apartment. It didn't sound like Jessie had declared a mental health day, when Cora and her twin brothers could stay home in pajamas, drink hot cocoa and watch TV.

Sasha stood in her socks at the end of the hallway, just inside the front door. Was Cora in the bathroom? Maybe she was in her bedroom. Cora had covered the windowsill with stickers and pasted glow-in-the-dark stars on the ceiling, something Sasha's mother would never allow. Jessie, Cora, and the twins would have listened to the radio from seven to seven-thirty, eating Pop-Tarts and waiting for a snow day announcement that never came. Sasha and her parents had done the same starting at six. Sasha's mother always cooked a hot breakfast of homemade fruit compote over oatmeal in the winter and wouldn't let Sasha skip school unless she had a fever. At Cora's house, even the five-year-old twins made their own breakfast. Sasha was welcome to pour herself a forbidden bowl of Cap'n Crunch or grab a Pop-Tart. Jessie never ate breakfast because she was always late for work, putting on makeup and sipping coffee in the bathroom.

Jessie was the best.

Sasha took off her backpack and leaned against the coats as the radio played a repetitive jingle from the kitchen. It was tragic to have only a snowstorm instead of a blizzard, even though Sasha had put a spoon face-up under her pillow last night. Her mother taught her to do that, something they did in Poland when she was a child (*as if we needed more snow*). Once Sasha told the others, they all did it. "Spoon up!" they had called out yesterday afternoon as they scattered home. Sasha still couldn't believe she had friends who did something from once upon a time in Poland.

You weren't supposed to admit it, but Sasha liked that Harrison was all girls.

Jessie was yelling at Theo and Henry in the kitchen. Now that she was twelve, Cora left first while her mother wrestled with the twins, whose snow things were never where they were supposed to be. The fun Jessie was the mother who pretended they lived on a boat where things were stowed properly during clean-up time. This morning, she was the mother who hated slush, hated her job, and hated WABC for not giving them a break. Who decided on the snow days? The President? Jessie hated him too.

Cora came down the hallway rolling her eyes, grabbed her sheepskin jacket and broken-in leather hiking boots. Sasha stepped into her purple snow boots and zipped up her puffy jacket, feeling overdressed and childish.

"Bye, Mom!" Cora slammed the door and they trudged down the stairs to the lobby, two turtles with heavy backpacks. Benny held the door open for them.

"Thank you, Benny," said Cora.

"Thank you," said Sasha.

"I walked along Riverside this morning," said Sasha. "Looking for the untouched parts."

She hoped Cora didn't think they were too old to collect clean snow where no dog had peed. Val and Cora had shown her how to scoop it up from under park benches, then hurry back to Cora's and sprinkle cinnamon sugar on top for snow cones. Everyone knew that Val and Cora were best friends. Sasha would never rate that high, but she had Cora to herself every morning. Val was always late to school and Lauren was dropped off by a car service.

Cora stuck out her tongue to catch a snowflake and grinned at Sasha. "Virgin."

Sasha stuck her tongue out as well. "Deelish."

Sasha didn't know why this moment kept coming back right after Cora died. The two of them saying *deelish* over and over, as if they were pirates grabbing booty from the air.

"Deelish!"

Cheeks shining, hair spangled with snow, they were off. They grabbed snow from the top of cars, packing snowballs as they ducked behind front stoops, running without looking for cars across the side streets. Sasha threw hard at Cora, who dodged, and the snowball landed *smack* against a strange woman's back just as she came out her front door. The snowball exploded and the woman turned around.

It was Miss Pierce, her red plaid coat cinched at the waist with a matching belt.

"What are you doing here?" Cora asked, as if teachers weren't allowed on the block.

"I live here," said Miss Pierce. "Seventh grade is old enough not to think your teachers live inside the school."

Sasha and Cora looked at each other. Of course the teachers lived inside the school.

"Don't know why they didn't give us a snow day," Miss Pierce said. "If I were the mayor, I'd make every snowstorm a snow day and send all the children to the park. It's healthy!"

Sasha and Cora started walking on either side of Miss Pierce. It was impossible that their science teacher could have an apartment in a brownstone indistinguishable from all the others on the block.

"It has a green door," Sasha told Cora later. "Number two-sixty."

Cora hadn't noticed any of that, but when they reached Harrison, Miss Pierce said, "I leave the house by 7:45 sharp."

As if she knew they would be coming again, even if they pretended it was by accident. They picked her up almost every day, this very Pierce-like invitation saving them from having to pretend it was all a grand coincidence.

But Miss Pierce never waited.

val

The clock that wasn't spinning backwards in the cafe read 3:00. Val finished her soup and bread in twenty minutes, forcing herself to keep chewing and swallowing. It was too easy for her to forget to eat and slip into a familiar, lightheaded remove from her own body. She was the only one sitting in the cafe without headphones or earbuds firmly in place. It's not that she didn't have both, but she believed what she used to tell her students: listen to the world. The bass drum thump when the barista slammed out used coffee grounds, the high squeal of the milk steamer over chiming bottles of flavored syrup, the chink of porcelain marking notations in the air.

She wished that she had been wearing headphones an hour ago, so she couldn't hear Olaf's owner saying he knew who she was. Was that a thrill for him? His own minor celebrity sighting? Now he would join Val's 3:00 a.m. whisper list: not enough money, no health insurance, no lover, no career, ugly, old, and gaunt in her cowboy boots and pea coat.

She had stopped for Olaf, not the man on the other end of the leash.

If he had kept his mouth shut, she might be able to eat her soup without every bite becoming an act of resistance.

"Name your demons. You fucking own them." Danny said to her once, then screamed, "Begone!" This made her laugh during one of those times when she didn't care enough to eat and couldn't get out of bed. Val was good at screaming into the mic, but not so good alone in her apartment. What would happen at Sasha's tonight? How quickly could she get Lauren to ditch the reunion dinner for a dive bar on Broadway? Why had Sasha decided to host this stupid thing and why had Val said she would come?

Because Cora died and Val wanted Sasha and Lauren to keep liking her despite all her fucked-up shit that drove Cora away. Pathetic. She couldn't even handle one boring cocktail party because she was afraid of what her former classmates would think of her. She left those people in the dust thirty-five years ago and now she was the one with ashes in her mouth.

Newsflash, said Cora. *Everybody's got ashes in their mouth.*

Val had to get moving. Throw her body into the storm and walk it off, find more dogs to talk to. Get Cora to leave her alone for five minutes. She put two dollars on the table for a tip, suited up and headed north toward Gramercy Park. The National Arts Club's nineteenth-century facade faced the square, its high windows and cornices outlined by the snow. Val had been to the great old bar inside, seen the stuffed black raven quoth *nevermore*, but the club was just like the rest of the neighborhood—private and rich.

A small group of children were building a snowman inside the fenced, gated park. She wondered about the nanny helping them roll the snowballs to make a bottom, a belly and a head. Did she hate her job or think she had a pretty good deal? This snowman would have a black top hat with an organic carrot for a nose. Nobody got into that park without a key. The only people with keys were the ones who could afford to live on the square or stay at the hotel. Upscale New York apartments were like that fairy tale where you open a room to find the corpses of past wives, though it was usually someone well-dressed, talking on the phone or lying in bed with shades drawn and shoes off in the middle of the afternoon. As a child, invited for occasional playdates with wealthy children from Harrison, Val didn't understand how all that money made people bone tired.

She had climbed the Gramercy Park fence with Lucian one night when he had a room at the hotel. Everyone knew the place was haunted. The Gramercy Park Hotel's final act was an eighteen-story jump from the roof by one of the owners. Val stopped halfway across the west side of the park and looked up. She couldn't see the top of the building in the snow. It was a long way down.

If you're going to do it, do it right.

Val and Lucian had shimmered that night at the Gramercy. "You're good at falling in love," Danny warned as they walked toward the bar after the gig. "My greatest talent," she said, sweeping one hand down to the toe of her boot, all mockery and deference. CBGB's wanted them back, their show at the Pyramid got reviewed by the Voice, and Cora was negotiating Val's first record deal with Slaughterhouse.

It was all because Val was in love.

She couldn't say this out loud, but she knew where the good stuff came from. The Joypoppers tumbled into the Gramercy at about 2 a.m. Lucian had played an earlier set, and by the time she arrived with the band he was well-oiled. They took the corner banquette and everyone who really mattered was there. Not just the managers and dealers (though they were there too, leading Lucian back and forth to the bathroom), but the musicians, lifting an invisible velvet rope for the scrappy Joypoppers with a bottle of Maker's Mark on the table. It was because of Lucian. It was also because of Val.

When they shut down the bar, Val pulled Lucian outside. They walked into the soft morning, and it was all she could do not to take her shoes off. She showed him the locked gate and they laughed at how people thought they could keep Val and Lucian out of any place they wanted to be. She held the iron bars as he boosted her up. skinny enough to fit between the spikes. She turned to give him a hand, but he was already halfway there, and once they reached the top, she told him to pretend the spikes were barbed wire, like the fences he'd grown up with in South Dakota. She swung one leg over, then the other, and dropped to the grass. Lucian ripped his jeans coming down. The park seemed bigger from the inside, low spreading trees, benches, and sanded paths. They lay on their backs, watching the sky turn blue.

"How are we going to get out?" he asked.

"We don't have to," she said. Nothing hurt anymore.

Val's phone buzzed in the pocket of her parka. She wiped snow from the screen to read a text from the curator of the show at the gallery. Val's heart lifted. They probably wanted to ask her something about the footage from the Joypoppers concert. Val was still a working musician.

Someone had told her that when Patti Smith made her comeback after dropping out of sight in the eighties, people asked what she'd been doing. "Laundry," said Patti.

Val flipped up the collar of her pea coat so she could read the text.

hey val. we just got a new curator. can't include joypoppers vid in march show

hoping for a second round.

thnx 2 u and Danny 4 yr help. great footage.

see u at the gallery

Oh. Right. The old bait and switch. Thanks universe. Why had Val let herself get so excited? It was just a tiny show in a nowhere gallery. Nobody would have seen it or written it up. Danny would shrug and roll his eyes at the time they spent digging up the old footage she paid to convert to digital. Danny would say it's still good to digitize their "archive" and hey, something else might come along. Just keep doing the work, keep writing, keep playing.

Or don't. Stop looking at her piano. Stop writing. Stop, drop, and roll out the window with all your pieces of paper left behind. Notebooks filled with handwriting. Shoeboxes of cassettes, CDs, undeveloped film. The best she could do. Val blew on her fingers to warm them up enough to text back.

no problem. have a great opening.

Did it sound like she really didn't care? Is that how she wanted it to seem?

no problem. maybe next time!

Was that better? Leaving the door open? Maybe she should cut the exclamation point. She hated false enthusiasm almost as much as the way people used numbers for words in a text. Which made her old. Who cared? How about:

fuck u asshole.

Cora started laughing as Val typed with one finger:

no problem. maybe next time. have a great opening.

Cora laughed harder. Val pressed send.

lauren

Everything was possible after soup noodles. The snow swirled around Lauren's boots as she strode toward Masha's school. She would pick up her girl and bring her home. Amy had to let her stay. They loved each other best in Masha's world.

Masha's new school was near the East River. Lauren had to map it on her phone. She'd only been there twice since school started and always forgot the cross streets. She used to watch barges piled high with black garbage bags steaming down the river when she was Masha's age; fat tugboats guided them through the current with seagulls dipping in until they dumped the whole load out at sea. Lauren had wanted to be a tugboat pilot, without a single thought about what it meant to toss the filth of an entire city overboard. She wondered if someone had to stand in the middle and shovel it over the side. Did they wear high green waders? Her father rolled those up in his suitcase for fishing trips. Or did one side of the barge lower down to let the sea sweep everything clean as a toilet bowl? Masha's school had construction paper cut-outs taped to the window. Green, brown, pink and blue children with overlapping circles for hands. Lauren walked up the steps, opened the double doors, and walked into that meat-and-cabbage school smell.

The guard looked up briefly from her phone, checked Lauren's I.D. and told her the students were in the gym for pick up.

"Where's the gym?"

A kid ran down the hall wearing a baseball cap and the guard yelled, "No hats!"

"The gym?"

This was a divorced dad question. The parent who doesn't know where pickup is, has to ask for the address of the pediatrician's office, and doesn't know where the immunization records are kept.

Amy probably knew why no hats.

Lauren walked toward the rising sound of children's voices and bouncing rubber balls. Her heart lifted as she went down a short flight of stairs. Masha would come running.

"Who are you here for?" asked the woman with a clipboard who looked too young to be a teacher. She ran her pen down the list of names. "Oh, Masha was already picked up by—" The teacher hesitated. "She was picked up by her sibling about ten minutes ago."

Lauren stared at the woman. How could Ash have gotten here first? She was five minutes early.

The teacher looked concerned. "I hope that's all right? Ash is one of the approved caregivers on our list. And you are?"

"Her mother. Her other mother." Lauren couldn't force a smile.

"So nice to meet you! My name is Esther, I'm the afterschool coordinator. Masha is such a sweetheart. So now I know the whole family."

Her perkiness made Lauren want to slam a rubber ball in her face.

"When did they leave?"

"Ten minutes ago. Girl Power was cancelled because of the snow. I hope there's nothing wrong?"

"No, no, nothing."

"It's so nice the way Ash takes such good care of her. You can tell how close they are. You must feel very lucky."

"Oh. Yes, I do. Thanks."

Ten minutes! They couldn't have gone that far walking at Masha's pace. Why didn't she see them on the way here? Maybe Amy told Ash to take a taxi home in this weather. Why did Ash pick her up? They had a babysitter and Ash was supposed to have a job. Lauren ran up the stairs and out the front door, past another mother zipping and wrapping her child in brightly colored snow gear. Lauren wanted her own bright creature so much it hurt to breathe.

She's safe, she told herself. Everybody's safe. Quit panicking.

She walked up Henry Street toward the donut shop Masha loved. It's where Lauren would have taken her after school if things were the way they were supposed to be. Donuts on the way to school and donuts on the way home. Could Masha and Ash have walked four blocks in ten minutes, even with the zipping and sliding and wrapping up? Every person on the street ahead of Lauren was the wrong shape and height. Old men with small dogs blocked her way, none of the other parents recognized her. The snow was starting to come down heavily again, streetlamps haloed in the thickening air. There was someone who looked exactly like Ash from the back, rounded shoulders and a black parka, but there was no child holding their hand. Here was the corner with the donut shop, steamed windows, shoveled sidewalk.

Lauren stopped with her hand on the door.

They were blowing onto their hot chocolates at the same time, Ash smiling in a way that Lauren was never allowed to see. Masha broke off a piece of her donut, gap-toothed mouth saying something that made Ash nod solemnly and break off a piece as well. The two of them traded, then dunked.

If Lauren walked in, Ash's face would become a blank screen. Masha would walk between them holding hands, but they would hardly speak to each other.

There was only one photo of Ash smiling at their absurdly small post-wedding party. How many people do you invite when the only child is so clearly unhappy? Lauren's parents didn't believe in gay marriage any more than they believed in gay people. Her sister, Diana, wanted to come, but that would only make things worse with their parents and Lauren told her not to bother. Sasha, Val, and Cora were there.

"We're your sisters and your mother," said Sasha.

"Not me, I'm your father," said Val, and it turned out pretty perfect after all. They all liked Amy. Her kid was a handful, but Ash was sixteen and right on track. Besides, they would be off to college in a couple of years.

Ash didn't like any early pictures of themselves displayed in the house, so Amy and Lauren put the older family photos away. Lauren was secretly relieved. She didn't like wedding photos even though she had wanted the marriage more than Amy did. She talked her into the whole catastrophe, as her bubbe used to say. Would Ash hate Lauren as much if she hadn't pushed for that particular brand of domesticity? Wife. Mother. Child. When Amy's sister Karen flew in from St. Louis for the wedding and asked how she could help out, Lauren said, don't let her kid ruin it for Amy.

Ash hadn't ruined the wedding. If Lauren walked into the donut shop right now, she would be the one who ruined everything.

Exactly how long could she watch her child from outside the door?

Lauren turned back down Henry Street to Clinton, imagining the old Lenape trail threading invisibly beside her for company. Why was she alive in the twenty-first century when she understood so much more about the seventeenth? Egrets, herons, ducks, and kingfishers nested along the original shoreline. Early maps showed streams running from the center of the island to an inlet right where she was standing. Lauren was such a nerd, she wanted The Historical to organize Lenape trail walks. Nobody else thought this was a priority.

"Let's let the Museum of the American Indian handle that," said Naomi delicately.

Lauren dropped it at work, but she was walking a bit more of the trail every year, following a map downloaded onto her phone. It was research, she told Amy on those nights when she called to say she wouldn't be home in time for dinner. So many family dinners avoided when all she wanted was Amy and home.

"But how can I do battle with Amy's child?" Lauren asked Cora the night of their last drink.

"Exactly," said Cora.

The couples therapist had warned Lauren and Amy against judging Ash's maturity by their age when they were going through a crucial gender transition.

"You're still the parents," Teresa said. "Ash may not show it, but they need a great deal of support from both of you."

Lauren stopped at the corner of Cherry and Clinton, an empty playground surrounded by bony trees, snow thick as summer leaves. The trail map on her phone floated through a tall, rectangular building where a string of fish hung by their gills from a broomstick across the fire escape. The wind sharpened between the buildings. Lauren tightened her scarf.

She was not a bad mother. She had chosen the children's happiness over her own. Wasn't that what adults were supposed to do?

She wanted to tell Amy how happy Ash looked when they thought nobody was watching.

sasha

When Miss Pierce answered the door Sasha felt like running away. She always forgot that Miss Pierce was old now. Smaller than she remembered, with dyed red hair, and wondering why Sasha had showed up at her door in the middle of a snowstorm. Did her sudden appearance mean bad news?

Sasha had been the one to make the phone call to Miss Pierce when Cora died.

Pierce gathered Sasha into a bony hug and closed the front door to the small entryway, snow scattering from Sasha's coat onto the tiled floor.

"Everything all right? Come in, come in!"

"Sorry I didn't call first. I was in the neighborhood and the weather's so bad, I thought I'd just ring the bell."

Sasha felt awkward, huge, and unexplained. What must her face look like?

Pierce led her up a flight of stairs. Everything was the same as the last time she was here. The aluminum mailboxes on the narrow first floor, the door beyond the stairs to the alley behind the building. It reminded Sasha of her parents' apartment building—metal bannisters, stone stairs with black and white hexagonal tile on the landing. Pierce lived on the second floor, facing the back. "You never want to be on the first floor or facing the street," Miss Pierce told Sasha when she was looking for her first Manhattan apartment, and she never had. Sasha took off her snow boots outside the apartment door.

The plain rubber doormat was new. Sasha hoped there was no new furniture.

Miss Pierce hung Sasha's parka on an empty coat tree. How many visitors did she have? Her life had seemed so glamorous when they were her students, off to the opera or a weekend in the country with "a friend." They always knew when she was leaving for the weekend because she wore her "country mouse" shoes to school on Friday. Those upscale tennis shoes were the opposite of her "city mouse" shoes, red loafers that Lauren swore were made from real alligator. They used to spin every hint into a melodrama about Miss Pierce and her "friend." Many of the teachers at Harrison were gay—it was a safe place to work, Sasha understood later.

There had been one affair between a senior girl and a beloved Spanish professor, who was fired as a result. The affair only became public after the girl graduated from Harrison, and nobody knew if anything happened between them before. Lots of girls had crushes but Señora Manresa was a favorite, and when she and the student remained a couple for many years after she was fired, it made Sasha's group, who had fought the administration against Señora's dismissal, feel righteous. Nowadays everyone would feel exactly the opposite and their old principal would be the righteous one. Miss Pierce never revealed anything private to the girls, even though everyone knew that the principal who fired Señora Manresa was also gay. Lauren had always been gay, and Val was gender fluid decades before it became fashionable.

Thinking of Val made Sasha wince a little bit. She knew that Val was only coming tonight as a favor to her, but would she be all right? Val was an octopus; she could spew ink all over the room.

"Tea?" Miss Pierce already knew the answer.

Sasha sat down on the couch. Miss Pierce's collection of small china dogs still paced along the mantel of a blocked-off fireplace. These dogs were Sasha's old friends, though a china dog collection didn't really fit Pierce, with her otherwise uncluttered surfaces and mid-century modern furniture. Bookcases lined an entire wall of the living room and continued into the small entryway. It felt like a gift that nothing had changed.

"All well?" Pierce turned on the electric tea kettle in her galley kitchen.

"Yes, fine."

"Oat cakes?"

Sasha would eat a whole box of them if Pierce kept filling the plate. Could Miss Pierce smell the onion and garlic from the bagel in her coat pocket? Sasha was afraid that a plate of oat cakes and strong Scottish tea might break her. Now that she was here, she had no idea what to say.

Everything bad happened in cold weather. Cora had left her all alone.

"Are you going to attend anything at school for alumni weekend?" Sasha forced the tremble out of her voice.

"Oh no, my people are all dead or retired. I don't want to be jealous of the new smart classrooms."

"Your classrooms were always smart," said Sasha. Miss Pierce gave her a look. She wasn't actually jealous of anything.

"I'm hosting a reunion dinner at my place tonight, just our class, the ones who could come."

"Dinner for fifty?" Miss Pierce brought out her tray with the old brown teapot, two cups and a plate of oat cakes.

"Twenty-four, buffet."

Sasha reached for an oat cake even though she knew she should wait for the tea to brew. "Should be interesting." Miss Pierce went back for milk and sugar.

"Why don't you come too?"

"Is that why you stopped by?" said Miss Pierce over her shoulder. "To invite me to the dinner?"

"I should have asked you sooner, I'm sorry. I sort of pulled it together at the last minute. Please come, everyone would love to see you."

"We don't have to pretend that I'm universally loved by my former students." Miss Pierce nudged the oat cakes to make room for milk and sugar on the coffee table. "But I'll think about it." She crossed her legs and leaned forward. "Tell me about you. Have you gotten a lot of research done?"

"Nothing. I've done nothing."

Pierce stopped pouring the tea. The cookie went dry in Sasha's mouth. Her bagel would be cold by now. Pierce reached for the glass sugar bowl with its perfect cubes and miniature tongs. In the silence, her sugar lump was a stone thrown into a pond; the tiny circles spreading out on the surface of hot liquid were predictable forms. Concentric circles, dissolving sugar, and the flooding scent of tea were discreet phenomena which merged to become an entirely new thing. Sasha couldn't help how her mind worked—or didn't.

"I have to give a verbal report to the prize committee this afternoon, it's not supposed to be too formal, more like an update. But I'm not ready and my notes are a mess."

"This afternoon? Before your dinner party?"

"I know."

"You always leave things to the last minute." Miss Pierce narrowed her eyes. "But then you pull off something completely unexpected. You were my very best student."

Sasha looked down, a flush rising up her neck. All through her slow march into research and tenure, grants and prizes, Pierce had attended every ceremony for Sasha that was open to the public, but this had never been said.

Sasha covered her face with her hands.

She had never wept in front of Miss Pierce. She had shone. It was her job to shine for Miss Pierce.

Did changing the surgery to Wednesday mean she was going to die?

"I'm sorry."

"There, now." Pierce's voice was calm. Was Sasha the only one who wanted to run shrieking from the room?

"I have some bad news."

The Undeniable was inflating inside Sasha's mouth, a stinking balloon of vomit, shit, and bad morning breath, none of which were allowed in her teacher's apartment. The cancer had spread everywhere and she was going to die, they just hadn't told her yet.

"There's a lump under my breast. They have to lop it off. Lop them both off, actually." Sasha fought the urge to giggle. Lop them off! She was a lop-eared rabbit! "My mother didn't have breast cancer but since both parents died of cancer in their sixties it's the right thing to do. I was supposed to have the surgery in a week, on Friday, but they just called to tell me they want to do it on Wednesday. Which is bad, right? It has to be bad."

Sasha knew she must look like a cartoon character, but she couldn't stop smiling and weeping.

Miss Pierce took Sasha by both shoulders. "You are not going to die."

"How do you know?" Sasha jumped up. "You don't know anything about it."

"It's going to be very hard and then it will be over, and you'll be fine."

"What are you talking about? I haven't told you anything yet!"

"I know there's more."

"You always think you're right!"

"No, I don't. But this time I am. Listen to me, you can train for this like an athlete. The treatments have come a long way since your parents' time and every cancer is different. I'll come with you to your appointments, as much or as little as you'd like. It can be done. I've been through it."

Sasha stopped.

"You have?"

"Four years now, cancer free." The lines deepened on either side of Miss Pierce's mouth as she looked at Sasha. "You have to admit that possibility coexists with the other."

"Why didn't you tell me?"

"I had the help I needed." Miss Pierce's hand shook when she lifted her teacup. "This is a wig."

"It is? But I thought—"

"I didn't like the way my hair grew back, so I just kept wearing the wig. I'm secretly quite vain, you know."

Sasha plopped back down on the couch. "I can't believe I never knew. I'm so sorry. I could have helped."

"I'm fine now." Miss Pierce patted Sasha's knee, almost motherly.

"My God," said Sasha. "I didn't know."

"This one is false," Miss Pierce said, pointing to one side. "I have a special bra to wear when I want to bother. I went out earlier to get some groceries, so I put it on. You'll be better off without anything."

"My hair and breasts are my best parts," Sasha whispered.

"Your brain is your best part. The thing to do is stay as strong and healthy as you can, and you will come through."

She went to the kitchen and came back with two small glasses and a tall bottle filled with dark brown liquid.

"This is called Nocino. It's an Italian cordial made from walnuts when they're still green. I got it in Umbria on a walking tour. The woman made this from her own trees and told me that because a walnut has the shape and furrows of the brain, it's good for the health of the mind. The mind leads the body, you know that."

Miss Pierce poured them each a draft. They touched glasses.

"To your good health," said Miss Pierce. "And the many forms of beauty."

They each drank it down in one gulp. Sweet and fiery.

"Sooner or later, everything happens to us," Miss Pierce said quietly.

Sasha held out Miss Pierce's balled up napkin. "I've snotted all over your napkin."

"Laundry does exist," said Miss Pierce. They both smiled, finally. "What time is the phone call?"

"Four-thirty."

"And when is the dinner?"

"People are coming at six-thirty."

"Do you have anything at all?"

"The caterers are bringing everything."

"I mean for the talk."

"My notes are in my bag. I thought I'd think of something this afternoon, as I was walking. I had this idea that I'd go to a coffee shop. But then I got the phone call from the doctor's office—and I came here."

Miss Pierce refilled both of their glasses.

"I hate the Genie. That's what I call the prize. I know, don't laugh, but really, it's like something came out of the bottle carrying a huge check that stopped me from thinking. And I don't want to use Cora or cancer as an excuse. It was happening before she died, but I couldn't tell anyone I was blocked, not even Cora. She was so proud of me."

"It's not so terrible to be the best, is it?" Miss Pierce said, handing her another napkin.

"It's awful."

Miss Pierce stared at her for a moment, then nodded. "Yes, I suppose it can be. The words are difficult."

"I've been struggling to put something down—"

"No, I mean the words 'best' and 'worst.' Let's leave them out of this."

Miss Pierce went into her bedroom and came back with a yellow legal pad, two ball point pens, and a box of tissues.

"Pop quiz?" Sasha sniffed and blew.

Pierce pushed her glasses up to the bridge of her nose. "I can't begin to understand quantum mechanics at your level, but I might be able to help you organize the sock drawer."

"Organize the sock drawer?"

"Show me your notes. Have another oat cake."

val

The Gramercy Park Hotel was right on the corner, and maybe they had a happy hour? One drink before the reunion. Fuck it. Val went through the revolving door and had no idea where she was. The piano was gone. The wooden bar gleamed anorexic, no bowls of nuts or popcorn. Two men perched on their stools with blue-lit faces, upper bodies curled over tiny screens.

The Gramercy looked like a bad face lift.

It's too sad to stay here, said Cora. *This place sucks, let's go.*

The wind pressed hard against the revolving doors back to the street. A woman wearing a white fur hat swirled in as Val swirled out. A dog started barking: Hey, over here!

It's a sign, said Cora. *You can take the bus across Twenty-Third Street and catch the subway uptown.*

"I know how to get to Sasha's!" Val yelled, like a full-on crazy person.

This snowstorm was starting to not be fun anymore.

Val ran for the bus at the corner. When she climbed aboard it smelled like wet dog. She looked at the driver as she swiped her metrocard, but he kept his eyes fixed on the huge windshield wipers. The bus lurched away from the curb. There was no option of changing to a car that didn't smell, like on the subway. In a solo seat toward the front, a furrowed man cradled a plastic bag on his lap. Darkness fell like a blackout shade.

The smell was stronger toward the back, and now, Val saw why everyone else was sitting up front. A dirty white pit bull lay across the steps to the upper level of the bus, calmly watching Val approach. Its owner occupied a double seat, leaning against a backpack. A line of blue-black dots divided their face down the middle, with triangles tattooed on each cheek. They wore so many layers of clothing it was hard to tell whether it was the dog, the clothing, or the body that stank the most. A crusty punk who could be twenty years old, or fifteen, maybe thirty. Val didn't recognize the crusties who camped out in Tompkins Square Park. Their dogs were easier to tell apart.

Val took a seat near the dog, breathing only through her mouth. "Can I pat him?"

"Sure, it's a girl."

"What's her name?"

"Clementine."

Val offered her hand. Clementine sniffed once and settled back onto her front paws. Val stroked her smooth white head.

"Aren't you a beautiful pup?"

The crusty smiled. They had good teeth, and looked more female than male. The skin above one eye was bruised.

"I don't know how old she is." It sounded like a question they'd been asked too many times. Clementine showed her pearly whites like Mac the Knife, pink and black tongue panting in and out. The crusty looked down the aisle at the bus driver and leaned toward Val, who couldn't help pulling back a little and holding her breath. She hoped it wasn't obvious.

"He almost didn't let us on the bus. But I guess he decided to ignore Clem because of the storm. I lost her emotional support harness, but the paperwork's somewhere in my bag."

Val rested her hand on Clementine's back, scratching between her shoulders and hoping she didn't have fleas.

"Cold out there," Val said. She wriggled her toes inside her boots. Her socks were damp, they'd dry out at Sasha's. She was feeling shaky and wanted to stay close to Clementine despite the stink.

"I'm glad he let me on," said the crusty. "I never pay. I don't believe in paying for public transportation."

"You broke?"

"I can walk. I'm young and I've got good boots." They twirled a pink snow boot.

"Better than mine."

They eyed Val's cowboy boots. "Yeah, those kind of suck in this weather," they said, a little dreamily. "But I wouldn't pay for the bus even if I had shitty boots or was old."

Val wondered if they had stopped themselves from saying *old like you*. It made her smile.

"Public transportation should be free," they went on. "We're the richest country in the world."

"Not anymore," said Val.

"Big trips you can hitch or take a train," the crusty said, getting wound up. "I'm going to hop a train down to Florida, get away from the cold."

"Really?"

"Yeah. I'm a traveler."

Val wished she could jump a freight with Clementine.

"What's your name?" she asked.

"Eleanor." So, they were a girl. Maybe. They looked younger when they giggled. "My parents named me after the Beatles song."

Val sang the first line.

"Hey, you've got a nice voice."

Val shrugged. "It's a sad song."

"Is it?" The girl looked surprised.

"Yeah, I mean, if you listen to the words."

"Oh, I never listen to the words." The girl leaned against her backpack. "I must have heard that song a million times and never listened to the words."

The bus wheezed to a stop on Fifth Avenue, two people got off, and then it was only the old man, the crusty girl, Clementine, and Val.

"You're wrong about that song," said Eleanor. "Weddings are happy, not sad."

"The song's about after the wedding," said Val. "Eleanor Rigby is picking up rice in the church *after* a wedding."

"Why would she do that?"

"Maybe she was hungry."

"Yeah, I'm hungry too. Have you got a dollar?"

Val knew this was coming. "I'll give you two," she said. "One is for Clementine."

"People always want to give to the dogs," said Eleanor, watching closely as Val unbuttoned her coat and took out her wallet from the inside pocket. Maybe she'd give her more because of the storm.

"What do the tattoos stand for?" Val felt like she had a right to ask since she was going to give her five bucks.

"These tattoos are the traveler's vow. You know what a vow is?"

"What kind of vow?"

Eleanor pushed her hat up and Val could see her whole face, baby fat cheeks and puffed-up eye. She might be eighteen.

"A vow of poverty. Like Saint Francis and those other guys. Once you get your face inked, you can never live inside the system. I mean, who would hire someone who looks like me?"

"Somebody might."

"Somebody won't. I tried, before I started traveling with Clementine. Even McDonald's wouldn't hire me."

"Fuck McDonald's," said Val.

"Yeah, sure, fuck Micky D, but they've got good dumpsters." Eleanor laughed and Clementine reached up to lick her hand. "Me and Clem live lightly on the planet. Less impact. I'm an all or nothing kind of person."

"Me too," said Val. Clementine thumped her tail.

The bus stopped at Sixth Avenue. It slowly lowered at the front like an elephant going to its knees. The light over the back door turned green and Eleanor snatched up her pack and grabbed Val's wallet in one quick move, jumping out the door. Clementine shot out behind her, no leash.

"Hey! Stop!" Val grabbed the back door, holding it open. "Eleanor! What the fuck!" Eleanor turned and Clementine grinned. The girl shoved the cash in her pocket, throwing back the empty wallet.

"Here!"

Her wallet landed in the slush. Val went for it, grabbing a corner just before it sank into the curbside puddle. When she looked up, the girl and her dog were gone.

The bus thrummed behind Val and the sounds of the city rushed in, back and forth horns, high pitched beeping from the crosswalk. Her feet were soaked but the wallet was barely wet. It all happened so fast.

"No!" Val screamed after them. "No!"

"Ma'am? Are you all right?" The bus driver was standing behind her in the open back door.

"She stole my wallet! That girl stole my wallet."

The driver's eyes flicked to the wallet in her hand.

"She grabbed it. Took the cash."

"And threw it back?"

Val opened the empty bill fold to show him. The driver looked back and forth at the people hurrying home dangling shopping bags, holding umbrellas, trying not to slip.

"You want to get back on? How far are you going?"

Val heaved herself up, legs shaking and boots dripping. "Just one more block."

The driver looked at Eleanor's seat. "I shouldn't have let her on, she smelled so bad, but I felt sorry for the both of them in this weather. She rode back and forth with me for about an hour, told me her whole philosophy of life. Her name's Lisa."

"She told me her name was Eleanor!"

"No kidding? What'd she say the dog's name was?"

"Clementine."

His face broke into a wrinkled smile. "She told me it was Sweetie. At least you got your wallet back."

Val took a seat near the front. Forty-five dollars gone. But the driver was right, she needed the wallet more than the cash. Maybe Eleanor-Lisa would buy a burger and fries to share with Clementine-Sweetie.

She loved this wallet. It was a gift from Danny after he came back from tour a few years ago. He bought it at a street market in Berlin, blue leather with a red striped lining. She put it back into the inside pocket of her pea coat. Her heart was beating too fast, too hard. Fuck the gallery show, Eleanor threw her wallet back because Val was an all or nothing kind of person. She still had her MetroCard, a Xerox copy of her passport, her ATM card, the ticket stub from her last gig with the Joypoppers, a four-leaf clover she had pressed between two of Cora's old business cards, and a black-and-white picture of the two of them vamping in some photo booth. Big hair and dark lips. And there was that one piece of paper she had folded over and over until it fit into the leather slot behind her expired driver's license.

lauren

When Lauren's phone rang, she answered without looking. It had to be Amy.

"Hi, can you talk?"

Diana. Oh God, not now. How could she get out of it when she had already answered the phone?

"Yes, everything okay?"

Probably some crisis with their parents. Her sister had found the assisted living place when the big house didn't work for them anymore. She took them to their doctor's appointments and managed the caregivers. Lauren had to remind herself to be grateful. Her parents had supported Diana and her two sons financially, so that she could be an artist who never had to work. The caretaking was more like a job with a salary.

"You don't want to be Diana and you don't need the money," Amy said when Lauren complained.

True. Lauren didn't want to be Diana, who moved into a "studio" their parents built for her in the back corner of their enormous yard in Westchester after she finished college and never left. It was a fairy tale cottage with a gas fireplace and window boxes. She raised her boys there with the excuse of the good public schools that came with her parents' address. Diana always had much better grades than Lauren; she took school seriously and could have done practically anything. Maybe that was the problem. The last time Lauren ranted about Diana, Amy said that Diana's photography was really good, plus she was a good mom and an amazing cook.

"Remember those mushrooms last Thanksgiving? The ones she foraged herself?"

"She wants to poison us, then she gets all the money."

Amy laughed. "I hope she makes them again this year. Don't forget how lucky you are that she takes care of your parents, so you don't have to."

"She won't let me forget it!"

"Still."

"I know."

Kiss cheek. Touch hands. They did all those married things.

"So . . ." Lauren could hear Diana sigh over the phone. "Things have been really difficult with Dad."

Lauren stopped listening.

What was there to say? That she was sorry Diana was their favorite? Her parents were a monster with two different heads.

"It's been really exhausting," said Diana. "Samwise is looking at high schools and we have to visit every single one or he won't get on the list."

Thank God Lauren's nephew insisted on being called Sam, though Diana named him Samwise and his younger brother, Frodo. They were Sam and Rubin to everyone except Diana.

"I'm actually worried about Dad. He's getting so moody. He's mean to Mom. It could be the beginning of Alzheimer's."

"He's always been moody and mean."

She could hear Diana trying to be patient. They both knew their roles by heart, but they never had much in common other than their genes, so what was the point of "working on their relationship," as Diana once asked her to do in some well-meaning sister therapy.

Diana was still talking. "I'm meeting with Dad's geriatric psychiatrist tomorrow. Maybe we should increase the antidepressants."

"Good idea." I'm just as mean as Dad, Lauren thought. Why not just put the old folks on an ice floe, split the money, and shake hands? Wasn't this why they had moved them into a place that went from assisted living to hospice to death?

It was already dark out. The sky at the end of Grand Street was turning orange. Street vendors lined the curb behind boxes of horned dragon fruit, teetering scales hung from chains, unintentionally weighing snow. People were out on the sidewalk doing their dinner shopping; restaurants and nail salons were still open. It was a village main street for a few blocks before you reached Soho. Maybe she and Amy could start over in this neighborhood, move ten blocks north to a completely different city.

"So, what do you think?" asked Diana.

Lauren had no idea what she was talking about. "You mean, taking Dad to see a psychiatrist? Should've happened fifty years ago."

"No, no, didn't you hear me?"

"Sorry, I'm on the street and it's really loud." It should be loud on Grand Street, but everything was tamped down by snow and twilight.

"Where are you?"

"Chinatown."

"In this weather?"

"I'm on my way to Sasha's. She's having a reunion dinner."

"The reunion!" Diana actually sounded excited. She'd always been a booster for Harrison. She couldn't understand why Lauren wanted out so badly by senior year. "I forgot it's reunion weekend. I've been so overwhelmed with this dad stuff."

This was Lauren's cue. "Thank you, Diana."

"That's okay," said Diana, though of course it never was and never would be. Lauren didn't need sister therapy to tell her that. "It's your thirty-fifth, right?"

"Yeah, can you believe it?" Oh God, could she please, please get off the phone.

"Maybe I should host a reunion dinner at Mom and Dad's house, when it comes around for my class," said Diana. "That would be really fun."

"Maybe, yeah."

Diana's voice was loud in her earbuds. "What do you mean, maybe?"

"It's just that, well, we might sell the house before your thirty-fifth reunion."

"Mom and Dad really don't want to sell the house."

"I know, it's just that it's such a big place, costs a lot of money."

"And I use it. I mean, me and the boys—"

"I was just thinking out loud."

"About what? Mom and Dad?"

"No, I mean, yes, not really. Sorry, I'm just distracted, it's so loud out here."

"Okay, well, I wanted to give you the Dad update."

Lauren stopped walking. "Listen, I'm grateful for everything you're doing, Di. I really am. I know it's a lot of work, plus the boys."

Diana took a beat. Lauren never thanked her this much.

"Are you okay, Laur? Amy and the kids okay?"

"We're all good. I just got back from a work trip. Kind of jet-lagged."

"Okay."

Cars honked and nudged their way past Lauren toward the Lincoln Tunnel.

"I know it's the first reunion since Cora." An empty speech bubble floated between them. "I hope it's not too hard for you guys." Diana meant it.

"Thanks."

"Say hi to Sasha and Val for me."

"I will."

Lauren stared at Diana's profile pic on her phone, the pain-in-the-ass-know-it-all-Daddy's girl. She had been careless of Diana.

Cora used to call Lauren "the turtle." Hard on the outside, soft on the inside.

One year, when Amy invited Diana to join them for Friendsgiving, Diana's boys gave all the guests dinosaur names. This was before Ash refused to come out of their room if strangers were present. Sam and Rubin drew place cards while the adults were cooking and drinking: Cora was a T-rex, Sasha was a triceratops, and Val was a pterodactyl. Lauren was hoping for a velociraptor, but Cora told the boys that Lauren was a Turtle-Saur. Amy reached for Lauren's hand across the table.

"If she's the tortoise, I'm the hare."

Lauren's heart unfolded just like that. Amy wasn't anything like the hare, but it meant they were in the same story.

Diana wanted to talk nothing but menopause when she came for dinner a few months ago. Amy and Lauren hardly ever talked about it, though Amy was in perimenopause, and Lauren was nearly done. Diana and Amy poured more wine, comparing Black Cohosh supplements, vaginal estrogen inserts, and Hormone Replacement Therapy. Lauren left the table.

"Where are you going?" Diana asked.

"She hates talking about it," said Amy. "She's really squeamish. For the last five years, she's pretended it wasn't happening."

"I'm not squeamish. It just doesn't affect me very much."

But Amy knew all about the quilt thrown onto the floor in the middle of the night, Lauren ripping off her T-shirt in a night sweat, anxiety pounding, unable to go back to sleep. Was she moodier than she used to be or had she always been kind of a bitch? It didn't help to talk about it.

"She wants to be a man," Amy said in mock horror.

"She always has," said Diana. "It's not too late, Laur!"

"I'm fine with Late-Life-Transitions," said Amy. "My daughter is my son and my wife is my husband. Could be sexy!"

The two of them laughed and tipped their glasses together while Lauren tried not to hate them both. It was good for Amy to laugh with Diana when she was so worried about Ash—but did they have to embrace this herbal, empowering-women bullshit around menopause? Lauren could care less that Orcas honored the infertile, elder females in the pod. She was a feminist lesbian, not a killer whale.

"I hated my period," she called across the living room. "Why should I be in mourning?"

When she reached for Amy in bed that night, wanting to apologize for acting like a jerk around her sister, Amy shifted her breast away from Lauren's hand. When had Amy started limiting Lauren to cupping her breasts instead of playing with her nipples? It felt like a concession when Amy turned toward her. Lauren used to put her hand over Amy's mouth so the kids wouldn't hear them having sex. Now she hardly made a sound. Was her disinterest all about menopause? Lauren wanted this part of it to be over. Once Amy stopped bleeding forever, would she take Lauren back?

She wanted to pretend that none of this was happening.

She really was acting like a man.

sasha

Sasha walked into her apartment and unfolded two new sheets of legal paper next to her computer. There was her revised outline in Miss Pierce's familiar handwriting. All she needed was to connect the dots.

Yeah.

Right.

Maybe.

Was it too late to cancel? She would tell them that the snowstorm had shut down the city and she wasn't able to get to her office, where she had her notes. But it was morning there. Members of the prize committee were already driving to some conference room, coffee and pastries set up off camera, tablets and laptops open. It wasn't snowing where they were.

She would have to put on something decent, and do her goddamned face, as her mother used to say. She opened her closet and picked out her favorite interview shirt, dark navy silk with tiny brass buttons. No cleavage, no hint of the small gold chain with a Jewish star she never took off, a present from her mother and father on the day she graduated from MIT. None of them knew this would be the last time her mother pressed an expensive bouquet into her daughter's hands and allowed herself to cry in public. Her mother's cancer was stage four when they found it.

Sasha never took off the necklace. She was like the girl in *Grimm's Fairy Tales* who wore a green ribbon around her neck. Sasha touched her index finger to the star and told herself that no matter how badly she did on this Zoom call, it's her boobs that were coming off, not her head. Miss Pierce was right, the brain leads the body. There would be some bad days, but she was going to be fine.

Maybe all we need is someone to tell us that we're going to be fine. She was going to start saying this to her students when she had no idea if they were going to be fine or not.

She secured the top button of her shirt.

She needed to dress like a serious person, but this top and her gold earrings would make her appear slightly more fashionable on the foundation website. She stepped back and looked in the full-length mirror. Her gray sweatpants and bare feet wouldn't be seen in the video; why not be comfortable? In the bathroom, she reached for her makeup and tipped her head back, dotting on foundation like the woman at the store had taught her. Tap gently into the skin, never rub. Not too much powder, it shows the wrinkles more. Just a little bit of glimmer.

Now we want our skin to be shiny? she heard her mother say. *Makes you look sweaty.*

Sasha spent so much money on the whole package, she had to learn how to use it.

Sasha twisted her hair into a loose bun. A bit of gel, and yes, there was more gray than dark brown, but it looked fine. (I love you, don't ever leave me, she told her hair). She ran some gel over her eyebrows then reached for the eye shadow recommended for olive skin. Sallow was more like it. But she used the eye shadow as instructed, bronze just above the eyelid, then mascara. It had to be waterproof in case her eyes leaked during the interview. When the woman asked Sasha if she wanted to try lash extensions her ego perked right up, but she beat it back down.

"I'm staring sixty in the face," she said to the woman who leaned in close with a taut thread between her teeth, expertly shaping Sasha's brows. "Lashes aren't going to make a huge difference at this point."

"But you don't *look* sixty-in-the-face," the woman said. When Sasha laughed, the woman shook her head. "You have lucky skin."

So maybe sallow paid off in the long haul? She knew there would be an unspoken comparison of how they were all holding up at the reunion tonight. Until the next day, when the few women who were actually friends dissected everyone else.

The face is not my problem, she thought. My problem is the Undeniable.

But if this was true, why did she care so much about the growing thicket of vertical lines above her upper lip, deeper curves between her nose and chin? Do noses really get bigger as the rest of the flesh falls back? Had she reached the stage where she should wear a silk scarf to hide her neck? No. There's nothing wrong with her neck, and she was going to be fine! She lipsticked and patted with a tissue. She wondered who had gotten work done in their class. These rich girls got it done so well it was hard to discern. Cora would have known exactly who nipped and tucked along the way.

Oh, Cora, Cora, Cora. Why wasn't she here? Or maybe she still was? The same way her mother stayed close, giving advice and cracking jokes, though Sasha couldn't smell her secret cigarettes covered by toothpaste. Maybe this is how it was with all of the beloved dead. Sasha would convince Val and Lauren to stay for a whiskey after everyone left. She would treat Val to a car service home and Amy would understand if Lauren came home a little late on the night of the reunion.

It would be the best part of the evening if it wasn't for the Undeniable.

What had Miss Pierce said? *Train your mind like an athlete.*

Fifteen minutes to go. Sasha sat on her bed and pulled on the silly animal socks that Cora's stepdaughter, Emma, had given her for Christmas. She was still Auntie Sasha. She could invite teenage Emma and Ben for hot chocolate *mit schlag* at the Neue Gallery with its newspapers on old-fashioned wooden spools. Cora used to take them there after school and text Sasha to come meet them. She would give Sasha a sly, thrilled look as the children studied the architecture of their pastry. *Look, I have children*! Cora's stepchildren had adored her. She was the lucky one, until she wasn't.

Sasha grabbed a pen and pulled her chair close to the desk. A screensaver of blue whales moved slowly across her computer screen. She logged into Zoom, blurred her background so that nobody would know she was in her bedroom, and clicked off the video. No need to look too closely. The socks from Emma had gray stripes with a little animal face on the front and tiny gray ears. She wriggled her toes.

All she needed to do was connect the dots.

"Doctor Kollwitz?"

"Yes. Can you hear me?" Sasha turned on the video and clicked off mute.

"Yes, yes, I can. Thank you. I will adjust the monitor so that everyone can be seen."

The woman on Sasha's computer screen was wearing a dark green scarf woven through with gold thread and large hoop earrings, touches of glamour contrasting with her stiff expression.

"Hold on, Doctor Kollwitz, I'm so sorry, but I'm having some trouble connecting with the others."

"Okay, no problem. I can still hear you." Sasha felt sorry for anyone expected to coordinate the tech side for academics who could barely figure out how to use Google Maps. Were the foundation board members seated next to this tech support person in a conference room? Or was everyone in front of their home computers, business wear from the waist up? (Imagine them all wearing plaid pajama bottoms, she told herself.) Why did people think Zoom presentations were a good idea? It was like looking down a long corridor into a badly lit room where nobody can hear you.

Sasha took a breath. Be patient. You've done hundreds of Zoom calls. Follow your outline. It's going to be recorded.

The woman glanced up at the camera. "I'm so sorry, Doctor Kollwitz, this is the first time we've worked with the new system upgrade."

"That's fine, gives me more time to think of what to say." Sasha hoped this might make the woman appear more relaxed, but of course, she was staring at a computer screen where Sasha was only one of many small, floating rectangles. Sasha could hear her fingernails hitting the keyboard.

"Damn!" The woman said, then covered her mouth, looking up.

Sasha shook her head, "I would swear a lot more if I was trying to do what you're doing." This time the woman did laugh a little, then bent her head.

"Are you all right? Can you still hear me?"

"Yes, I can hear you, Dr. Kollwitz." The woman straightened up again, head balanced perfectly on her spine. She must have done ballet. Sasha had taken ballet classes as a child and could always recognize it.

"I'm sorry," the woman said, rather formally. "I hardly slept last night. My daughter is sick."

"I'm so sorry," Sasha said, feeling her American warmth gushing inappropriately toward someone who must wish she wasn't at work today. "I hope she's feeling better?"

There was a pause long enough for Sasha to remember that not every child gets better. Her right hand started to move to the Undeniable like a touchstone. Stop! This wasn't about Sasha and she was onscreen. The woman tapped the corners of her eyes with a tissue, fixing two perfect wings of eye make-up without a mirror. Was there a box of tissues on the table in the conference room?

"She will be fine," the woman said. "I simply haven't slept. I am sorry, I know how busy you are, and we're already running late for the meeting."

"I'm not busy," said Sasha. "Not really busy at all. Are you alone there?"

"Where?"

"There, in the conference room."

The woman looked confused. "I'm not in the conference room. I am in the technology office."

"Okay, well. I'm glad you're alone. It's terrible to cry in front of strangers."

"But my coworkers are not strangers," the woman said. "You and I are strangers. Please forgive me. You are our honoree."

"I won't say anything to the board about any of this," Sasha said. "They're strangers to me."

The woman stopped tapping the keyboard and looked at Sasha, nothing showing that she had been crying. "This should only take another minute," she said quietly.

It felt wrong to watch her and wrong to turn off her camera. Sasha closed her eyes.

"I'm afraid that I'm going to have to call an AV technician," the woman said finally. "The system error is beyond what I can do from here."

Sasha's heart lifted. Trumpets sounded, a REPRIEVE! She had needed to be scared enough to pull her talk together, and now, she wouldn't have to do it. Sasha sent up a quick prayer for cancellation. Of course, this woman didn't want to talk about her daughter to a stranger. Sasha hadn't really wanted to be a mother. Was that why the Undeniable had appeared? Because her breasts never completed their reproductive task? She had asked her oncologist this, who looked surprised by the question.

"More likely that there was a female ancestor whose genetic blueprint was lost—"

"So, it's a Holocaust thing?" Sasha had asked, sounding angrier than she meant to.

The doctor, younger than Sasha, took a breath. "It's not really possible to know what caused this malignancy. It may be a combination of factors, but we do know the best steps for treatment."

Malignant was an interesting word. An adjective that grew into a noun.

"How old is your daughter?" Sasha asked the woman on the Zoom screen.

"Five." Her face lit up as if her girl was standing right next to her in that room with nubbled gray carpeting on the wall and a dark, flat screen suspended behind her.

All these sad, neutral spaces.

"My mother is with her. She texts me once an hour. The doctor said that it may be something to do with her appendix. If the fever doesn't go down today, she will have surgery."

"Like Madeleine," Sasha said without thinking, but the woman smiled for the first time.

"Yes, like Madeleine. She loves that book. We are hoping for this kind of solution. A storytale ending."

"I hope so, too," Sasha said, jotting down *storytale*, her new favorite word.

"Ah! We are ready! I am sorry, again, Doctor Kollwitz, for the long wait."

"It was a pleasure speaking with you," said Sasha.

Sasha pulled her legal pad closer and picked up her pen. No trumpets, no reprieve.

"They're your ideas," Pierce had said when Sasha tried to thank her. "I just put them in order like a shopping list."

"Are you ready?" She hadn't realized the woman was waiting to let her into the larger Zoom room.

"Yes, thank you. I will be thinking of you and your daughter." Sasha realized she had never asked the woman her name, but now everyone was ready, how to ask?

"Thank you."

The screen broke quickly into seven rectangles, and she disappeared. Here was Kristof, full of apologies for the delay. After a round of greetings and her formal introduction, Sasha began to speak about the Invisible World, drawing circles around the word *storytale*.

val

Would Cora stop talking to Val when they got to Sasha's house? Would she ever stop? There were so many people hearing voices in New York. Val was simply tuning in to a different frequency.

The uptown train rattled into the Twenty-Third Street Station, its bright red number leading the way. Today was the first time she'd been mugged since she was a teenager, but Val couldn't really get mad. Eleanor took what she needed like a dog grabbing a hunk of meat. The doors opened onto a half-empty car, and Val picked a seat near the door. The back and forth rhythm of the train was comforting. Danny had given her *The Tibetan Book of the Dead* when she was in her Buddhist phase, the closest she came to a system of belief except rock 'n' roll. One late night, they decided that the subway was their bardo. Each stop was a stage of purgatory, every street exit a gateway to the next phase of existence. Everything kept happening in the bardo: love, violence, envy, sex, revenge, greed, desperation, and ignorance all mashed together. You couldn't stop the train whenever you wanted to, the only way through was to accept your current reality, especially if it happened to be August, in a car with no air conditioning. All these souls going through a metal turnstile that never stopped spinning.

Val and Danny were high when they thought it up, waiting for the L train after a gig. But it still made sense to Val in the morning. A smooth stone of analogy to keep in her pocket. After she quit teaching, Val spent a lot of time riding the trains.

At Ninety-Sixth Street, a man walked into the car talking nonstop. He looked about twenty, wearing snow boots and a decent coat. There were white stains down the front as if he'd fallen into the slush. He was speaking to an empty water bottle. Everyone kept their heads down. Val wondered what he saw. Skeletons holding glowing screens? Humans with animal heads? If she were an animal, Val would want to be Juno. I'm just like this water bottle guy, she thought, talking to ghosts, putting heads on people and skeletons in the seats. The man was using the empty bottle as a microphone.

Don't look at him, Cora said. *I'm the one in the bardo, not you. You should be more careful.*

But Val couldn't help herself, and the man stopped right in front of her like she knew he would. He pulled the water bottle closer to his mouth, holding it to his lips like a pop star. So, it's a wireless mic, thought Val.

Only you would say that, Val. It's a fucking water bottle! said Cora.

The man took a deep breath, dropped to his hands and knees, and kissed the streaked gray floor of the subway car at Val's feet. Lips pressing against layers of gum stamps, paper wrappers, dried saliva, spilled coffee, crumpled tissues and the infinite soles of shoes.

Was he kissing an altar covered in white cloth, gold chalice, and candles?

Val couldn't ignore him or make him invisible. She put her head in her hands as the train slowed into the next station, waiting for the man to smash the back of her neck when she wasn't looking. Empty water bottle landing like a club or a knife. The man got to his feet and walked off the train, singing. He had a great voice. Val wished she still had money in her wallet so she could give it to him.

Living like the water bottle man, Cora whispered, *good song title.*

When she got off the train at Sasha's stop and started walking toward the exit, a hand touched Val's shoulder. She didn't bother turning around, so sure it was Cora.

"Val?" It was Lauren. "We must have been on the same train." Lauren's eyes were desperate.

"What's wrong? What happened?"

"It's Amy. I've fucked everything up." Lauren was trembling through her down coat. Lauren was the one who always knew what to do, so much taller and richer than Val. Val hugged her and another pair of arms wrapped around them both. Beloved ghost.

"I miss her," Lauren said in a voice too small for her body.

Cora's arms tightened around them. They swayed together on the platform.

"Me too," said Val.

"What?"

"Cora." Cora's arms disappeared.

"Cora?" Lauren pulled away.

"Did you feel it? Her arms holding us. Just now."

"What are you talking about?" Lauren took a step back. "I miss Amy, not Cora."

"But—"

"I miss Cora too, I mean, yes, but no." Lauren looked at Val like she was a stranger. "I didn't feel anything."

They turned at the sound of an oncoming train heading into the station on the downtown side. Snow fell through the grate above the tracks in a rectangle of white.

"Let's go," said Lauren. "We're already late." She turned toward the exit, striding up the steps in her sleek European boots, parka zipped tight. Val walked behind her, angry and foolish with her pea coat unbuttoned, gripping the slick metal handrail for balance.

sasha

Sasha drew a chain of question marks turned upside down like stairs on her yellow legal pad. Maybe only a stepladder, but it was a start. What if it really was possible to interpret human behavior as Qubits? The motherboard of a quantum computer as a giant loom with our decisions for threads, human choices as particles of change. She could look for patterns, avoid first answers, and craft more complicated questions. If she had to throw it all away, there might be something shiny in the trash heap.

There was a gleeful hum inside Sasha's favorite organ. She had an idea!

I'm too old for this, Sasha thought, stepping into the shower and tipping her head back so that her hair wouldn't get wet. Procrastinating up to the last minute, like she was still in high school. She smiled as she turned off the water and reached for a towel, stepping around her clothes on the bathroom floor. She had sweated right through her nice shirt but managed to talk for forty-five minutes as if she was sure of the importance of what she was saying. Kristof was impossible to read, but there was only a brief question period, and they threw her soft balls. She gave them the headline they needed: "The Invisible World." Now, they could write their pull quotes for the website.

Sasha hated the sound of her own voice, but she could ask them for a transcript. She would be able to write her final report by next fall. She didn't have to prove anything; a series of questions is enough. Exactly what Miss Pierce said when Sasha was in eleventh grade at Harrison; what she now told her own students: *You don't need the answer to ask interesting questions*. Thank you, Miss Pierce! Maybe it was the walnut liqueur? She'd buy a bottle.

Sasha put on her robe and went to the bedroom closet, taking out the dress she had worn only once for the prize ceremony. Floor length black silk, fake pearl buttons down the center. She tossed it on the bed and flopped back, smashing the dress in a sinful wallow. Storytale, she thought again. This was one of the rungs on her ladder. It wouldn't make sense to anyone else. Had she written it down? Yes. Everything important landed in the margins of her legal pad.

The doorbell rang. It must be Hannah and Kiara, come to set up the food and the bar. Alex would be here soon, carrying trays of food with one of her helpers. Sasha pulled the belt on her robe tighter and stepped into her house slippers, then stopped. This was the longest gap of time without thinking of the Undeniable since her diagnosis. She had taken a shower without reaching up to see if it had simply disappeared. Thank you, she whispered to her brain.

She might make it through.

"Coming!" She called, walking toward the door. And there were the girls, snowy and smiling. The coat rack was in the hallway, just as Anthony had promised.

"Sorry we're a little late, the snow slowed everything down." Kiara pulled at her boots. "Can we leave these out here?"

"Yes, perfect."

"We brought other shoes for tonight," said Hannah, the worrier.

"Of course, no problem, come in! Come in!"

The girls placed their dripping boots side by side outside the door like good children and allowed Sasha to kiss their cold, plump cheeks. Nothing could be better than Hannah and Kiara. They would remind the women of their own college-age children, only kinder. She waved the girls into the apartment ahead of her. They had worked for her before, some book party she hosted for a colleague or end of year dinner for the postdocs she was mentoring. The flowers had been delivered; bottles of white wine were stacked head to tail in the refrigerator. The counters were spotless and ready.

"Are the caterers coming soon?" asked Hannah.

"Any minute. I'm sure it's the weather."

"What should we do first?" asked Kiara. "Do you know where you'd like us to set up the bar?"

"Yes. No! I had this ridiculous Zoom call this afternoon, and I'm a total disaster. You have to help me choose what to wear!" The girls shook their heads (typical Sasha!) and followed her down the hall to the bedroom. The line of dresses in her closet was stupidly thrilling.

"Look at all those dresses! They're beautiful," Kiara said.

"But none of them fit," said Sasha. "I gained weight over the holidays."

Kiara started flipping through the hangers. She was the one headed for a fellowship at Harvard, though she claimed to spend most of her time watching stand-up on YouTube. Hannah had to work for it while Kiara's mind recognized systems automatically, like Sasha. She would still have a harder time since she wasn't only female, she was Black. Why not watch a lot of stand-up?

They would both have careers. Sasha could make sure of that.

"What are you in the mood for?" asked Hannah.

"A glass of wine. Seriously, this is a disaster."

"Dress first, then wine," said Kiara, pulling out a blue pleated rayon. "I promise we'll tell you if it doesn't look right." Kiara held it up to her twenty-six-year-old body in the full-length closet mirror.

(You will never look like Kiara in that dress, Sasha reminded herself.)

"It's the right length," said Hannah. "As long as it's not too clingy below the waist."

"It's too clingy," Sasha moaned. "I am the great whale."

"Try it on," ordered Kiara.

Sasha took the dress into the bathroom, leaving the girls to discuss her other choices. The soft material slipped over her head, and she sucked in her breath for the side zipper. At least it had pleats. Was rayon too warm in case she got a hot flash? She was wearing her best bra for comfort and cleavage—not bad. She held one boob in each hand. "This is your last night out," she whispered. She made them nod back at her in the mirror and laughed aloud.

"Does it fit?" Kiara asked through the door.

What a fool Sasha was! She opened the door and Hannah and Kiara started clapping. She turned around for them to check how it hung from her hips. They could put her in whatever dress they wanted. It was all about her glorious bosoms. In her forties, they gave her lower back pain and needed more infrastructure, but it was impossible to imagine them gone. In ninety-six hours, the landscape of her body would be altered. Any high school physics student knows that a solid can transform to gas in response to pressure and temperature. The sun is an example of plasma, Miss Pierce explained in eleventh grade, the most common form of visible matter in the universe, an ionized gas moving freely into different shapes and volumes. Sasha's breasts would become something like the sun. She gently nudged each one into prime position.

No matter what she wore, they were always the place that men looked first.

Now, they'd have to look at her.

Sasha turned around again, pretending to be worried about how the dress looked from the back.

"Hoop earrings!" said Kiara, and Hannah picked up a pair of low-heeled Ferragamos.

"Iconic and comfortable," she said.

The girls were right about everything, as usual.

reunion

Sasha circled with her second glass. Every time the door opened, she thought it was Val and Lauren. Where were they? Had they met early for a drink? Why hadn't they come to the house and helped her pick out what to wear? She was afraid that the only ones who mattered wouldn't come.

"Eat! Eat!" She sounded just like her mother at their annual holiday party, shouting into the living room as she flipped potato latkes and shared puffs of a cigarette out the window with Aunt Marina. Sasha's job was to place layers of paper towels between the latkes and pretend her mother wasn't smoking. Latkes with applesauce, sour cream, and slices of pork from a cartoon-shaped can. A menorah in the window next to the tree. The smell of hot oil and her father's famous mulled wine with nutmeg, cinnamon, and cloves. The whole apartment smelled like the land of plenty.

"When we arrived here, we had nothing," said her mother.

"We were fine," said her father.

Sasha kept the Jewish Holidays cookbook when she emptied her parents' apartment, the loopy colorful script on the spine throwing a party next to the formality of Joan Nathan. I am the loopy script, Sasha thought, as she passed through the kitchen.

Prosecco, red wine, white wine, sparkling water, lemon wedges, a basket of cloth napkins next to a wire container of heavy stainless-steel knives and forks, a vegetarian and a meat lasagna, green salad, grilled asparagus, garlic bread, hummus and olives, carrot and celery sticks, a large clay platter with soft and hard cheeses, green grapes and table water crackers, cold poached salmon with capers and fresh dill, pots of grainy mustard and fancy mayonnaise.

Could it get any more Waspy?

Despite the storm, eighteen women showed up. Sasha would look at her email for the weather-related apologies later. The ones who came really wanted to be here; some had come all the way from the West Coast and were attending events at the school all weekend (how could they stand it?). Miss Pierce arrived right on time. Sasha seated her in a place of honor in the middle of the couch.

"The call went well. I'll tell you all about it later. I'm getting you a single malt. You saved me this afternoon. How can I thank you enough?"

"You can't."

They clinked glasses. Pierce had given her two more rules when she was looking for her first apartment: always have a bottle of single malt in the liquor cabinet and keep track of your own money. Sasha's mother had different rules: Get an apartment close to the subway, never touch hard liquor, and who exactly do you think will keep track of your money, if not you?

The door opened and Val and Lauren walked in—together. Sasha spread her arms wide.

"Can I spend the night?" Lauren whispered. Sasha pulled back. Had she been crying? Lauren never cried.

"Of course you can. What's going on?"

"It's Amy, I'll tell you later—I may not need to stay over."

"Please, Lauren. I want you to stay," Sasha looked at Val. Whatever this was, Val already knew about it.

"I wish Cora was here." Sasha pulled them close, trying to ignore a surprising resistance from each of them. "I want to hear about everything, but there's all these people. I wish they were already gone and it was just the three of us."

Val and Lauren were here. The three of them would get each other through whatever came, including the Undeniable.

"You spend the night, too," she said to Val, who nodded warily, looking past her into the living room.

"Who's here? Will I recognize any of them?"

"We're the only ones who look exactly the same," Sasha said a little too loudly. "Come in, get a drink, there's too much food!"

Sasha swept triumphantly back into the living room with Val and Lauren linked on each arm. Val looked at the photo of the four of them in the center of the bookcase and held Sasha's arm tighter. Sasha squeezed back, placing Cora gently inside a balloon they could tap around the room with their fingertips, each girl waiting her turn to bop Cora back into the air above them. The hum of voices increased. Sasha waited until Val and Lauren had each been given a glass and her glorious grad students refilled the others. Then she tapped her glass, and for some reason, everyone got to their feet.

"To Cora," said Sasha. "May her memory be a blessing." And there were her father's lips speaking the Kaddish over a bird wrapped in newspaper. They raised their glasses.

Val listened for Cora's voice. There was nothing. She had to be here, didn't she? Val couldn't turn the key to her song machine without Cora there to listen. Maybe it didn't matter if she stopped writing music. Was that what Cora was trying to tell her in that long silence before the accident? There was a sharp breeze from the window cracked open behind the flowers. Val looked hard at Sasha and Lauren, catching their eyes over the rim of her glass. When she was sure they were looking, Val kneeled down and poured the rest of her wine onto Sasha's thick Persian carpet. The wine was a still pond until the surface tension broke and a dark red circle spread out on Sasha's rug. Val remained crouched near the ladies' well-fitting shoes. Nobody moved.

"How very Greek," said Miss Pierce. "A libation to the Gods."

Val looked at Sasha, daring her to get angry.

"A libation to Cora!" Sasha said loudly. She would not allow Val to tip everything over this early in the night with her dramatics. Hannah appeared beside her with salt and seltzer to pour onto the wet spot. Sasha was surprised that she didn't really care about her expensive rug anymore. As far as she was concerned, that stain could last forever. If she changed her mind, she'd call a professional rug cleaner.

"Thank you, Hannah," said Sasha. "Everybody sit!" She made space for Val and Lauren next to her on the couch, opposite Miss Pierce.

Val sat on the floor in front of them instead, watching the wine turn the salt crystals pink. Nobody would look at her and maybe these women thought that she was as weird as ever, but what was really crazy was pretending that things were normal without Cora. Miss Pierce got it right away, even Sasha and Lauren got it. Cora would have loved it. Val could tell that Sasha was secretly glad there was a crisis with Lauren and Amy. Of course, Sasha wanted them to stay together as a couple, but tonight she wanted Lauren and Val to have a sleepover with bowls of microwave popcorn in her king size bed. Val wanted to be as loyal as Sasha, but how could she spend the night when she didn't think she would last another hour in the same room as Lauren?

Sasha didn't know about Cora on the subway platform.

Cora smiled at Val out of the photograph of the four of them on the bookcase without saying a word.

Lauren was squashed next to Nora Danforth on the couch. Leave it to Val to make a dramatic entrance, she thought. Pouring wine onto Sasha's rug was so rude and strange, almost as strange as thinking she felt Cora's presence in the subway station. It was all about Val, as usual, though Cora would have appreciated everyone's mortal coil tightening around the living room. Sasha must be upset. It was a beautiful rug and she loved her things. Lauren forced herself to turn to Nora, who looked surprisingly chic and interesting. Late Life Lesbian? Lauren took another sip of wine.

When Sasha looked up, she saw Val staring into the room of chatting women with an expression that terrified her. Whatever happened with Lauren and Amy, was Val going to be all right? Would they stay over? What if Lauren stayed at a hotel instead? They both thought this dinner was a terrible idea, they hated Harrison, they hated her, they were only here for Cora, who brought Sasha into the group last of all. Sasha was never cool (smart didn't count), never funny (except as a sidekick), never sexy (except for those boobs), never, never, enough.

The photo of the four of them was right next to a small sculpture from the Jewish Museum, a reproduction of something by Louise Nevelson.

Sasha had splurged on the sculpture as well as the catalogue. All she remembered now was that when someone asked Nevelson how she managed to look so fabulous well into her seventies, Nevelson answered, "Fucking, dear, lots of fucking."

It reminded her of something her mother and Aunt Marina would have said, holding their cigarettes out the window. The women of Nevelson's generation had the best comeback lines. When did funny replace witty? That was the kind of thing Cora would say, and Sasha missed her so much she had to drop her eyes and concentrate on her lasagna. She heard her mother's voice again, *Eat! Eat!* But now it sounded far away, down the hall, at the bottom of a stairwell.

Hannah and Kiara were pouring more wine, helping refill the platters in the dining room and speaking to everyone as if they already knew them and might someday date one of their children. Sasha had introduced them as her two most brilliant graduate students. What must they think of these middle-aged women who poured red wine on the carpet and then pretended it never happened? Was it manners or privilege? Sasha was never asked if she wanted to go to Harrison—once she got the scholarship, she was going—and here they were thirty-five years later. These were the ones who still answered emails with Harrison in the subject heading.

I love this party.

I will always get to look youngest at the reunions!

Where did Nora Danforth get that profile? She looks like one of those Steiglitz photos of Georgia O'Keefe. And her hair is so smooth, the perfect blend of gray, black, and silver. Maybe she got a blowout for the reunion. At school she wore those clear, thick-framed glasses and kept her hair in pigtails.

Oh! She's happy!

According to Val and Lauren, everyone except me was miserable at Harrison. I stopped paying attention to Nora after the fourth grade Jacks tournament. I beat everybody with my lucky superball, the clear one with a Snoopy inside. I love Snoopy the best, even if Val thinks I'm more like Lucy because I'm so bossy. If I'm Lucy it's because I had to listen to all her problems and tell her what to do! If I'm Lucy, then Val's the worst combination of Schroeder and Pigpen.

Val can't leave early now that we're finally all together.

Does Nora Danforth remember the Jacks tournament? I organized the whole thing, put a big chart on the wall, and we took over the sixth-floor hallway. The teachers hated the balls bouncing all over at recess and the jacks crunching under their sensible shoes. But they couldn't stop us and I practiced all the time. I even taught the twins how to play. Nobody thought Nora Danforth was worth worrying about. She sucked at gym.

I was sitting opposite Nora on those red and black linoleum school tiles, both of us on our knees or crisscross applesauce. Didn't they used to call it 'Indian Style' at Harrison? I hate us. I really hate us. Do I still have to be us now that I'm dead?

Nora tossed the jacks for the first round, and I could tell from the way her ball bounced that it was almost as good as mine, then she raced through her turn without dropping a single jack. Everyone started watching, a circle of girls blocking the hall in their matching uniforms. Penny was in front with her crew cut hair and droopy socks. She didn't play but followed every move in the tournament. It took until high school to figure out that she was gay.

"Your turn," Nora said, as if it was no big deal. But I could see right through her. She'd been practicing, too. I knew that Paula Salinas wanted me to lose. She towered over the rest of them, hoping I'd mess up. The best athlete in the class except for me. She didn't like it if anybody could beat her at anything. She used to chew wads of notebook paper because gum wasn't allowed. I bet we'd be friends now. We both used to push to the front of the line.

On the next round, we had to flip the jacks from one hand to the other and still catch the ball. We had only ten-minute breaks between classes, so every round was a speed round. The bell was about to ring. I scooped them up and caught the ball. One jack fumbled off, but I had them.

"I win."

"You dropped one," said Nora.

"I dropped it after."

"No. Before."

"After!"

"You fumbled," said Nora, and I could feel Val moving in closer behind me.

"Let's go," Penny said to Nora. She didn't want to be late to class.

Nora hesitated. She knew that me and Val didn't care if we were late to class.

"We have to play another round at lunch, best of three," said Nora.

"No, you don't," said Val, and kneed her in the back so hard that Nora's glasses flew off, skittering down the hall. She got a bloody nose.

"Cheater! I won!" Nora yelled, tipping her head back and pinching her nose with her fingers, defenseless without her glasses. Val and I looked at each other as everyone ran off but Nora. The bell rang for the second time.

"Don't be such a baby!" I said. I picked up Nora's glasses and Val brought some toilet paper from the bathroom. I didn't want to be mean. I wanted to win.

Mr. Schultz came out to the hallway. "Paula said that somebody got hurt out here. Don't you girls have to be in class?"

"It's just a bloody nose," Nora said, head tipped back.

"I'll take her to the nurse," I said, butter melting in my mouth. Nora wasn't going to tell and Schultz didn't want to get anywhere near girls and blood.

"I'll go with them," said Val, but Val wasn't as good at not getting caught as I was. She already had a reputation. So, it was just me and Nora walking down the hall to the nurse's office. I could see students' blurred reflections through the opaque glass panes on the classroom doors. Nora gulped and snuffled with one hand on her nose and the other on her glasses. A piece of toilet paper hung past her chin.

I reached for the door to the nurse's office.

"Are you gonna tell?" I asked.

"You cheated. Paula and Penny were there when it happened."

"Okay, fine. You won," I said. "If you want to cheat—you won."

The nurse gave Nora an ice pack and made her lie down in the office. She took her glasses off and wiped her eyes with the back of her hand. It's not like I was happy that she was crying. I wasn't happy or sad. I only knew that it was my idea to have a tournament and I couldn't lose. I ran back to where the teachers had let me tape the tournament results on the wall. I'd written the names of the players on the poster like a family tree. Teachers liked what they called my 'initiative,' but I'm not sure they liked me very much. I tore the poster off the wall and ripped it into pieces.

I'm not that girl anymore. None of us are. A lot of those girls are here tonight and probably nobody remembers the tournament except for me and Nora. I hope she forgot. I really am sorry. And it's not just because she's happy and I'm dead.

I'm watching her lean in to talk to Lauren, and I can tell that Sasha's glad that she went ahead with this dinner for our class, even though something big fell apart on the asphalt on October ninth. I had to come to the reunion. It's lonely out here in the Bardo, and I'm waiting to find out what price I have to pay to get out of going through all these things twice, like the man said.

Do you get the reference, Nora?

Doesn't matter. You win.

"Does everyone have what they need?"

"Yes, yes, Sasha! We're fine!"

Sasha tapped the side of her glass again. All these faces lined up for their class picture in braces, in the yearbook, in gym clothes, hiding in the bathroom during a school dance, grabbing lunch trays, letting their hair go gray, dying it dark or light, thinned or fattened or tightened cheeks.

Who were these people?

"I'm so glad you could all make it," she said. "In spite of the weather—just like Harrison, we never get a snow day." The women laughed and Miss Pierce nodded like a general at the front of her troops. "But here we are, and I thought, since we may not have a chance to have a real conversation with everyone, maybe we can just go around in a circle and say what's happening in our lives."

There was a silence and the wave of faces washed back, floating the women, light as fish, over Sasha's thick Persian carpet. Lauren put her phone away, Pierce leaned slightly forward, and Val let her hair fall over her face. Sasha hadn't planned to start a circle, but it was a good idea, wasn't it? She always made her students take turns speaking in the first few weeks of the semester to get everyone's voice in the room.

Of course it was a good idea.

"There's plenty of food, too much food!" Sasha spread out her hands. "Please, get more if you'd like." But these women were the kind who didn't allow themselves to go back for seconds. Hannah and Kiara were quietly taking plates and refilling glasses so that nobody had to get up.

"I'll start." Sasha looked around the circle, smiling as if she knew what she was doing. Val curled up tight, wrapping her arms around both legs. Had Val really cut thumb holes into the sleeve ends of her sweater so that she could cover her hands? Yes, she had.

"Of course, nothing is the same without Cora."

Everyone's eyes slid over to the photo on the bookcase.

"That's the last time I saw many of you, at the funeral, and I know it meant a lot to Jeff, Emma, and Ben that you came." Did Jeff and the kids even notice the Harrison loyalists at the funeral? "So many of us have also lost parents over the past few years." Heads nodded. Sasha was adrift now that death was in the room. But wasn't it always? Should she say something else about Cora? No, she would cry.

"I wouldn't say I'm slowing down." She knew that everyone was thinking of the fucking Genie. Would they ever know about the Undeniable? Not something for the annual class notes. If the cancer got her, she wouldn't be there to see the announcement. "Sixty on the horizon, and still so much more work to be done. I have wonderful grad students to help with my research, you all met Hannah and Kiara. Honestly, they keep me sane."

Now the ship was righting itself as the girls smiled at her, doing their job.

"Teaching is so important to me." Why was she saying that? She loved her students but the last thing she wanted was to teach two sections next semester, when her leave was over. "It makes me grateful for the teachers we had at Harrison, like Miss Pierce."

Miss Pierce shook her head, smiling. She wouldn't stay the whole night, but Sasha knew she was pleased by these multi-colored heads of hair nodding at her, glasses raised and tipped. It was time for Sasha to pass it to the next person in the circle. Miss Pierce hated sentimentality and it already felt like they'd been in Sasha's living room for a long time.

Sasha was the only one who couldn't decide to leave early. She glanced at Lauren, who was tapping her phone again, right here! Right now! Sasha wanted to slap the phone to the floor no matter what was happening with Amy (who was too good for her anyway). Let Lauren go to a hotel. Did she even care about Sasha? Val pressed her hand gently on Sasha's foot, as if she knew that she was floundering. Had it been three seconds or three minutes of silence? Sasha launched herself again, the great blue whale of lopsided enthusiasm.

"I'm so glad to be here with all of you, thank you for coming."

"Thank you for having us!" Wasn't that Jenny Heller raising her glass to toast Sasha? Now it was Sasha's turn to shake her head as they raised their glasses, and what was the harm in that? Lauren put down her phone and leaned her head on Sasha's shoulder. She was having a terrible time with Amy, not Sasha. She and Val would spend the night and tell each other the truth.

"Thank you, but no toasts," Sasha said. "This isn't—that wasn't a toast, let's just keep going around the circle. I want to hear from everybody!"

She turned to Nora Danforth, who was sitting next to Lauren. The George Washington bridge was holding the view in place out the window, tugboats and barges sliding steadily by the little red lighthouse in the snow. The evening would pass.

Nora's face was slightly frozen (Botox?). She had been a pale, awkward girl. She still looked slightly off-kilter despite her smart gray bob. Who had told Nora that she could pull off a large silver necklace on the outside of a high black turtleneck? Maybe, Sasha told herself, it's time to stop judging everyone like they're still in sixth grade. Sasha sipped her wine. They all seemed to like her idea of taking turns talking about their lives.

Keep it real, was what Cora would say.

"Well," said Nora. "This is the year I decided I don't want to be married to my husband anymore. My son, Stephen, won't speak to me, and I can tell you all about that after one more glass of wine." Hannah and Kiara paused in the doorway to listen. Uncertainty rippled across the room. How many of them were divorced by now?

"Why won't your son speak to you?" Lauren asked, as if this was some kind of Bull Session from middle school: Never Have I Ever. Just because Lauren had a terrible relationship with Ash—but Nora didn't seem to mind. She looked at Lauren with a fixed smile.

"He hates me."

Why was she telling them this?

"Actually, he lives on an ashram. Isn't that funny? They don't like anyone but the guru. We live on Long Island, and the ashram is in the Catskills. I went to visit him even though they don't like parents to come. It used to be the Borscht Belt, remember *Dirty Dancing*? Now it's prisons, ashrams, and monasteries. There's signs along the highway warning you not to pick up hitchhikers." There was something professional about Nora's face, mulberry lips, and smoky eyeshadow.

"I went up for the day, you know, to be supportive, and Stephen pointed out someone who was walking the guru's dog. They all dress in earth tones, orange and brown, and here was this black and white pinto pony of a dog, maybe a Great Dane? The trees were brown, the grass was brown, the clothing was brown, even the buildings were beige, like the stairwells at Harrison, remember? Anyway, Stephen told me this huge, spotted animal was the guru's dog, and something about the way he said it, I couldn't help myself." Nora started giggling and couldn't stop.

They all wanted her to keep going. It was terrible.

"I asked Stephen, who's the person that gets to pick up the guru's dog's shit?"

Lauren laughed harder than anyone, ignoring the side glances of all these women wearing long tops over black pants, low-slung shoes they could wear in a snowstorm because they took a taxi door to door. Sasha wondered if this whole thing was starting to go in the wrong direction. Were Lauren and Nora bonding over rotten children? Pierce was practically glowing. Maybe she wouldn't leave early, thought Sasha. It was finally getting interesting.

"Stephen hasn't spoken to me since. He'll probably outgrow it," Nora said. "I mean, he's twenty-four, they can still outgrow things, right? Oh, and I should have said this at the beginning—he isn't called Stephen anymore, he's been given a new name—Ashima-something, I always want to say *asthma*, but I'll get it right someday. I'll report back at the next reunion!"

"You can take a make-up test," said Miss Pierce, dry as a bone. Nobody else could have said it. It was too wonderful and horrible to watch Nora giggling on the verge of hysteria. Somebody had to shut her up and Miss Pierce was the only teacher in the room.

They were all back in sixth grade.

One of the Jennifers was next. There were four in their class, but Jennifer H. was the only one who came to the reunion.

"I'll pass," she said quietly.

"No! No passing!"

Jennifer H. looked surprised behind her wire-rimmed glasses. "Really?" Age hadn't softened her lines, horse-faced and intimidating in a tailored jacket.

Everyone looked at Sasha. Was passing allowed? This was her game. Sasha hadn't meant to start anything weird.

"I don't know," Sasha said. "Nobody has to speak if they don't want to."

"No passing!" Lauren said sharply.

Maybe it wasn't Sasha's game.

"Very well." Jennifer H. steered above the fray, chilly and amused. "I live in Portland, Maine, with my wife, Victoria. Our daughter is in graduate school, our son works in real estate. I run a foundation that helps women transition back into the workplace after time away." She smiled. "I know that Harrison was never exactly in favor of 'time away' from anything, but many women have been managing the home, or were incarcerated, or struggle with single parenting. We have a lot of families hit by the opioid epidemic, so my work has been focusing on that lately. Trying to educate the community, not to mention law enforcement."

Jennifer stopped speaking and folded her hands in her lap.

Miss Pierce swirled the last of her whiskey, bored. Who could live up to the humble brag of Jennifer H.?

Fine, leave, thought Sasha, suddenly enraged at Miss Pierce. You don't have to like her. I don't like her either but at least she does good work in the world even if she wants an A+ for it. Sasha wasn't putting on a show. This was only a reunion dinner. If Nora was her mother, Sasha would have gone to an ashram and changed her name too. They could all go to hell as far as she was concerned.

Val caught her eye. Could she tell how angry Sasha was? Was she leaving soon? Val often left without saying anything. A thief's goodbye. Sasha shook her head slightly, hoping that Val could read her mind. She'd happily kick the rest of them out if only Lauren and Val would stay.

Val couldn't take it much longer. How could Sasha have started this terrible circle? These women were part of where she came from, though she hardly recognized most of them. Was Cora here, listening to everything? You got me here, now what am I supposed to do? Val asked silently. If Cora's voice stopped forever, what happened next? Val drank too fast, ate too fast, and fought the urge to go into Sasha's perfect bathroom with the flowered wallpaper and stick her finger down her throat. She hadn't done that for years. She told herself to sit tight and the urge would pass, like quitting smoking. If only Sasha hadn't put that picture of the four of them in the center of the bookcase. Cora's wedding wasn't that many years ago. Did the photograph mean that Val would never be that happy again? Danny had told her to start microdosing. Cora had told her to go running and do yoga. Change was inevitable. Why couldn't she get it?

That picture was taken when Cora still loved her.

If Val really stepped over the line the last time they saw each other, it was because she didn't know there was a line. Not with them. Nobody here knew that Cora had frozen her out for eternal punishment except the four of them. Not counting Cora's dickwad husband, Jeff. Maybe Dickwad talked Cora into cutting her off. He never liked Val because she'd gone down on Cora twenty years before he came along.

Yeah, well, Val wasn't the only one.

And fuck you too, Cora. Don't talk to me if you don't want to. Go haunt Dickwad. I'm gonna get a lot of great songs out of this and you'll wish you still had me on the label.

She never actually said that to Cora. She only wished she had.

Maybe.

Val had to get out of Sasha's living room or she might do something irrevocable. But she was transfixed by this circle. There was Nora who looked like a wax doll and spoke like a real human being. Smug Jennifer H. and the rest staking their claims one by one.

"I love mentoring," Annette Hanson's gray and black clothes draped like an ad for Eileen Fisher. "I've finally gotten to the point where I'm truly comfortable with who I am."

Really? They mostly didn't mention husbands or partners, despite the wedding rings. Was everybody married, whether gay or straight? Settled?

"My interns are amazing," said Annette. "So much talent."

How had they built these lives that looked like dioramas to Val? She could see Annette Hanson behind a large pane of glass with matching King Charles Spaniels. A Christmas tree with tasteful white lights and the smell of cinnamon in the air. Though that wasn't quite fair to the spaniels.

Was there nothing left but envy of what Val never thought she wanted?

"I'm leaving," Val whispered to Sasha, who gripped her hand.

"No, wait."

Paula Salinas was next. Class president, a jock with long legs that looked like they could cover a city block in three strides, like the giant in a fairy tale. Her hair was wound into a smooth gray knot, face beaming above a chic version of a monk's habit, black cotton, high collar. Paula's wrists were clustered with silver bracelets.

She raised both hands with a tiny cymbal crash of jewelry. "At this point in my life, I am on a new path."

Paula's voice was deep and scratchy, though she was too much of a jock to be a smoker. She looked around the room, those wide green eyes had always been part of her success. "I'm a medium," she said. "A psychic. I work out of my home in Kingston. I haven't been in touch with many of you over the years, but I felt called to come here."

Sasha tightened her grip on Val's hand, trying not to laugh. She didn't know that Val heard voices too.

"I also have a new name." Paula turned to Nora. "I know it's hard for people who have known us all our lives to accept this kind of change, but

I was never really a Paula, that was the name my parents chose. When I turned fifty, I changed my name to Sigrid."

"Do you have a guru?" asked Nora.

Paula (Sigrid) shook her head. "I have guides."

"What do they tell you?"

Nora was serious, but Sasha was fidgeting behind Val on the couch. Was she trying not to lose it? They used to laugh so hard they had to squat down in the hallway at Harrison with a heel dug into their crotches, pretending to tie a sneaker, holding the position until they could stagger to the nearest bathroom, pee and laughter flooding. The sweaty, rubber smell of the Harrison gymnasium with its metal cage over the wall clock. The slamming of the ball that Paula Salinas threw harder than anyone, effortlessly marking them out in dodgeball.

Val let go of Sasha's hand. She didn't feel like laughing.

"My guides tell me different things," Paula said. "I tried to ignore them for a long time. I mean, hearing voices? Not something you want to tell people."

She locked eyes briefly with Val. Did she know?

"I worked in nature conservation for twenty years. I was good at management. It must be the Virgo in me."

Paula's lightness was infectious, despite her testimony about guides and mystical powers. Even Miss Pierce was smiling. Grinning like a vulture, thought Val, circling over the bodies in Sasha's living room, ready to pluck their last bits of flesh. But Paula was smiling right back at Miss Pierce. Could she really be this unconcerned about what they thought of her? They should forget this stupid circle and ask her to interpret their natal charts, thought Val. Would she be willing to do it on a sliding scale?

"I began to hear one very specific voice in my head," said Paula. "It didn't stop, in fact, it made a great deal of sense—except for the fact that I was hearing a strange man talking and nobody else could hear it. Eventually, I had to quit my job and accept that this was, indeed, happening to me."

"Like Joan of Arc?" asked Miss Pierce.

"Not exactly Joan of Arc," Paula said, ignoring her tone. "Though I am engaged in a certain kind of battle."

"Maybe more like the Lord of the Rings?" asked Sarah Bailey from across the room, and this time everyone laughed, Paula most of all. Would any of them ever be able to call her Sigrid?

"There are actually a lot of us working energetically to create a sort of net to hold humanity intact as we enter a dark cycle. I know this all sounds very WooWoo. I give readings. I have a website: SigridInsights.com."

Paula settled back with her hands folded together, then turned to Elizabeth Hoffman on her right.

"My name is still Lizzie," said Lizzie Hoffman.

Laughter burst their polite silence. Little Lizzie Hoffman had the line of the night! The women wiped their eyes, trying to catch their breath, while Lizzie perched on the edge of the couch, owlishly happy. Was she funny?

"More wine," Sasha gasped. Hannah and Kiara moved among them like nymphs as the women lolled back in Sasha's expensive furniture or tilted their wooden chairs on the back legs, the way they were never supposed to do in class.

"To the Saturn Return!" Paula toasted them in her deep, minister's voice. Was this her Guide talking? Wasn't Saturn always returning or was that Mercury retrograding? Who cared! Val raised her glass with the others and repeated after Paula—she was still class president.

"To the Saturn Return!"

Now everyone would go home with a story about the reunion.

Val tugged Sasha down toward her. "I want Sigrid to give me a reading."

Sasha kissed Val on the top of her head, and Val pressed her fingers to the spot to keep the kiss from flying away.

Something was loosening.

When Lauren got up and went toward the front hall with her phone in her hand, Sasha wondered if Lauren had heard Val and what she thought of Sasha's fleeting, motherly kiss. Lauren had barely spoken to Sasha since she came in, but that didn't mean anything, did it? When things were bad at home, it was probably easier to talk to Nora Danforth, whom she hardly knew. Sasha still felt jealous. She had lost track of her own party. The women shifted in their seats. Some got up to sniff around the buffet, use the bathroom and check their phones, though they were all too old to use the babysitter as an excuse. How could they feel so fulfilled when the world was on fire? Sasha was as guilty as anyone, fanning out the food, the wine, the flowers, the view of the Hudson. The circle in her living room coiled and uncoiled. Taking turns to talk about their lives was either the best or worst idea she ever had. Would Sasha have told them all about the Undeniable if she hadn't gone first? She had no idea how many of them were being honest or how much she cared.

Sasha would never tell about going to Rebecca Benedict's house for a sleepover, where her father felt under Sasha's long T-shirt as she stood next to him. She was watching television while Rebecca was in the bathroom. He was lying on the couch and never looked away from his newspaper as he reached up to press his hand against her name-of-the-week underpants. Sasha stood perfectly still, waiting for Rebecca to come back.

She didn't want to be impolite.

When the family ate breakfast the next morning, she couldn't stop staring at the black hairs on his knuckles. She had never noticed Rebecca's father before, flying by the grownups in their own bright world of dress-up and sock puppets. Sasha never went to Rebecca's house again, even after Rebecca cornered her, cheeks flaring, in the school bathroom. I thought you were coming for a sleepover? I'm not allowed, she lied. Rebecca knew she was lying. Was that long-ago fight why Rebecca hadn't come to the reunion?

Sasha never told anyone about the hairy hand, or how she started to think about skin as spandex manufactured to cover the blood and guts and goo dripping out of holes in their bodies. Most of the girls in her class weren't allowed to come to Sasha's house. Nobody even knew how to get to Queens.

Lauren sat on the toilet, calling Amy.

Pick up, pick up, pick up, pick up, PLEASE pick up.

"Hi, this is Amy. You know what to do."

BEEEEP!

"Mommy Lala?"

Lauren was Mommy Lala. Amy was just Mommy.

"Masha! Mashabear. How's my bear?" Lauren's heart tightened.

"When are you coming home?"

"Soon." The longing made it almost impossible to speak. She wanted to kiss her until Masha pushed her away, all happy and annoyed.

"We're making cookies. Mommy's hands are all covered with dough so I got to press the button on the phone."

Amy's voice was muffled under Masha's panting breath. "I want some dough, Mommy, just a little bite. Ash, you want some cookie dough?"

"Can I speak to Mommy?"

"Not so big, Ash. I want some too!"

"Sweetheart, can you pass the phone to Mommy?" Nobody was listening to Lauren.

"I want the big spoon, same as you—no!"

"Masha? Amy? Hello?"

"Hi." It was Amy.

"Sweetheart, please. I love you so much. I have to come home. I'll leave right now, I have to see you, the kids—"

"It's not a good idea."

This was Amy's fake voice, the one that didn't mean it. The one she used when she didn't want to upset the kids.

"Come on, it's me. We can't let this happen."

"Not tonight."

"When? Please, Amy—"

The call ended. Lauren stared at her blinked-out phone. She would kneel on the bathroom floor and pray if that would make Amy call her back. "Please," she said aloud. "Please."

"What can I help you with?" asked Siri.

"Shut the fuck up!" Lauren threw the phone on the tile floor. She pressed her fists into her eyes. Didn't Amy know that Lauren could have listened in on her life forever?

When she picked up her phone, the screen was shattered. Perfect. Lauren placed it carefully next to the sink and splashed water on her face. She had a six-year-old child. She had counted Masha's breaths when her perfect skull fit in Lauren's hand. She wasn't allowed to give up. Lauren cupped her hands under the running water and sipped in handfuls, splashing all over the sink. When she opened the bathroom door, two women she didn't recognize were standing there with strained expressions. How long had she been in there? Didn't Sasha have another bathroom?

"Guess we can't hold it as long as we used to." One of the women said cheerfully, squeezing her hands together.

Lauren tried to smile as she moved past them. She hated these women with their low maintenance hairstyles and jokes about middle-aged pussies losing their clench. She didn't want to think about any of it, menopause, perimenopause, or how you just couldn't hold it after having babies. Amy had two babies and she was tight in all the right ways.

She stood in the doorway to the living room, dreading that empty spot on the couch next to Sasha that was saved just for her. Val's ragged, startled look only made her feel more guilty for wanting to leave. So what?

Lauren wanted the future, not the past.

Sasha patted the cushion next to her. Why was Lauren standing in the doorway instead of coming back to sit with her and Val? Lauren didn't move and something about her expression made Sasha's insides open and close like a jellyfish. It was Miss Pierce's turn in the circle.

"I think you're all doing just fine. B+."

Everybody laughed. Pierce never gave A's, except to Sasha.

"Make sure you exercise every day and stay curious." Pierce nodded to the person next to her. That was it? Work out and stay curious? She's setting an example, keeping it short, thought Sasha. Her cheeks ached from forcing a smile and she had no idea what time it was. Was the reunion over yet? Hannah and Kiara were setting out trays of cookies, there were tea and coffee urns in the dining room. The breeze from the barely open window picked up, pressing in the cold scent of lilies. Their orange pollen could stain the couch. Sasha would move them into the kitchen before she went to bed. Did the flowers make the room smell like a funeral? This was another thing they would have to adapt to, seeing each other at funerals more than reunions. If things didn't go the right way with the Great Lop Off, she could be the next to go. *ADAPT, MIGRATE, OR DIE* was the banner Miss Pierce taped over the door to her science classroom at Harrison. A long line of *Homo erectus* marching toward *Homo sapiens*. Sasha would try to adapt, but why was Cora the first one gone? She would have loved hearing all these . . . Confessions? Pitches? Stand Up?

All of the above.

Sasha had to stop herself from winking at Cora in the photo. She'd maybe had a bit too much to drink, started too early, but it was her house and she had done her Report to the Academy. Who cared what people thought about her talking circle? It was Penny's turn, and she looked just the same. Short brown hair, crew neck sweater. She never got rid of that small black mole on her chin. Penny used to make sardonic remarks about the teachers without moving her lips, so she never got caught.

"I don't have anything to say. I don't do anything!" She held up her hands. "I have no kids, I'm not married, my job is boring, I have nothing to add."

Because it was Penny, they all pushed. "Come on, say something!"

"What? I've lived in the same apartment forever. It's very cheap and I basically do nothing. I volunteer at an animal shelter and have too many pets for the size of my apartment. I still have a land line. I warm up a can of tomato soup almost every day for lunch, occasionally a sardine sandwich, but the smell makes the cats go crazy. I'm very boring."

Everyone was so happy that Penny was still their Bartleby. They were all just the same.

"Honestly, I hated Harrison," said Penny. "I was bullied the whole time." She looked around the room in the sudden silence. "I mean, they didn't call it bullying then, not the way we do now, but I was scared to go to school every day, at least until high school. Plus, there was the racism and abuse that everyone ignored. I used to get shoved against the wall and kicked by Angela Sanders every time we had to go to assembly. She was in the grade above us, remember? She did it every time and you all kept walking past us down the stairs. And what about the way Mr.

Chollet made us sit underneath his desk, squatting between his knees when we made a mistake in grammar or pronunciation? Or the gym teachers who lined us up, stripped down to our underpants, taking photos behind that big black screen at the beginning of every school year? I don't think that was about checking our posture."

"The school destroyed those photos," said Jennifer H. "There was an email about it."

"Of course they destroyed them!" said Penny. "It was totally perverted! Not to mention that song we sang every Christmas, worshipping England as if it were Jerusalem. As if it's good to be England or Israel!"

"Oh, please," said Miss Pierce. "That song was written by William Blake. He sat naked in his backyard; he saw angels in the trees."

"All I remember is the line about dark satanic mills."

Everyone in the room could hear the school song: *and did those feet, in ancient times walk upon England's mountains green?*

No, Cora used to whisper in assembly. *They did not.*

"I love that line," said Sasha. "About the mills."

"That song is like everything else we learned at Harrison," said Penny. "Sort of beautiful and sort of heartless." She pressed a cocktail napkin to her eyes. "It doesn't matter."

Wait. This was Penny, whom they loved. Funny, sharp Penny, who was always the first to shrug things off. Nobody could look at each other. They were sitting too close together in this overheated room. It was like someone crying on an airplane as the person next to them dug into microwaved Salisbury steak.

"You're right," said Val. "That place was fucked up." It was the first time she'd spoken in the circle. "How come you came tonight?"

Penny balled up the red paper napkin in her fist. "I know this may sound crazy, but I was glad to be invited. Harrison's still part of my bookshelf."

Penny's face was shining, freckled and translucent. She didn't look embarrassed to have cried in front of them. Val nodded like it all made sense to her.

"Thank you for inviting me, Sasha. I was kind of surprised. The four of you were so snotty at school," said Penny. "Always thought you were too cool for the rest of us. But that was a hundred years ago." She turned to Val. "I couldn't believe it when Cora died. I'm so sorry she's not here."

"Me too," said Val.

Lauren couldn't ignore Sasha's bewildered glance. Come on, they all knew that they were mean in high school. Cora was the meanest (and funniest) most of the time, but the four of them created a certain kind of monster. Lauren always liked Penny (she'd never seen her getting beaten up in the stairwell), but it was high school. Did nobody understand how long ago that was? Sasha's eyes darted around the room, looking like she was asking everyone to please be okay. Maybe Lauren should go to a hotel tonight. Oh, why did she always want to leave when she hated being alone? Amy was the only one who understood that push and pull. Lauren had worn her out with leaving. Cora would have given her instructions on how to get Amy to take her back. If Lauren went back to the couch, she'd have to look at that photo of Cora pulling the four of them close for the camera, locking arms like she'd never let go. Amy took the picture. That was how Lauren used to look at Amy.

Cora's wedding day had been so happy it hurt.

Lauren forced herself to go back into the living room and sit next to Sasha on the couch.

Someone had to go after Penny. Susanna Porter, the one whose parents rented a charter bus on graduation night so the whole class could get dead drunk going from party to party. Did her parents think renting a bus meant that people would want to go to graduation parties with Susanna? Even then, it had seemed like a cruel waste of money. Had anyone gone on the bus? Or was it only teenage Susanna in a too short dress and high heels flap-flapping down the sidewalk, the bus lumbering behind with blind, tinted windows?

How had any of them survived their parents?

How would Masha survive if Amy never let Mommy Lala come home?

"My mother passed away in the fall," Susanna said. "As many of you know. Thank you for the condolence notes, it really meant a lot to hear from you."

At school, Susanna's nickname was Olive Oyl from the Popeye cartoon, because she was so tall and skinny, but there was something forthright about Susanna. She didn't mind being called Olive Oyl. Or maybe she did? Then Lauren remembered that she was the one who first made up that nickname. She called Susanna Olive Oyl in the lunchroom, in gym class, when they were lining up to go to the park in partners, two by two. Lauren was the worst one.

"I'm sorry that I called you Olive Oyl," Lauren said. "It was really mean."

She could feel the room holding its breath. Were they all supposed to apologize to each other now? Lauren hadn't sent a condolence note when Susanna's mother died, and now she was apologizing for what she did in middle school?

"Did you start that?" Susanna shook her head. "I don't even remember. Everyone called me Olive Oyl. I mean, Olive Oyl is way better than Popeye. He's dumb, but she just pretends to be dumb. Plus, that was the first time I had a nickname. Do you remember what you said to me the first day I came to Harrison?"

"No." Lauren could barely remember Susanna.

"You told me that I would never be popular because I was no good at sports. I don't know how you could tell! I was actually pretty good at track," said Susanna.

Some of the others looked at Lauren as if she had something wrong with her. Had she missed something when she was in the bathroom calling home? This was turning into an AA meeting where people drank wine instead of coffee. How many people did she have to apologize to? What if she lay down on the floor of Sasha's living room and let them spit on her, kick her, dump food on her?

If she let Amy do that, would it be enough? Was it what she wanted?

"You were right," Susanna said. "I wasn't popular and basically hated gym. Anyway, now I'm an ob-gyn at Mount Sinai, and I brought something for everyone." Susanna reached into her shoulder bag. "A little party favor in my capacity as a doctor."

"Party favors?" Miss Pierce perked up.

"Coconut oil. If you're not using it yet, it's time to start." Susanna held up a little plastic jar, small enough for airplane carry-on toiletries. "You may have noticed something that happens to most of us at this age: the incredible shrinking vagina."

"Oh my God, are we really going to talk about our vaginas?" asked Nora.

"She's a gynecologist," said Lizzie Hoffman. "She's allowed."

"Wait, I read that article somewhere." Penny was back from the bathroom and looked as if nothing was wrong. "Was it in the *Times*?"

"That was a great piece," Susanna nodded. "Vaginal dryness can occur post-menopause, and chances are we're all nearly done with our periods by now."

Lauren started to get up from the couch, but Val trapped her by leaning back against her shins. It was the first time they had touched since the subway platform. Lauren fought the urge to kick her out of the way. Why did she hate everyone all of a sudden? All she could hear was Amy telling her not to come home.

"It's a natural part of the aging process. The walls of the vagina lose elasticity, but this can slow it down. Not everyone should use estrogen vaginal inserts or HRT. For example, if you've had breast cancer, hormones are not advised."

Sasha expected everyone's heads to swivel toward her, but they were all listening to Susanna like good students. Maybe she wasn't the only one in the room with breast cancer. Sasha took another sip of wine. Her torso would be bone smooth post-surgery. A good look for her fifties. She'd buy tailored suits.

Susanna was still talking. "You put a small gob of coconut oil inside, morning and night—and don't be afraid to give yourself a little self-massage down there, your body is your oldest friend, it needs you to take care of it."

"Stop!" Nora covered her ears.

"Stretch the walls of the vagina with your index and middle finger for about two minutes. It can be easier to put one foot up on the toilet seat, like inserting a tampon. Very simple and completely safe. Morning and night, like brushing your teeth."

"I already use coconut oil on my teeth!" Paula said. "I rub it onto my gums. My dentist says it's excellent for gum health."

"You can add this to your routine." Susanna handed Paula the first jar.

"Are you a board-certified physician handing out snake oil? We are not here to discuss vaginas," said Miss Pierce.

Susanna smiled and handed Pierce a jar. "It's never too late for good vaginal health."

"It is for me!" Miss Pierce passed the jar to the person sitting next to her.

Susanna ignored her (were they allowed to ignore Miss Pierce?) and kept handing around the jars. Everyone took one (Lauren took two), and some unscrewed the lid and took a sniff before slipping it into their purses.

"It's organic," Susanna called out. "Most grocery stores carry it. I have more than enough, since some of us didn't make it here tonight. Anyone want another?"

Paula raised her hand. "One for the top and one for the bottom!"

Sasha pressed her hand against her mouth. "That guy! My Tinder date!"

"You're on Tinder?" Nora asked.

"Not anymore," Sasha said. "But Lauren, Val, you remember the guy—" She turned to the rest of them. "I met this guy. He was youngish, really cute."

"She was crazy about him," said Lauren.

"No, I wasn't! It was only a couple of dates, but yes, he was cute—"

"You said gorgeous," Lauren interrupted.

"You made us look at his profile picture," said Val.

"Okay, he was very handsome."

"And younger," said Lauren.

"And younger, so what?" Sasha looked around for Hannah and Kiara, but they were in the kitchen. She lowered her voice. "The first night we had sex, okay, the only night we had sex, I started bleeding—I mean, a lot—I thought maybe I'd torn something down there!"

"You might have," said Susanna.

"He was so freaked out. I mean, he was a 'big' guy."

Now the whole room was giggling. Sasha shouldn't be telling them this!

"I made him go out and buy pads at the bodega. I mean, how sexy is that?"

Now even Val and Lauren were laughing. All was forgiven. The whole class floated on inner tubes down rivers of coconut oil.

Sasha looked at Susanna. "Do you think?"

"Probably," said Susanna. "Did you go to your gynecologist?"

"I was too embarrassed. Eventually the bleeding stopped, or slowed down. I went home. Never saw him again."

"Try the coconut oil," said Susanna. "It really helps, and you might consider buying a vibrator. They make great ones now. Never be too embarrassed to go to the gynecologist."

She put the unclaimed jars back into her bag. "Thank you again for the condolence notes," she said brightly.

Val shoved the jar of coconut oil into her pocket like she would ever have sex again.

Now was the perfect time for a friendly lab mix to sniff its way around the room, black tail swinging. What was Val going to do when it was her turn to talk? This was not Val's pack. She belonged with Juno and Sheila and Bertie; she belonged with Eleanor Rigby on a freight train heading south, smoking hand-rolled cigarettes. Val would have planned something if she knew this was going to happen. She could have brought her guitar—no, that would be pathetic. She could never be as guileless as little Lizzie Hoffman.

"You're always standing outside yourself," Danny once said to her in the middle of one of their fights. "When are you just in it?"

The only time she stopped watching herself was when she was onstage. The problem was that she wasn't gigging anymore. The problem was she couldn't get hired or keep a band together. The problem was money. It takes so much longer to do things when you're broke. The time it takes to wander the grocery aisles looking for items in the food coupon newsletter, then they're all sold out. No matter how hard she tried to be smart about it, Val came home with random groceries. A bag of rice and Nutella. She was better at planning her way around a menu at a restaurant, pretending not to be hungry or want another drink. There was also the problem of too many clothes and not enough interest in food. She had a hard time letting go of outfits. Her costumes were her armor, the leaky cowboy boots she wore tonight when she had perfectly good snow boots for walking the dogs.

Too proud, too arrogant, too old.

Val was flushed and sweaty. She wondered if something bad was actually happening to her. Something like a heart attack. That would be news for the annual class bulletin. She started to pant quietly through her mouth, working through the pain in her chest, hoping nobody noticed. Sasha caught her eye and from the way her expression changed, Val figured she hadn't been able to hide her panic as well as she thought.

She was out of practice with humans. The earth was a ship burning at sea and here she was counting rolls of contentment on people with good bone structure.

Beatrice London leaned over to her. "Is it true you walk dogs? Can I give you my card? Our dog-walker just quit."

Beatrice's business card had a line drawing of an unrecognizable object and listed her as senior analyst. Val panted through three more classmates who shared their contractor and renovation problems. Lauren looked like she would bolt if she wasn't spending the night. But Val couldn't sleep over, she just couldn't. Sasha would take care of Lauren.

How had Beatrice known she was walking dogs?

It was Lauren's turn. Val was next.

Maybe her heart would seize up and she wouldn't have to speak.

"I didn't know we were going to do this circle," Lauren said. "But I have something to read."

Everyone looked pleased, a poem? Something funny from one of the yearbooks?

"Since this is the first time we've gathered since Cora. I'll read something from her."

Nobody moved, though a couple of them dropped their gaze as if they were in church. Cora never went to church! Val wanted to scream. Lauren and Cora were the biggest drama queens even if Val was the one onstage. Would everything be okay with Cora by now? If Cora was here, why wouldn't she talk to her?

"I didn't have time to go home," said Lauren. "But I have these pictures on my phone. I took them after Cora died and I never deleted them, not sure why, but—" She looked at Val. "You remember how we used to write notes to each other in the margins of our textbooks? During class?"

Val nodded.

"I still have my old Spanish book," said Lauren. "I looked through it again for the first time after Cora died, when I was trying to get rid of things, deciding what 'brought me joy.'" Lauren rolled her eyes but kept going. "Me and Cora sat next to each other for an entire year in seventh grade. That brought me joy, but I can't even show my old Spanish book to my daughter, the notes are so dirty!"

People were smiling, this is the kind of thing that was supposed to happen at reunions. "Remember the pornographic library?" Even Miss Pierce nodded. Everyone knew about the library in Cora's locker: *Rubyfruit Jungle*, *The Godfather* with page thirty-seven well-thumbed, *Lady Chatterley's Lover*, which was so boring nobody read it.

"I took pictures of some of the pages from my Spanish book to show Amy—she's my wife."

Did saying "wife" out loud make it unbreakable?

"Anyway, since we're all together, I thought I'd share some of my favorite notes from Cora." Sasha reached down and squeezed Val's shoulder. It was going to be okay. This was the perfect thing. Lauren gave Val one of those "you're going to love this" looks, and started reading Cora's note aloud:

"SO I went to Val's, and we were super hungry after school, but her MOM wouldn't get out of bed and all we had for a snack was RAW SPAGHETTI out of the BOX!"

Val had told the story of the raw spaghetti lots of times, but hearing Cora tell it in a note from seventh grade made it sound worse.

"SO we tried to make fried rice, like from a Chinese restaurant, but the rice just stayed hard. It tasted all burnt!"

Val left that part out when she told the story. She and Cora didn't understand why the rice didn't get fluffy and soft when they poured it from the box into a frying pan. The rice grains crackled and smelled like burnt toast. They had finally given up and taken two spoons, the glass sugar bowl and a jar of Skippy back to her room for peanut butter lollipops dipped in sugar. These were the semiotics of Val's childhood, Skippy peanut butter and a cut glass sugar bowl her mom picked up somewhere. Did Cora write about that too?

Now, Lauren was acting out her and Cora's voices. "Then *I* wrote, sideways in the margin, GROSS! OH MY GOD!"

Val fixed her mouth into what might be a smile. Lauren flipped to another photo on her phone and enlarged it so she could see the writing.

"So THEN—" Lauren looked around the room. "Cora wrote this part in all Caps—SO THEN—"

Now everyone was laughing with Lauren, as if they really knew Cora. As if they knew anything.

"We watched TV and when we went back to the kitchen to get a glass of milk, there were roaches EVERYWHERE! We ran into the living room to give them time to scatter, counted to ten, then went back into the kitchen. It was so GROSS!"

"I mean," Lauren was speaking in her own voice now. "This was New York before 'Combat.' We all had roaches, admit it!"

Val tried laughing harder than the others, but it sounded more like barking. Was she really barking like Juno? Was Lauren done? Was Cora done? Val got up, wishing she could go on all fours, reaching for the back of one of Sasha's folding chairs as the room rose up in a roar of laughter behind her. The women stretched to the ceiling in cartoon shapes, dresses and fashionable slacks trailing behind. Val ran her hand along the wall all the way to the bathroom. Maybe they thought she was drunk.

She wished she was drunk.

When she closed the bathroom door, she couldn't get the seat up fast enough. Her finger down her throat and vomit spattering the inside of the toilet bowl. All that lovely warm food right up out of her lovely warm tummy. Just like the old days.

She leaned her cheek against the cool tile floor. She had spent so much time pretending not to be hungry.

I wish Val could see me sitting on the toilet smoking a cigarette. I just fig-

ured out that I can smoke in the Bardo. It's the best. All those years wishing I could smoke again, and the first time I want a cigarette after I'm dead?

Boom! Delicious.

I don't think Val can smell it, which is too bad 'cause I know she'd love a cigarette right now. Poor baby. I want to hold her hair out of her face and get her a damp paper towel like when she went overboard in the club days. She always smelled like cigarettes and vomit by the end of the night.

It feels like another shift is happening. It could just be the cigarette.

I guess she can't hear me anymore, but I'm going to try.

I wasn't really making fun of you, Val. Your house was just so far from Pop-Tarts and Cap'n Crunch. You know I loved your mom, even if she was a little scary. Hey, I'm a little scary. You always laughed when you told that story. You even told it to strangers, right down to the cockroaches. You thought it was a badge of honor growing up rougher than the rest of us, with a different brand of neglect.

I know. You're the only one allowed to tell it.

I want to slip my hand under Val's head. Cushion those bathroom tiles while she closes her eyes for a minute.

Then she can wash her face and forgive us our trespasses.

Does anybody still know the story of Saint Francis and the wolf? There was a wolf who was terrorizing the town where Francis lived before he was a saint. Just another bad boy from a good family who threw it all away. The wolf wasn't just killing the occasional duck, duck, goose. It was getting the old folks and children. Anyone it could grab as they walked along the paths or went out into the fields. Nobody could catch the wolf, and pretty soon, there was no walking or weeding. The wolf got bigger and fatter, its coat the color of wet clay.

Saint Francis went outside the walls of the town and asked the wolf, why are you doing this? What do you want?

The wolf said, I'm hungry.

If I feed you every day, said Saint Francis, will you stop eating people?

Yes, said the wolf.

All the people laughed at Saint Francis when he put out meat for the wolf, once in the morning and once at night.

Who trusts the word of a wolf? Besides, a wolf can't talk.

But the wolf left the people alone.
We all grew up hungry, Val. Talk to the wolf.

Sasha wanted all these people out of her house.

Where did Val go? The bathroom? Out the front door?

Lauren was leaning over Val's empty spot, showing the photos from her old Spanish book to Beatrice London, the two of them giggling at her phone as if nothing was wrong. Who the fuck was Beatrice London? These women had been chosen by the school, not each other, thrown together because of their brains. They had no hearts. She had to say something to Lauren. She should go after Val.

A familiar pain started at Sasha's sacrum and moved in rivulets across her lower back.

"Coffee and dessert!" Sasha pushed herself up from the couch. "You can't leave me with it or I'll eat it all myself!"

She led the way into the dining room in the rising chatter. Sasha reached for a mille-feuille overflowing with cream. She would enjoy her own goddamned party. "Yes, there's decaf," she heard Kiara say. Thank God, the girls were still here. Her students were her family now, not these well-brushed women she didn't know anymore. Some of them would slip out the door, watching their waistlines and gathering identical puffer coats from the rack in the hallway. Most of them were half in the bag after all that wine. A few would stay long enough to slosh coffee and sweets. If Val came back, she could skip her turn. Sasha didn't care. She couldn't tell them about the Undeniable now that Lauren threw Val under the bus. Val would flee if she hadn't already. Sasha was too angry to tell Lauren anything except where the sheets were for the pullout couch.

It felt like two in the morning.

Had Sasha liked the other girls better when Cora was alive? They were always a closed system. In quantum mechanics, closed systems are time dependent and vulnerable to external forces. Cora's break with Val was a probability and her death was the Lucretian swerve, but they lost each other long before that. It really did all come down to probabilities, chance, and time. Simple and elegant. Sasha looked across the living room at Miss Pierce.

"Help me remember," she said. "Quantum probabilities and closed systems. It's important."

Miss Pierce looked as if she thought Sasha was drunk, "I'm going home." But she didn't get up off the couch.

Fuck them all. This was a very expensive pastry from the best bakery in the neighborhood and she was going to enjoy it on her own couch, in her own living room, on her own fat ass.

Lauren didn't want to spend the night anymore, but where could she go? Sasha would be too upset if she left. She had made them all laugh, hadn't she? Sasha gave her a weird look when she read Cora's notes, but someone had to bring Cora's voice into the room. Val seemed as fine as she ever did. Everyone knew the cockroach story. Val told it herself enough times. Wasn't "Raw Spaghetti" going to be the name of her first album before Cora talked her out of it?

Lauren didn't want to think about Val. She wanted to think about Masha. She felt better since she spoke to Beatrice London, of all people. Beatrice was a life coach now, whatever that meant. Life coaching was such a soft target, but without really meaning to, Lauren was telling Beatrice everything. Lauren was glad the others had gone to the sugar trough. Glad that Val had left the room.

"What are you doing here?" asked Beatrice. "You love Amy. You should go home and tell her. It's time for a grand romantic gesture. You have keys, don't you? To your own apartment? Your daughter wants you home and you love your wife, that's the most important thing to you both. Fuck the mediator. Go home and tell Amy you can't live without her." Beatrice spoke with absolute conviction. What would that be like?

"This isn't a movie, Beatrice."

"Wrong, it *is* a movie," said Beatrice. "Remember the end of *When Harry Met Sally*? Billy Crystal running back to that stupid party because he was about to lose the love of his life? That's what you need to do. What about 'you had me at hello'? You're the guy who runs back at the end of the movie."

"*Jerry McGuire* is the stupidest movie, totally sexist, and what about the Bechdel test?"

"It's the greatest movie, and of course I know about the Bechdel test, I went to Oberlin."

"You did?"

"Look, do you want to pass tests or stay married?"

"Amy hates that movie. What if she won't let me in?"

"If she won't let you in, you say it in the hallway. What else are you going to do? Keep texting like a teenager? Penny's right, the four of you were total snots in high school, but you're fifty-something years old! It's time to move-on-dot-org."

"Move-on-dot-org?"

"You guys had your little clique, fine. I'm really sorry about Cora, but you're still here. Nobody's the same person that they used to be."

The past was so exhausting.

Beatrice pulled out a tissue and handed it to Lauren. "Sometimes we just need permission," she said more quietly. "Tell Amy that you love her *and* her child, even if they're a little shit. You know what else? Masha might turn out to be a little shit sleeping in the living room when she's twenty-five. You don't want to be alone for that."

Beatrice snapped the rubber band she wore on her wrist because she was quitting smoking.

Lauren stared at her. "You're better than our couples' therapist. If we'd talked to you, we might never have gone to mediation."

"That's what everyone says." Beatrice snapped her rubber band. "Jesus, I wish I could have a cigarette."

Val walked back into the living room looking like hell, skinny and pale. Lauren felt a little jolt. Had Val eaten anything? Of course she'd eaten, they were sitting right next to each other and Val had shoveled it in. Lauren hadn't really done anything wrong by reading Cora's notes out loud. It was a joke! Beatrice hadn't said anything about it, so it must have been fine. Maybe Beatrice was right about everything. Lauren would order a car and drop Val off at her place, then go home—did "no" ever actually mean "yes" or was that the patriarchy talking? She would bring home a couple of desserts from the party wrapped in paper napkins. Something sweet and creamy that she and Amy would lick off their fingers, unable to save any for Masha and Ash even if they tried.

Why did Val keep looking at her like that? Cora died when she wasn't supposed to, that was the problem.

Val pulled a folded piece of paper out of her back pocket. "I don't have a song," she said. "Or any notes from Cora about Lauren's fucked up family."

Everyone stopped talking. There were large gaps in the circle now, the people who left after saying thank you to Sasha and no to dessert. Miss Pierce arranged her petits fours geometrically on a paper napkin.

"You don't have to say anything, Val," said Sasha. "It doesn't matter."

"It's my turn."

She unfolded the paper like origami, flattened thin as tissue.

"It's not a song, but it's the last thing I said to Cora, so I thought I'd share it. I've kept this in my wallet ever since Cora died." Val squinted, holding it out at arm's length, too vain for glasses.

"I almost lost this tonight," said Val. "Kind of a long story. It's a bunch of text messages to Cora that I printed out and deleted from the phone so I wouldn't keep reading them over. Then the phone broke. So maybe it's good I printed them out." She looked at Sasha and Lauren. "Or maybe not. Anyway. Here goes:

hey cora
quick drink after work?
i cn come uptown if u want
i know its late but need to talk

im here are u coming
they won't let me have a table without u
Cora?
K going home now

Lauren says im harassing you
so i won't txt anymore

why talk to her not me?

Cora its me

i get u cant help me w new manager agent Jeff whatevr
forget it
just
trying all positive reboot like u said
thats me all positive
hahaha
u've helped me plenty and i thought
no harm no foul
thats all

hi ok no more texting
feel like an idiot
over and out

im sick of yr voicemail
im not gonna walk by yr house like a dumped gf
OK maybe i did

hellooooo
are u still mad ;)
dont be a hater
<3

lauren says yr still mad
sasha says u need break

gonna be near yr office today
is a month enuf time?

its been 7 hours & 15 days
OK a lot longer but couldnt resist

are u there god it's me margaret
525,600 minutes
but whose counting
C?

i still dont get
i mean
i know i asked u for new manager recc
but
u might not be seeing these msgs
dont know if u blocked me
good country song huh?
u blocked me but
i keep writing to u
cant you hear it w pedal steel
Cora?
C?
C?

"I thought you burned it," said Lauren.

"I was going to."

A smudge of whipped cream quivered on Sasha's upper lip. She reached for Lauren's hand, then stopped. She meant to reach for Val. Why couldn't she get up off the couch? Val looked at Lauren as if she was a stranger. Sasha's heart started beating too fast. Why couldn't she make things better?

"Burn it," Paula said. "A text like that should always be burned. Bad energy. Cora is here with us." Paula got to her feet. "I've felt her presence since the beginning of the night."

"Sit down and don't be tedious," said Miss Pierce.

Paula closed her eyes, arms outstretched with her palms facing up. "Cora? Are you here? What do you need?"

"I don't know what Cora needs," Beatrice London said to Val out of the corner of her mouth. "But Paula's right. You've got to get rid of that text."

Val looked past Paula. The dark window was streaming close-up shots of Cora's face superimposed on the lights from Jersey. Cora gazing into Sasha's well-lit room, her half-smile with those slightly buck teeth that she never got fixed. Then the camera zoomed out and Cora was sitting behind the women with their backs to the window, her arms wrapped around her knees, watching Val watch her. Val knew exactly what Cora was thinking without her having to say it. This was how they sat on the radiator cover in Cora's room with a bowl of popcorn between them. This was how they partnered in gym class, sitting on the floor with their legs spread apart, wrists locked, feet pressed against each other's ankles, stretching their hamstrings. Neither of them willing to let go first.

Paula opened her eyes. "Cora didn't mean it. You don't need her anymore. You don't need her permission."

"Fucking right, I don't," Val snapped.

Paula took Val's hands between her own. Val could feel Cora's fingers wrapped around her and Paula's, her knuckles like fish spines. Cora's hands were warm, not cold, and Paula's eyes widened as she stared at Val, gripping hard. If Paula felt it too, maybe it didn't matter whether this was a summoning or a longing. Cora's hands tightened. She had taught Val how to link hands and wrists to make a seat of bones. The four of them took turns carrying each other down the hallways at school.

"Bring me a candle," said Paula, without looking away from Val.

Lauren went for one of the ivory tapers in the dining room.

Sasha could hear her mother spitting over her left shoulder three times fast, pupupu, to keep away the evil eye. Val didn't care what she looked like anymore. It made sense that Paula's cheeks were wet. This was a mirror exercise.

"Are you sure you want to burn it?" asked Lauren, holding the candle.

"Cora loved you," said Sasha.

"I know," said Val.

"I didn't mean to—" Lauren started, but Paula interrupted.

"Give me the candle," she said, taking the candlestick from Lauren with one hand and holding tight to Val with the other.

"Now," said Paula to Val. "Do it now."

The ash went flying up.

Cora's hands let loose. Val stared at the ceiling with her mouth open. Wind scattered snow against the window. Ash drifted onto their creased faces as their waterproof mascara started to run.

"Look!" Sasha said, catching a piece of ash on her palm. "It's like the cookie wrappers in science class."

Miss Pierce always brought Italian cookies into science before the holiday break, pale blue paper twisted around hard macaroons that cracked between their teeth. Pierce told them to crumple the paper wrapping, then roll it into a cylinder. Each girl set it on fire and made a wish. The paper shot up to the ceiling and turned to ash. Everyone saw the cookie wrappers flying up from their Bunsen burners at the same moment.

This was supposed to teach them the scientific principle of—joy?

"Oh, Cora," Sasha gasped. "You were so mean!"

Now that was a great party!

I loved every minute of it. Sasha, you really pulled it off. All those women walking home through the snow with their girlhoods unwrapped like Italian cookies.

If you do the math, we spent more hours together between the ages of six and seventeen than anyone else in our lives. A school like that's not normal, but maybe it doesn't fuck you up any more than your parents. It's funny how we don't think about it, and then it's all that matters. We're a dying breed, but who isn't? It's our lungs, not our feet, making the last beat as we spin the turnstile to the other side. Maybe that's why so many of us choose fire over the body's slow, composting return. I'm going to shoot straight up without ever hitting the pavement.

Goodnight Paula, and goodnight Nora.
Good night Beatrice, and goodnight Susanna,
Goodnight Miss Pierce with your breast strapped tight,
Time to go home and turn out the light.
Good night Penny with your crew cut hair,
goodnight to the lilies scenting the air.

"Finally!" Sasha closed the door.

Cheeks kissed, scarves wrapped, leftovers put away and desserts left out at Sasha's request. The elevator descending for the last time bearing Kiara and Hannah with their envelopes of cash.

Val was sprawled out on the living room floor with Lauren. When Sasha walked in with the whiskey, they stopped talking.

"What?"

"I was apologizing," said Lauren. "I thought it was a classic Val story, but—"

"Not your story," said Sasha.

They both looked at Val.

"I mean, yeah." Val sat up. "You didn't think. That's all there is to it, right? Not thinking. I don't really want to talk about it anymore."

Sasha poured out three glasses of whiskey.

"Don't pour this on the carpet, Val. It's really expensive."

"Sorry about that."

"No, you're not. Neither am I," said Sasha. "I've had that rug forever. It was the right thing to do." Sasha held up her glass. Now, the three of them could look each other in the eye.

"When you called to tell me about Cora," said Val to Sasha. "I wished it was you instead. Either one of you."

The air stilled.

"Me too. I wished it was you or Lauren," said Sasha.

"I thought you'd be the one, Val. I mean, you're always rehearsing," said Lauren.

"Do we all hate each other?" Val asked. She started coughing and laughing at the same time. "What would Cora say?"

"She won," Lauren said. "She always wanted to be first."

They all started laughing because it was true.

"What the fuck happened tonight?" said Val.

"Paula and Beatrice grew up to be goddesses and seers," Sasha said. "Who would've guessed? Least likely to . . ."

"But they were right," Val said. "You know they were right."

"What really happened with you and Cora? She never told us, not really." Lauren said.

"I don't know."

"You guys had lunch that day before Sasha's talk at Columbia," said Lauren. "Then you didn't come to the talk." Sasha looked at Val. The holes in her jeans showed her bony knees through the black tights she wore underneath.

"I asked if she would put in a word for a new manager, recommend me to someone. I'm such a fuck up. I hated asking her, you know? I had to really work myself up to it. Then she just brushed me off. Something about her being at a certain level now, what it would imply—like I was getting a contract with Sony or something. Then she went to the bathroom. I've gone over and over that fucking conversation. I wake up at three in the morning, etching it in stone. But I don't really remember what I said anymore, or even what she said. Plus, it's probably true. What do I know about the business side of anything? One lunch in one restaurant. We ate lunch together at school, five days a week for twelve years. So many breakfasts at all-night diners after gigs. If Cora was still here, she might not remember either."

Val took a sip of whiskey and looked at Lauren. "Was there really only a box of spaghetti in the kitchen cabinet? Maybe we ordered Chinese that night. Maybe there were only a couple of roaches when we turned on the light. Everything that ever happened is a matter of opinion. I mean, really? It's nothing but the dash."

"What dash?" asked Lauren.

"The dash between the dates. You know, on a headstone. It's a whole person's life, but all we know for sure are the dates. Play and Stop." Val smiled. "I'm not rehearsing anymore."

"What does that mean?" Sasha asked carefully.

"I'm going to take a break from music. Some of the new songs are good, but I want to write stories, maybe poetry, maybe both. Cora always said I was a poet. All I've ever done is put one word after the other. I think I'm going to write a story about an old woman who never gets out of her bathtub."

"That's me," said Sasha. "I never want to get out of the tub."

Lauren reached for Val's hand. "If you disappear on us, I'll kill you myself."

Val held out her little finger. "Pinky swear. I hate you guys."

Lauren hooked her finger with Val's. "Hate you too."

Sasha hooked in. "What about when we're old?"

"Don't worry, we'll still hate each other," said Val.

"I know I was going to spend the night," said Lauren. "But I've got to see if Amy will let me in."

"You still haven't told me why Amy—"

"I know, I will."

Sasha wasn't as disappointed as she thought she would be. Val would go home too. Maybe it was the whiskey, but Sasha believed everything now. She nodded at Lauren. "I'll give you a set of keys just in case. You can let yourself in. But before you go, I have to tell you guys something."

Sasha pressed her fingers against her right breast, searching until she found it. Lauren and Val leaned forward. They bent their heads together.

You should take off those uncomfortable shoes, Sasha, maybe just fall asleep on the couch now that everybody's gone. I'm covering you with the scent of those lilies you forgot to move to the kitchen. Go to Scotland with Miss Pierce, she's stamping the snow off her boots right now, annoyed, overtired, and secretly thrilled with the whole evening. Go ahead and unzip your dress, sleep right here in the living room. You're allowed.

The streetlights are coming through the window for my lost mother knitting a shroud out of a sail. The ocean is pounding at the edges of the city for Jessie the Brave.

And Lauren, standing in the hallway outside your apartment with the key in your hand. Grab your heart with both hands. Squeeze hard. Open the door.

Val, sweet Val, here comes the downtown train. You can watch the windows filled with strangers flip by in the opposite direction. You don't need to hate that picture of the two of us anymore. Me in a cowboy hat and ripped jeans, you with your long hair and band T-shirt, walking down Christopher Street in eighth grade, the coolest of the cool. We're the ones who eat the pulp and the rind, forgetting nothing and remembering it all wrong. You're still my first love.

It's lighter than you think.

There might be a song in it.

acknowledgements

There are many people and places whose support, conversation, and time have sustained me in the writing of this book. It has been my great fortune to find a home with the mighty Red Hen Press: Kate Gale, Mark Cull, Piper Gourley, Rebeccah Sanhueza, Tobi Harper Petrie, and Monica Fernandez. These extraordinary and dedicated individuals, along with the rest of the Red Hen team, are the reason you are holding this book in your hands. Thanks also to Marisa Crawford and Ben Crisp for helping me get the word out with dedication and generosity. Endless gratitude to my agent, ally, and friend, Jennifer Carlson. It is hard to express my gratitude for the nurturing, refuge, and support given to me by Civitella Ranieri, Dora Maar House, the American Academy in Rome, and the Virginia Center for the Creative Arts. I am forever grateful to the Bard College Institute for Writing and Thinking, which has taught me so much and given me a place to grow as a teacher and a writer. My thanks and profound respect to my former colleagues and students from the MFA Program at Fairleigh Dickinson University, where these pages were first read and graciously received. Thanks also to my editors at *The New York Times*, *The Yale Review*, *The New England Review*, *Two Coats of Paint*, *Bookpost*, *The Los Angeles Review of Books*, and *Lit Hub* for publishing my work across genres. Thanks beyond reckoning to Marisa Silver, Louis Begley, Anka Muhlstein, Rene Steinke, Minna Zallman Proctor, Padma Viswanathan, Katherine Barrett Swett, Fernanda Eberstadt, Charles McGrath, Nancy McGrath, Peter Trachtenberg, erica kaufman, Michelle Hoffman, Joan Silber, Kaveh Akbar, Lauren Groff, Jennifer Collins, Erin Cox, Evan Dunsky, Lisa Zimble, Eva Dunsky, Martha Cooley, Alice Mattison, Annik LaFarge, Tim Weiner, Kate Doyle (TWC 4ever), and especially Jacob Buhler. Gratitude beyond everyone and everything to Ken Buhler, Pesha Magid, and Rebecca Magid. Always.

biographical note

Rebecca Chace is the award-winning author of five books: *Talking to the Wolf*; *Leaving Rock Harbor*; *Capture the Flag*; *Chautauqua Summer*; and *June Sparrow and the Million Dollar Penny* (for children). She adapted her first novel, *Capture the Flag*, for screen and television with director Lisanne Skyler; it was awarded the Tony Cox/Showtime Award for Best Screenplay Short Film at the Nantucket Film Festival. She is a contributor to *The New York Times* and her nonfiction essays have appeared in *The Yale Review*, *The New England Review*, *The Los Angeles Review of Books*, *Guernica*, *Lit Hub*, and many other publications. Fellowships include Civitella Ranieri, MacDowell, Yaddo, Dora Maar House, American Academy in Rome (Visiting Artist), and others. She is a Faculty Associate at the Bard College Institute for Writing and Thinking.

www.rebeccachace.com
Instagram @rebeccachace1
Substack @rebeccachace
facebook.com/rebecca.chace.7

www.ingramcontent.com/pod-product-compliance
Lightning Source LLC
LaVergne TN
LVHW091140080826
845145LV00008B/2206
9781636284620